# The Heart
# of the Order

# The Heart of the Order

## THEO SCHELL-LAMBERT

Published by Little A, New York

www.apub.com

Amazon, the Amazon logo, and Little A are trademarks of Amazon.com, Inc., or its affiliates.

ISBN-13 (hardcover): 9781477829530
ISBN-10 (hardcover): 1477829539
ISBN-13 (paperback): 9781477828328
ISBN-10 (paperback): 147782832X

Cover design by Gabrielle Bordwin

Library of Congress Control Number: 2014956067

Printed in the United States of America

*For Zoe*

# JUNE

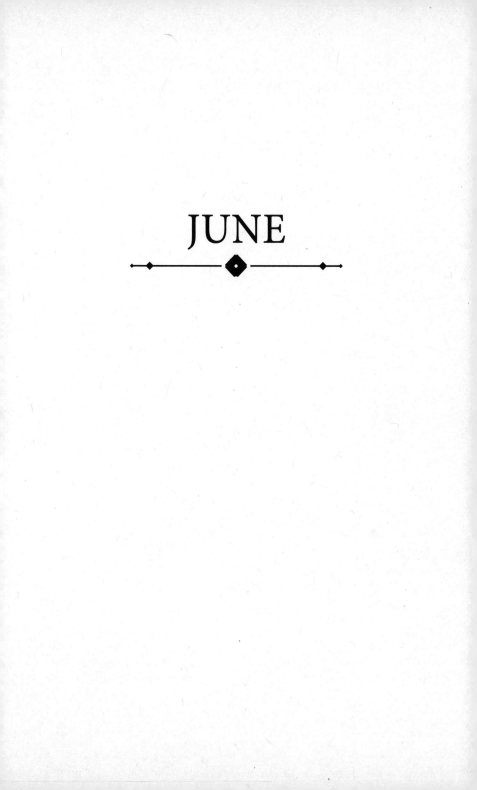

## Thursday June 3

I remember it clearly. Is that too obvious to mention—a useless way to begin? Were you in doubt that a man who makes his living with his arms and legs, his ankles and hands and rotator cuffs, would recall the moment that one of these—a cruciate ligament, they told me later, the doctor said point guards have problems with them—made a loud noise and quit working, in front of 22,471 men, women and children? See, I even remember the crowd size. They'd just announced it, answer B on the JumboTron quiz.

You may be acquainted with the words they use to describe these noises. Whenever it's bad, some witness in the vicinity—it always seems like a third base coach—talks about hearing a "pop" or "snap." Which is ironic I guess, because mine was more like a crackle. Or maybe it was a crumple or a crinkle, I don't know, I wasn't really focused on the wording at that particular moment. When your knee comes apart, it sounds like a knee coming apart. It sounds like a conversation you had with your wife about the mortgage.

Okay, this last part is only speculation. I'm not married, not even close. It's just that when you spend enough time in locker rooms, certain words start to run together—the body parts and the surgeries and the things they'll take away live in the same part of your brain or something. Quadriceps and motor yacht. Tommy John and 6,500 square feet. Mercedes and bursitis, but that almost rhymes, so it's a different thing. Hamstring and Hamptons—that too.

But this thing I remember: it occurred in Cincinnati, on a warm night for the first week of May, a heavy breeze cutting out to my station in left. The Cincy stadium used to be called Riverfront. Now it's just in front of the river. Pick things up in the bottom of the sixth. Tie game, two outs and a man on second, a 2–0 count on their second sacker, who's a lefty and a guy with pop, but going the opposite way. These are all important points, I'm not just trying to "set the scene." Because being a leftfielder I would normally have been playing a lefty hitter toward center, a good eight paces from where I was at that moment. And maybe this even had something to do with it. You make your living standing on the correct patch of grass, it's engrained somewhere deep in your muscle fibers to play a lefty toward center. And then one night you're on another patch of grass a few feet away, and the air just feels different over there. It's like you're trespassing or something. This hesitation creeps into your first step, and the first step is everything to an outfielder.

2–0 on their second sacker. Our SP5 is on the hill, a fastball pitcher pitching in a fastball count, so about 22,463 know what's coming. But it's still only 2–0, not 3–1 or 3–0 or anything, so it doesn't have to be a *panicky* fastball. Just something hard and no-fuss with a dash of location. Location to taste. A blue-collar pitch, a pitch they haven't improved on in seven decades. But the thing is, it's also the sixth inning, which in the modern game is this weird flux time, this sort of unsolid ground. The pitching talent is starting to deteriorate in front of your eyes, but it hasn't yet been replaced by other talent, because that would mean admitting the night has gone wrong. And so you basically start moving backwards through the minor leagues. The guy's throwing AAA sliders, then AA curves, and if the manager doesn't start placing his calls to the pen you'll all be back in rookie ball, stuffed into a bus for an eight-hour ride across some state's panhandle. The sixth inning messes with the laws of physics—I swear if you brought a toilet in the dugout the water would go down the wrong way.

2–0. Our tosser hurls said fastball, only he no longer has the stuff to make it true to itself. The pitch that comes at the plate is in the throes of an identity crisis, a 3–0 groover that's strayed into the wrong count. Yet even at this late moment in the fate of the thing, so many details could be different. Their 2B could be a worse hitter, and freeze. He could be a better hitter, and send it 417 feet, beyond the concern of all of us on the field trying to bend destiny, because it's just history out there, just what happened and when. There could be no one on base, fewer than two outs, an other-than-tied score, or just me in my usual locale, any of which saves me from having a shot, but not a very good one, at making a critical catch of the ball he subsequently ropes over our third baseman's head, toward a herd of half-interested relievers in the pen. You hear of incidents like this being "frozen in time," but I can now safely report that they're not. Because as I'm running I somehow register one thing other than that arc of gleaming majors white, and that is our lefty specialist's jaw going up-down, up-down on his plug of tobacco. And I even record, I swear, a little dribble of brown juice descending from his lower lip toward his soul patch. So there was one thing, anyway, that wasn't in the same spot when the moment ended as when it started. He should probably have been in the game.

Whatever Rice Krispies effect my knee comes up with starts right around the time nicotine hits whiskers, sound at some point turning into feeling and throwing me into a half-assed elbow-first slide. If you've ever seen a career American League pitcher try to run the bags in the Series, you've got a pretty good picture of me at that instant. Yesterday I watched the replay for the first time. Not my finest moment from a grace standpoint. I guess that's how you know it's bad—no one's razzing you for sliding like a pitcher.

The first guy who shows up is our third base coach, Billy. I swear, these third base coaches are everywhere, someone needs to look into this phenomenon. Though I guess I did end up pretty close to his office. Everyone calls Billy "Billy" even though Williams is actually his last name, not his first. Ballplayers, right? If someone had called Ted Williams "Billy" he'd have cracked him over the head with the nearest fly rod. I guess it helps to have Hall of Fame talent. Our Billy is a fifty-one-year-old ex-utility infielder. He didn't stand a chance. Not that I don't have my own nickname issues.

Pretty soon center, short, and third have turned up too, and even the Cincy baserunner, I guess he went ahead with scoring—hey, might as well—then turned right around and trotted out to join the gang in shallow left. They told me later the 2B in question just parked himself on third to wait the thing out. I suppose he felt enough guilt not to try and score, but not so much to hold himself to a double.

Some guys are better company than others during these sorts of incidents, and it's not necessarily who you'd expect. In my experience the tough guys are the least helpful, like an injury is somehow an insult to their code of living. But fragile types like closers are, shall we say, lacking a certain empathy. Give me a good setup man by my side, he knows what hardship is. Of course in the end it doesn't really matter, nothing that gets said by someone without an M.D. is going to count for much at that moment.

Speaking of which, if not getting teased is the first sign you're in deep, the second is the sight of those trademark khaki pants and that tucked-in polo shirt—I think all the team doctors in the majors must have stock in the Gap or something. You see the khakis first if you're the one on the grass, always with that big pager clipped on. This part has confused me for some time. There is clearly better technology now, so why still with the pagers? Maybe it's just tradition at this point, part of the image. Like us with our stirrups, which are not exactly the latest in athletic sockwear.

Our guy is the best in the business, I couldn't have been in better hands—or maybe that's just something Billy said in the postgame presser. They turned it on in my hospital room, which was nice enough, though I'm not sure why they thought it would be my first choice in programming. He has a name, but does it surprise you at all that we only ever call him "Doc"? I can tell you that when you're lying there on that field it's just comforting to have someone around from a different line of work entirely—someone who doesn't know the first thing about fungo bats, who probably watches televised tennis if he watches sports at all.

You've seen how these things play out. Doc crouches next to me for a while, everyone on the field logs some time doing nothing, which is what they'd be doing anyway, that's what baseball is. This is just a different version of it: a sort of sad nothing, but also more reflective. Like before they were on a plane that was on time, and now they're on a train that's been delayed. Then the cart, the standing ovation, the whole bit, all of which seems so obvious, but I can't exactly walk off and the crowd can't exactly not salute my courage. Billy's everywhere during this, clearing a path through the clubhouse to the ambulance, tossing off clichés to any reporter requiring one. "We're just gonna take it day by day," "Xandy may be short on speed, but he's never been short on heart," et cetera and et cetera. I guess a catastrophic knee injury is the exact opposite thing in the world from yanking your ear three times to indicate a hit-and-run, so his interest was piqued.

I stayed in that hospital for precisely forty hours—10 p.m. on Monday till 2 p.m. on Wednesday. I think medical professionals and team officials get confused with a situation like mine, they don't know how long to keep you there or how they're supposed to treat you. It's like they want to match the shittiness of your situation with some really high-end hospital care, lots of shouting of "stat" or whathave-you. But obviously there's no need for anything to happen stat with a busted ligament, if anything the problem is the opposite. So they just keep you there for a dignified 1.5 days, coming up with enough tests that you don't feel forgotten, then they send you to the airport in a hired Town Car wearing the best brace money can buy.

That was twenty-nine 2 p.m.'s ago now—May 5th that day, June 3rd this one. A whole leap month for me to ponder things. Only available one year out of four. When they gave me my honorable discharge, one technician commented that the tear wasn't as bad as it could have been. Though that's true of anything, when you think about it. I guess it was minor as far as tearing a CL goes, but pretty major on the question of whether your knee is torn at all. I suppose if the playoffs were famously called "November baseball," I might not be out for the season.

As I write this I'm sitting on a patio chair I didn't purchase, two feet west of some sliding glass doors at the rear of a house that isn't mine, in a part of coastal Florida that seems to have more than its share of lagoons. One of these constitutes my view. A few days ago I saw an alligator floating by, only about thirty feet from where I'm currently reclining. I didn't notice him at first—it just looked like there was something off with the surface of the water, and the offness was shaped like a six-foot reptile.

A short drive from here is a rehab facility that specializes in my kind of injury. Our Assistant GM's brother has a house he doesn't use in the offseason, and don't things have a way of working out? The place itself isn't too bad, though. In fact, it's kind of growing on me. I like coming out back in the early evenings when the heat starts to fade, and the sun gets ready to juice itself into the lagoon like some local orange. This chair and its neighboring ottoman are about right for a guy in my condition, being designed for the sort of lounging I now do out of necessity. I can prop up my leg and all its hardware and feel like a tax lawyer just kicking back by his grill. The off-white cushions complete the effect, though I'm sure the color has some more complicated name. "Eroding Dune," or something.

I guess the patio is sort of my clubhouse right now, where I while away the hours before a contest I won't be playing in. The roof hangs over a bit, so I'm able to keep my typing hands cool while my legs are in the sun. Though I kind of like to get that tropical sweat going—somehow it makes you feel like you're in America but also like you're somewhere else, which I find sums up the South Florida experience in general. Sticking out into the ocean like that. A little later the mosquitoes get pretty thick. If you want the symmetry, you can say they start to come in earnest right around 7:05, just as my nine is jogging onto some knoll of 1⅛-inch grass. But as a pre-game spot, it's close to ideal. And since it would appear I'll be passing a fair share of days out here, I figured I'd spend some of them writing down my thoughts on the whole thing: "On Life and Baseball and

Season-Ending Injury," by Blake Alexander—"Xandy" to his team-mates. The "X" isn't silent. Don't think of this as a personal journal, exactly. I'm not writing it for my health, though I would if that worked. I type for you: the passingly curious, the casual fan. You know just enough to realize all you're missing.

Well lesson one is that a ballplayer lives by his game-day rituals, and that's sort of how I'm viewing this keyboard: my new superstition. I used to face aces. Now I face an Acer. It's funny, though. I'm just thinking again about the night in question. With an event like that, pieces of it seem to trickle back to you later—aspects you hadn't even thought to consider. And you know what just occurred to me? The ball—I never did see what happened to it. Isn't that ironic, in a way? I'm sprinting like anything for this little round object, then twelve feet away my leg goes to jelly and the object of my affection, in some overly true way the cause of the whole thing, just loses its ending forever. Just keeps on heading up that foul line, and upstairs in some Cincinnati of my mind, never gets caught, never lands.

## Friday June 4

You might be wondering why ballplayers are such suckers for routines. I think it goes to the whole boredom thing. Baseball *is* boredom, if you want to think of it that way. Boredom cut up into shapes and sizes, summer evenings of boredom beginning at appointed hours, staged on fields of specific dimensions. Boredom reclaimed from the gods via the sale of hot dogs. Go to enough ballgames and you start to realize that the plays aren't the real game, they're just the organizing principle. The real game is the stretching for the plays.

So the thing you have to do, to make all those buckets of boredom make any sense at all, is use the powers of superstition. You surround the game with activities and get obsessive about them. Identical room service orders of chicken penne, ordered at identical hours. A 2:10 dip in the hot tub, followed by three-side rummy played to a Beatles backdrop—Lennon songs only. In A ball, everyone hears some story: the shortstop who lost a 4 p.m. hand of five-card stud on a terrible bluff, then went out and hit for the cycle. For weeks the guy insisted on making a bad bluff every day at 4 p.m., losing half his paycheck but hitting circa .380 for the month of July and earning the call-up to AA. And you think about that the next time you see a prospect flying through the system.

The thing to understand is, this isn't about killing time between games. It's about making sure game-time stands for something. You have to crowd the game into its time slot—that way it needs to happen right then, and that way it's for real. I've always been a middle-of-the-road ritual guy: yes on the music part (only Zeppelin before the game, and only the odd-numbered albums), but no on the same meal every day. I need a little variety in my diet, and I like to try out local delicacies when the opportunity presents itself. Ballplayers are America's foremost business travelers, after all, racking up points at Courtyards by Marriott, Rotundas by Hyatt and Gazebos by Westin and what-have-you, and we enjoy generous meal stipends in towns with fine culinary traditions. My knee went soft on a belly full of Cincy chili, and I haven't once had the thought that things would have been different if I'd opted for chicken penne. Well, until right now.

Down here they have me on a routine too, though it may just be a schedule. It starts with physical therapy, every Monday, Wednesday, and Friday at 8:30 a.m. at the Para Atlantic Rehabilitation Center. You'd think they'd call the place PARC, but no one seems to. It's housed in a local strip mall, between a sandwich chain and a Publix supermarket. The white lines in its parking lot are pristine, almost like foul lines. Funny, isn't it, how licensed medical treatment can take place anywhere? In New York City they do plastic surgery in row houses.

The two therapists who work with me are named Jenn and Erik. Jenn is tall, with a whole pile of red hair that she keeps in a ponytail. Elaborate commercials could be staged around this ponytail: Jenn getting home from work, walking in the door, and yanking off her hair tie to let loose just a river of red. You can't help but think of this when you see her. Jenn went to a college whose name sounds a lot like the Para Atlantic Rehabilitation Center—Nearby Coastal County College, or Atlantic Area U., something like that. In my mind this college is the sort that mails out brochures featuring those statistics unique to small schools in beautiful areas. More beaches within a five-minute drive than tenured English faculty. More square feet of swimming pool than living alumni. I feel dead-certain that the place has beautiful, perfectly lined parking lots, that Jenn has spent her adult life surrounded by gorgeous asphalt. Erik is of medium height.

Jenn has an eight-year-old son who sometimes spends the morning at PARC when his dad can't take him. Jenn had a four-year marriage somewhere in the middle of those eight—a topic that has come up more than a few times during a lunge series, to stony looks from Erik, or maybe it's just that he wears wraparound sunglasses indoors. Jenn mentioned the other day that the youngster has no interest in baseball. She said this apologetically, like it was something she'd been needing to get off her chest. I told her not to worry, my son has no interest in physical therapy! but the joke fell flat about three different ways. "You have a son too?" she asked.

Therapy goes until 11. Afterward I've usually worked up a pretty fierce appetite, so I hobble my whole operation into the supermarket and pick up something for the grill. "When on a patio . . ." The seafood selection at the Publix is actually pretty impressive. South Florida has all these fish types that just *sound* like they're from here. Dorado. Grouper. Turbot, with the silent "t." I guess this is true of other regions as well. In Minnesota, where I'm from, we get smelt and pike, and I'd argue those names summarize the upper Midwest pretty nicely. Fish that could've been made by General Motors.

Next it's back to the lagoon, an attractive drive of eight minutes and two causeways made significantly more difficult by the fact that I've had to become a two-footed driver. For me, driving is now a problem of lateral motion. The knee is allowed to go north-south, but east-west must wait till the All-Star Break—leg as broken compass. Conceive of this: Xandy Alexander, son of 5.2-liter Pontiacs, lurching through semitropical intersections in a borrowed forest green Volvo sedan. A real sight and a half. I realize I'm now sounding exactly like I'm supposed to. When it comes to cars, I guess I'm the ballplayer you've always read about.

Tuesdays and Thursdays are pool days, which involve approximately none of the leisure you may be picturing. The pool I use is on the campus of Five Palms Junior College—not Jenn's alma mater but their bitter rival, you figure—and kind of amazingly it isn't even outdoors. The implication being that this state is so full of sunshine that it's gotten a little annoying. That pleasure is something the region is infested with, like alligators. Like most of the towns around here, this one follows the Palm Beach Modified format. Technically, I'm just over the border into East Palm Beach.

The pool exercise is so exhausting that pleasure quickly becomes a distant memory. I "run" endlessly in the deep end, flotation belt tied around me, and it's a good assumption that I get soaked in sweat, though I end up splashing my face just enough that I can never really tell. One funny thing about baseball is that we wear belts while we play. At the end of my pool workouts, I am often struck by the sensation of wanting to take a nice refreshing dip in a pool. On the drive between the pool and the lagoon, there is only one causeway.

I'd like to tell you that there's a lot more to it than that—that I have a number of further commitments beyond therapy and the local swimming hole. But in truth, there is not a single day in my week in which I have to commute somewhere in both morning and afternoon. My entire life as an employee right now is dedicated to the incremental mending of my own body, which becomes a stranger notion the more you dwell on it. I bring my lunch pail to a sofa in the living room, and I let tissues deep in my leg regenerate for a few hours. Punch out, consume a sandwich and a can of regional soda, then get back on the clock for a few more hours of hard healing. Just like my father, with his Bachelor of Science degree from a land-grant university. My right leg the iron mine, location of billable hours.

All this gets us into interesting territory. A ballplayer is an American hero of at least some sort, even for those who don't go to games. I don't think you'll argue with me on this point. And yet he is the definition of a deadbeat: he actually gets his pants soiled by sliding into a patch of dirt tended for his personal use, then gives them to someone else to clean. He is constitutionally lacking in class. The bum of this story should be Jenn's son's father—that's how stories work. But the man runs a podiatry practice that by all accounts is thriving. They broke up amicably. If you'll forgive my using cars to make one more point, he drives a Toyota Camry.

And now it strikes me that I've left out something obvious. I've described Jenn and Erik, but I haven't said the first thing about myself, or anyway the third thing. If I had to pen my own scouting report, what would it say?

Blake Alexander, LF.
Carolina Birds of the National League's South Division.
Place of Birth: Duluth, Minn.
Height: 6'1"
Weight: 195
Hair: Sandy
Nickname: Xandy
Eyes: 20/15
HR/SB: 16/6
Eyes: Blue
High school: .478 AVG
College: Briefly considered
Eyes: Really more of an azure
Bats/R. Throws/R.
Below-average average. Around-average looks.
Strong through trunk and hips. Quick wrists.
Slow of foot. Fleet of mind.
Classic pull hitter. Classic push bet. Decent upside.

*Saturday June 5*

Every weekday, within ten minutes of 12:30 p.m., my agent calls me on my cell. Today being a Saturday, someone's logic indicates that no call is necessary. Maybe I should have included this in my description of routines—I'm not sure whether it qualifies.

"Hello?" As though I don't have Caller ID.

"Xandy? Xandy it's Jeff!" he says, playing his part in the make-believe. Always good to get that squared away.

The purpose of this phone call is to assure me that I have not been forgotten, that I am not just a number to Dynastic Sports Management of Sherman Oaks, California. Lately this has started to have the opposite effect, sort of the way the tropical plants in Jeff's office actually make it feel less personal. It has started to seem like Jeff has a to-do list on his mobile device, and once he calls me and that side-armer on the O's with the elbow problem, he can go to lunch. I don't resent him for this. I suppose there's no point suggesting that he mix up the time of the call so as not to give himself away. In my short time on the patio I have developed a theory that Dynastic Sports Management was supposed to be Dynamic Sports Management, but I guess "dynastic" makes just enough sense for no one to care.

Last night I watched Carolina play for the first time since Cincinnati, which must count as some sort of milestone in the psychological part of my recovery. I wasn't avoiding the games on purpose. Our Assistant General Manager's brother didn't opt for the comprehensive cable package, so I had no way of seeing games played in our home park, which is up in the heart of downtown Raleigh-Durham. But now it's interleague play, and the team is on the Gulf for a weekender with the Rays, and a station in West Palm is carrying it. Actually, I'm surprised we're even getting the game here, us being on the Atlantic side and Miami having a team of its own. You'd think they'd divide these things coastally.

My going on the sixty-day DL—read: "the worse DL," not that I'll actually be back in sixty days—meant the organization could dip into the minor league talent pool. My replacement is everything I'm not, which technically means nothing but is noticeable. Southern, played college ball. Fast and a great glove, whereas I have been called a "deliberate" runner and am known, when I'm known, for my arm. They have him hitting second—the spot for contact hitters, not usually trusted to the young. I found myself when I started hitting sixth, just outside the heart of the order. Last night he went 1 for 4, tagging a clean single to center in the top of the fifth. An exact wash of an evening, not good and not bad, a deferring of all decisions till a later date. My Birds dropped the contest 5–2, under a light rain. Boredom being played out on time.

Another night, another save situation. The weather, and whether it was a factor. It's been striking me that one of my issues down here relates to information. Baseball is really about computing, about making tiny adjustments in reaction to tiny drops of data. It's a game of tinkering, and literally every statistic—an mph of wind, a pitcher's ERA in away night games west of the North Platte River—is usable once it is known. But daily now I'm surrounded by surplus stuff: extra facts I'm not sure how to respond to. Truths just drifting around, undeciphered. The growing season of the lime tree at my feet. The brand of Erik's sunglasses. The smell of Jenn's shampoo.

This always was my issue when I walked off a field prepared to my exacting specifications. When I exited the locker room and entered city limits. I wanted to keep playing baseball out there, could always let a loss go but not the thinking I'd brought to it, the angles on the game. To be a leftfielder on the unmown grass of a city.

"What are you thinking about, Xandy?"

Well, the wind. (A problem when you're indoors, I'm aware.)

But I'm starting to adjust. I'm getting accustomed to this new climate, which is fair now but I guess won't be soon. To the layout of this development, which this morning I realized like a thunderclap is just a plain grid they bent at the edges, then sprinkled with cul-de-sacs. You only see it when you don't look. But I can sense so much getting wasted, just washing right over me. This is unimaginable for an outfielder.

## Monday June 7

No writing yesterday. The Lord's day. Xandy's day. By early afternoon I found myself feeling restless, so I decided to test the limits of the term "athletic activity." Everyone is always talking about how fishing isn't a real sport, so I drove down to the bayside pier and found a place where I could rent a little skiff. I won't lie, the purpose of the trip was less fresh seafood than canned American pilsner. That and the pleasures of speed and mobility, two things my life has lacked of late.

The guy renting boats recognized me—only about a biweekly occurrence down here. Which is to say, it's now happened twice. The first time was in line at the deli counter at the Publix. The woman standing in front of me—bleached blonde, one baby and a dozen cans of frozen orange juice concentrate in her cart—turned and did the standard peering double-take in my direction. "You," she said, tilting her head slightly and jabbing a finger toward my chest. "My *husband* likes you." She delivered this line like her husband was the only one in the household who felt that way. Then she proceeded to name a NASCAR driver known for his ill temper and taste for bumping opponents' fenders. "I thought you guys were up at Pocono this week."

*You're right,* I thought but did not say. *I totally forgot about my race.*

This is pretty much how the average professional athlete experiences his or her fame. Being misrecognized on behalf of someone else. Once you get past about a four-mile radius from the home ballpark—shrink it to 1.5 miles on the road—you start melting faster and faster back into the ranks of the unknown. First you're recognized as who you are, then as some participant on your team, then as a player of your sport, then a member of the larger sporting community, and finally just as a face that's been on television, imprinting itself on eyes as they journey from CNN to QVC. The thing to understand here is, she wasn't wrong that I was famous.

But fishing-boat rental man actually knew who I was, down to the level of suggesting that a fresh evaluation of my skill might be in order, in light of the new sabermetric stat models. "You can't run, of course," he said, in the middle of a longer speech on the state of the pastime in the expansion era. "But now they're saying that running is overrated, that stealing just isn't worth the risk." The wisdom of a leathery sixty-year-old in a shed full of rusting tackle. Do I even need to point out that this is the language of crime?

Out on the water, I put a worm on a hook, issued some line, and parked for a while. I reclined in the cockpit seat with a six-teen-ounce beer in my left hand, looking out across acres of blue. Water and fields are supposed to be opposite things, but as I sat there gazing, I had the thought that there was nothing it reminded me of so much as a baseball diamond, and not just because it sparkled. It was all that open space, I think. Not just the quantity of space, but the theme of it, the way space was what was being illustrated. I cast and I reeled. I cruised past white bungalows with docks out back, a plume of spray trailing me. Speeding without a gas pedal in sight. Sunday, 3 p.m. Elsewhere relievers were being readied, healthy OFs were swimming through power alleys. I have no idea if the fish around here eat worms, but I can report that none did yesterday.

## Tuesday June 8

I'm realizing I should provide a proper description of this house. The truth is, it's typical to a degree that in other circumstances it wouldn't be worth mentioning. Any ballplayer would instantly recognize its expensive, underused feel—we are the masters of the ignored Viking range. Countertops featuring whole hectares of shining gray marble, imported I'm sure from a highly specific town. Then the "island" in the middle, like the floor is a lake and you need to take refuge. Real islands have fruit trees, and kitchen islands have fruit bowls. The blue pattern on the Sub-Zero fridge is the same as what's on the walls, which you also see a lot, and which always suggests to me contracting collusion happening on a frighteningly deep level.

So the kitchen was clearly done recently, but the house must go back to the early '80s, which seems to be when they started conquering the local lagoons. As with most of the homes in the neighborhood, the front yard pretty much got mailed in. You proceed up a short path to the front door between this and that example of hot-climate flora, behind which the house is half hidden. There isn't a blade of grass out front, just small white stones on both sides of the path. This would horrify the devoted turf builders of greater Duluth.

The house itself is white, stucco, one story as I mentioned, but deep and pretty spacious. Flat roof, green shutters and trim, tile floors throughout. Semi-tropical standard-issue. I suppose you would call it an open floor plan—or partway open, ajar—in that the dining room, on your left as you enter, isn't a room so much as an area, blending into the kitchen behind it, which in turn becomes the living room off to the right. There are two steps down into the living room, or living region or whatever, but I don't think the one-story description is threatened by this detail. It's surprising the landscapers were even able to produce these couple feet of grade. There are no hills down here, I mean none. You sense a general flatness, of course, but I'm not sure people realize the extent of the condition. Illinois gets called flat, but Florida is just "hot." But I looked it up a few nights ago. The highest point in the whole state is only 345 feet, up near the Alabama border. Barely a home run tall. They've got the marker there and everything, but instead of a grand vista there's just a mezzanine view of a field. Did you know Duluth is called "the San Francisco of the Midwest"? We're built right onto the side of a steep slope, rising up from the lake. Still, I would not read too much into this if you're planning a visit.

On the subject of interior décor, I don't have much to contribute. But let me just say that there is more of a tendency for an object in this house to glisten than you'll find in my own places of residence. Bright gold fixtures in the bathroom sink and on the Jacuzzi. In the living room, a glass coffee table, a silky leather sofa in still another shade of off-white. Everything so close to white, yet so far. The thing is, my professional life is full of shine. Gleaming bats, aluminum charter buses with windows tinted into shaving mirrors, leather cleats brought to a polish that would pass muster at Parris Island. At home, I prefer my furnishings to have some grain. Canvases and twills, worn wood and rough stone—these are my materials.

And on the mental tour of the house, this leads us out back to the patio, through the sliding doors behind the brackish water where kitchen and living zones meet. I have led us to me, the young man with the knee brace typing away on a laptop. *What is he writing about?* the tour guide wonders. *What did he do to that leg?* Don't worry, I'm now settling back into my limbs. It's an interesting thing, though. We professional athletes get used to seeing ourselves through other eyes, but we also have bigger blind spots. Like in utilizing this skill, we lose some of the sensations generally felt by private individuals. Yesterday at therapy, Jenn asked if it had hurt. My catastrophic knee injury, she meant. And I realized to my amazement that I had not once considered this, though now that she mentioned it, it had, and like hell.

*Wednesday June 9*

This morning, after my session, I had a meeting with the head of PARC, Jens Nielsen, M.D. Ph.D. Jens as in the plural of Jenn, but pronounced with a "y," and a man. It's only confusing when you see it written down. A tall sort with a shaved head who, I've noticed, seems to put on his white coat only when he's setting up a conference call. Roaming the halls of the Center, he wears a tailored suit.

He informed me—and my agent and our AGM, patched in from California and Carolina, respectively—that he and the rest of the staff here at the Para Atlantic Rehabilitation Center are extremely pleased with my progress. This was intended to lift everyone's spirits, but it sounded so much like what they always say in these situations that it actually had the opposite effect, at least on me. I was pretty sure Jeff felt the same. "Oh that is -reat to -ear!" he piped up, his letters getting gobbled by static, and I could practically hear his attention start to drift. Bad cellphone connections have a way of saying things that people can't.

The rehab game is all about words, you figure out pretty quickly. "Pleased" and "thrilled" and "ecstatic" all mean something slightly different, but none of them mean what they actually mean. For example, no one is ever *dis*pleased with progress, which kind of takes away your faith in the dictionary they're using. At worst, everyone is just "encouraged." Anyway, my knee and I are so far away from athletic locomotion that it's hard to get too exercised about outperforming on the week. It's like making great time to Newark on the drive from New York to LA.

Besides, my real mile markers aren't the comments of the director, but the facial expressions of Erik and Jenn. If I was worried that they'd be too starstruck to do their jobs, I can lay that fear to rest. Erik in particular seems to view it as a moral failing when I slow down at the end of a set, or can't complete a full range-of-motion. Like I am confirming something he has long suspected of my kind. I think he looks at his muscle tone and mine and just can't quite process what happened to his own majors dreams. It can be hard to wrap your head around, when you've got the sunglasses but not the talent.

This morning, he had me doing step-ups, which are where you ascend and descend a small stool repeatedly, like you kept starting to climb something and then changing your mind. And it's tiring, being that indecisive, and after a while I started thinking maybe I would just commit to staying on the ground, and I started to gasp something to that effect, but before I could present my logic, he jumped into a story about a home run he once almost hit fifteen years ago.

Anyway, this is the point I really want to make about my physical therapy: it is *hard*. Hard in a genuine way that you don't really expect, or I guess just don't think of. In modern sports circles, injuries are seen as chunks of time. You're out for the season. You'll go away for a spell, and then we will see you again. During that period, you will complete a series of tasks. And the thing is, it's fake time. Time gone missing. The world on pause. I was raised Catholic, and I can't help but notice certain similarities. I must go away and say seventeen thousand Hail Marys, then I will return and we'll pick up where we left off. The actual experience is nothing like this. You feel it all in a very direct way. Knee exercises are extremely difficult, because your knee is broken. You wonder if you will be able to complete them, and consider what will happen if you can't.

I don't know the best way to put it, but it becomes clear pretty early that you stay inside your life with a situation like mine. The game clock doesn't get turned off, like it's an extra point in football. Which sounds obvious enough when you write it down, but this is one of the big surprises. Playing pro ball is such a big thing to do, such a *public* thing, that hours spent off the field really can look like blank space. Even players get sucked into this, so I'm sure it seems that way to fans. I almost want to pin every sweat-stained workout shirt to a wall, to mark off the real efforts I produce within these calendar days. The spectrum of body odors. On the other hand, maybe I should just mount a stopwatch on the mantel, which I'll run whenever I'm sitting on the ecru sofa with my hands folded on my lap, at 11 a.m. on a Tuesday, completely sweatless, mending.

*Friday June 11*

Sometimes, when I am driving with two feet around East Palm, songs will pop into my head, like they're suggesting themselves for a soundtrack to this experience. Lately, for reasons I haven't tried to understand, these have tended to be the later hits of '70s classic rock stars. "I'm No Angel" by Gregg Allman. "Treetop Flyer" by Stephen Stills. I won't have heard them on the radio or anything, they'll just bubble up from some dark corner of my brain. The Stones' "Saint of Me." CSN's "Southern Cross." Songs about party girls in polluted beach towns in the offseason. Alimony and Cuervo Gold and mermaid tattoos. Guys who used to be cool becoming sleazes in their forties. There's a certain relevance here that I don't like. An injured pro athlete roaming a development in a borrowed car is a creep, on some level, and I sort of wish my mind would come up with different music.

Driving, at least, I am starting to get the hang of. I've found it helps to think of my injured leg, which has accelerator duty, as an implement attached to my waist rather than a normal limb of my body. It occurred to me this morning that instead of seeing myself as healthy, I'm pretending I'm an amputee. And of course, a brake foot needs to put in the hours to get the force out of its system, to work through those first itchy hard-stops. It's amazing how skilled a motion that really is, what a carefully mixed beaker of firmness and restraint. It's chemistry, and there is no way to teach or rush it, as my father would be the first to tell you, having spilled coffee on his Saturday jeans through two offspring before going beverage-free for me, the third. I finally shook out my last left-foot yip last Tuesday, at exactly 3:15, four stop signs from the lagoon.

Siblings of professional athletes: an interesting subject in and of itself. You almost can't read about an All-Star catcher without coming

across a human-interest piece on his brother, the third baseman—
the real talent in the family, everyone always said. The kid with the
golden arm who just never had the desire. Or he had the desire but
he didn't have the heart—there was a congenital defect in a forgotten
valve. This wasn't the case in my family. Drew and Katie Alexander
are, respectively, a biologist on the University of Minnesota's main
campus and an operations manager for the Duluth Department of
Transportation. This is exactly what they both planned to be, and
both enjoy regular chuckles at the fact that their little brother's baseball dream worked out, that their last name gets abbreviated in the
hallowed basements of Fenway Park and Wrigley Field.

The open secret is that none of them really expected me to go
this far. They are realists, my family, and simply too good at math.
Or in the case of my mom, who teaches middle-schoolers their
grammar and vocabulary, too firm about what stories can be told. At
some stage in the ascent of any prospect, never mind a 24th-rounder,
something goes wrong. Gridlock at your position in High-A, a bum
shrimp cocktail in the middle of spring training. And if you're not
visibly designed for success on the diamond, and I am not, this is all
it takes. Something always goes wrong, only in my case, it . . . didn't.
I closed in on the highest level of my sport at the end of a five-year
succession of small upsets, none of them ruffling any feathers at the
time. And then one year, the Birds made their last cuts in the last
week of March, and they tacked the list to a corkboard a few beach
towns over, and my name just hadn't been typed into that particular
Microsoft Word document. (Was it saved as "finalcuts.doc," I wonder, and what was the secretary's max WPM?) I didn't "make it" to
the majors, I can see that clearly now—I just never got stopped.

Not that it felt that way at the time. Back in A ball, the Show
was kind of like an object in a telescope: I knew it was far away, but
it was also detailed and bright and seemingly in reach. But this was
just a delusion that never got proved wrong—sort of like how heads
of companies think they got there because of their leadership skills,

then go out and charge forty thousand dollars a pop on the lecture circuit. The real view is from the MLB backwards, through the telescope the wrong way. Squint and try to see Blake from Duluth, then all the mouthfuls of minor towns. Corpus Christi, Cucamonga, bowls of vowels. D F N Q, a train of consonants to a ballpark in deepest Brooklyn. He's just a distant speck so small your eye doesn't even know it's noticed it. There are interesting parallels to the way my fame works now.

*Saturday June 12*

It's occurring to me that with all my commentary on what's bizarre and surprising and complicated about being a professional baseball player, I may be giving the impression that I don't really care about the sport—that I don't have the so-called "passion for the game." This is not true. There are plenty of players who *do* feel this way, I might add. Who run their fly ball routes like paperboys. But for me, if nothing else, my sport is different from everything else. Allow me to make a brief case for the pastime.

I strongly believe that any discussion of what sets baseball apart has to start with the gear. In baseball, unlike in most North American team sports, you get to make key equipment decisions even in the highest professional league. What color bat to use, and what type of wood. What brand of mitt, and how to care for the leather. And here you can apply certain lessons from your upbringing. The things your father told you about the respective properties of those woods, the various tradeoffs of hardness and spring. The times he took you to the hardware store for glove treatments, and the pronouncements he there made: avoid linseed, which makes the mitt look great at first, then cracks it—a short-term oil, all flash and dazzle. The point is, you actually truck all this onto the playing surface with you. Your own knowledge, your own history.

And then there is your hat, the marker of personality. You can curve it as you please, or give it an ounce of tilt. You can even be one of those guys who wears the same hat all season, even though it's already toxic by May, and every fan in the field boxes will know you are one of "those guys" because they'll be able to see that white EKG line of sweatsalt around the fitted band—a fitting image, since it's tracing your body's own style of mineral loss. They'll see the sickly color fade that by July can break even the hardiest Detroit Tiger navy. And that will be in large part why they paid extra for those seats. The ballplayer's hat is *his*.

My point about baseball is that it's really you out there, being you, showing everyone what you prefer. You even chew your favorite things in baseball, throughout the most important, athletically demanding moments of the contest. You are saying, "This game will not interrupt my daily habits." And the sport would not ask this of you. Coaches join in the chewing, but beyond that they're a funny case, because for them the personality scenario is actually reversed. A basketball coach displays his taste in tie patterns, but baseball managers must stuff themselves into the playing suits of the young. They are forced to pretend they can't let go of their youth. And in protest, they embrace the sameness. To a man, managers don't curve their brims, they just don each new one straight from the box.

I haven't even gotten to the game itself. The game is an elegant thing: a masterpiece of distances and spacings, a 99.9% functional math proof. It can only work exactly as it is, as more than one sports historian has pointed out. Pitching and hitting and fielding all holding each other in check, not unlike the branches of the United States government. I guess you could say I savor all this in reverse. I like the tricks that have been invented to throw *off* the whole fragile balance, to get into the game's dark corners of measurement and timing. The shift, the hit and run, the "wheel play," in which the shortstop covers third on an anticipated sacrifice bunt, allowing the third baseman to charge the batter's box and grab the lead in the race to own time. He is giving away ground in terms of deep infield coverage and bag-manning for a shot at winning the play before it even begins—at having the bunted ball in his hand so early that it's like he's playing a different, poorly designed game.

But of course, once everyone knows how they work, plays like the wheel or the suicide squeeze pay for themselves in risk. What *really* interests me is that 0.01%, those little flaws that would take down the whole game if not specifically addressed. The black holes in baseball's logic that force the rulebook's hand. Take bunting with two strikes. If you bunt foul on a two-strike count, you're deemed out by strike-out—baseball's version of the TKO. This makes no sense based on the sport's master plan, it is a rule glued crazily on top of other rules, no one really comfortable that this was the best they could do. But it was necessary because it turned out that bunting a ball foul was simply too easy for a professional hitter. He could stick the bat out and touch the ball thirty times in a row if he didn't have to push it straight, and pitchers would tire and scores would get run up and contests would go for six hours. Baseball would become like one of those games they play at English boarding schools, where actual winning becomes so luck-based and besides-the-point that the whole thing ends up just being a lesson in management of an empire. Not having the one rule would literally ruin *the entire sport*. I enjoy this.

This isn't to say that I don't appreciate the more traditional, crowd-pleasing elements of my game: the swinging strikeout with men on base in the ninth, the home run drilled off the brick wall of a long-shut cannery whose sign they just repainted poorly. I get pleasure out of these things too. But when you get down to it, what gets to me now about my co-worker's homer off an ex-factory is the way you look at that moment. I've given this some thought. As spectacles go, your side is much more impressive. 22,471 people, to pick a number, all getting religion at once over something my colleague has just done. Can you blame a ballplayer for wanting to watch you back?

*Sunday June 13*

Yesterday was my sister's birthday. I forgot to call her, maybe because this was the first year in a decade I didn't have a game that I expected would make me forget to call her. No need for my mind to start itching with forget-anxiety on the night of the 10th. The result being that I sat around scratching a dry patch of skin under my brace, watched several lizards climb the kitchen screen, enjoyed a dinner of two boxes of macaroni-n-cheese and three Bud tallboys, then passed out on the couch before the Marlins game hit the seventh-inning stretch, zero phone calls to Minnesota having been made. I've noticed that the Marlins have no stretch traditions— no recording of "God Bless America," or guest singer intentionally butchering "Take Me Out to the Ballgame," like at Wrigley. Even the Birds do something for the stretch, though usually it involves a UNC basketball star from the '70s waving from the press box, and they don't give him a mike. I'm pretty sure the fans in Miami don't even substitute "*Mar*—lins" for "home team."

June 12th is just two days before Flag Day. My relatives all seem to have birthdays on or very near minor holidays. Is this an actual phenomenon? My dad was a Groundhog Eve baby, and every few years Columbus Day falls on Drew's date of birth. A blessed bunch, I tell you. I guess if we weren't American, we'd be nothing special at all.

Anyway, I am in the Alexander family doghouse today: conspicuous lack of call from Katie, but wakeup calls from mother and brother informing me that my error had gone into the ledger. I got to her around 12:15 CDT, after she and her husband, Todd, returned from morning mass. Leaving my apologetic message during the service, thereby reminding her I am a hopeless heathen, was probably not the best way to get back into favor. "What are you *doing* down there anyway?" she asked me. When you miss a birthday call, you always risk becoming the subject of the conversation.

It was a fair question. My blockbuster Saturday night may indicate a certain failure to engage with the local community. But it's tricky, the sort of social life a player can or should pursue during a rehab assignment. Plenty of guys have gotten themselves into serious trouble while on hiatus from the diamond or pitch or court. I don't mean sleeping with married women, I mean felonies. I don't think of that as my style, but then again I'm sure they don't either, and you can see why it happens. Not having enough to do is only a small part of it. Pro athletes get used to extremes, and I think some of them just don't adjust to the scale of daily life. Not a good idea to swing for the fences in a local watering hole.

When I'm with the team, I'm actually a fairly social type. I'm not a big club guy, but I enjoy making the rounds of the more upstanding bars with a couple like-minded teammates, and I have my favorites in each city in our league. Charlie's in Atlanta. Chuck's in St. Louis. Apostrophe 's' places, you know the type. All of them named after some enterprising guy who worked his way up from dishwasher to buy the joint, then got famous serving free suds to Mickey Mantle. A mutually beneficial deal. If there's not an old picture of the Mick behind the taps, Jimmy of Jimmy's shaking his hand and two floozies on his arm, I won't stay! I exaggerate, of course. A Polaroid of Whitey Ford will do.

So I like to go out, but I don't get too crazy with it. You won't be reading in my memoirs about the time I hit for the cycle while still in excess of some states' legal limits. There are always exceptions, however. One of my first years in the league, July 4th fell during our annual jaunt to play the West Coast teams. The 4th was a Sunday that year, and the date of our third game out of four against the Giants, an XL final series of a tiring trip. Now, I should point out that one of the downsides of playing ball is the schedule. We play on weekends, we play at 1 p.m. after cross-country red-eyes, and we *definitely* play on major American holidays, going to a ballgame being a majorly American activity. But we too want to have that sort of day off, gift of our nation, free for some serious partaking. And I'll just say it, we have more money to spend on our entertainments than you do, so the frustration goes double.

In this case, we had an afternoon game that only went 2h20, so by 4:30 we were all showered and out of the ballpark and feeling like sailors on leave. Probably the wrong way to picture ourselves, since we had another 1:05 first-pitch the next day. But when you're 24, you're liable to get swept up in patriotic fervor. Our third sacker at the time grew up in the Bay Area, and he was keen to show off for his old high school buddies, so he'd arranged for a yacht to take interested parties out on the water. Sixty feet—same as mound to plate, I remember thinking, plus or minus a six-inch bowsprit—with two bartenders, various unsteady carriers of appetizer trays, the trump card being our own private fireworks guy, who set up on the stern. . .

I woke up the next morning to the sound of seagulls near some boat word: a port'le, a fo'c'sle. Talk about apostrophes. Still the only time I've had a truly crushing bender before a game. That's always something I've taken seriously. What's funny is, if you saw me on the field that day (1 for 4), you probably would have had no idea. You simply wouldn't have been thinking about it. You just go to a ballpark, and inside it are ballplayers, and they haven't come from anyplace (in a speeding cab) and they aren't going anyplace after (to the team charter, with its airsickness bags in team colors). If you saw a ballplayer in street clothes, you'd notice him looking green, wincing as he slogged through a coffee. But—and I've verified this with non-playing friends—it's impossible for the layman to see a hangover inside a uniform, your brain just can't piece that together.

*Tuesday June 15*

I'm writing inside today. A big thunderstorm rolled in about an hour ago—one of those mean two-tone jobs that look like a computer simulation, where the cottony edge of the cloud bank starts folding back into the gray and the whole thing just spins, spins. We got one yesterday, too, turning up about three minutes after I'd gotten my leg all situated on the ottoman, which lives hard by the shade line. It came straight out of nowhere. By the time I realized I wasn't as hot as I should have been, fat drops were already bouncing off the slate. I limped my laptop inside, sheltering it beneath my chest because the water was blowing under the overhang, and when I turned and looked back through the glass, the whole surface of the lagoon was a riot. I'll wager no amateur can sniff out a June thunderstorm better than a major league leftfielder who plays his home games in the former Confederacy, but these coastal types are some different breed, they have no future, just boom, are there. Or maybe I'm losing my touch.

So the rain stopped me yesterday. As I've said, this writing project is something new for me, and I hadn't really thought of it existing past the patio. That's where it resides. But today I was ready to adjust, and I'm now making a go of it on the sofa. I don't know how much importance to give to the things you actually see while you write. I am certainly not a landscape painter, letting you know about the vista I'm beholding. And it seems to me that when you're tapping on a keyboard, a sort of artificial horizon line rises inside your head—like that read-out in the cockpit of a plane. You see in front of you, inside of you. Still, certain parts of your setting must seep in, thoughts that form three thoughts away from the sight of an alligator. What I'm trying to say is, there are a remarkable number of golf-related items in this room, I mean from a signed photo of Greg Norman ("Best

Wishes, The Shark") to a stack of instructional swing DVDs to a "While You Were Out" notepad cut in the shape of a noted dogleg left.

Living in someone else's house really is a strange thing, and I'm starting to think it gets more strange the longer you're there, not less. It isn't really what you'd expect. It's not the sleeping in another person's bed that's weird, or the using their shower. People have a surprising capacity for stuff like that, we just understand it comes with the territory. We have to get past it to be functional, to stomach hotels. No, what's weird is how you start to get used to that shower's particular sounds, how you learn the special way to twist the nozzle to get all the water coming from the head. You start to think about the person in their house, doing those things, *knowing* those things, and that's what is creepy and too intimate.

There's something more to it too, I think. On some level, people start to seem pathetic when you really get acquainted with their residences. Hear me out. What happens is that an absent homeowner, i.e. the Assistant GM's brother, turns into the sum total of the evidence of his hobbies, of the running toilet sounds that you now know live in his ears, and then it just spirals. You feel embarrassed by his decision that this place, this view, was good enough for him, represented the level of pleasure he felt he could aspire to, the level of taste. I think this would occur even if the home were truly elegant. There could be virgin-wood floors and a wall of diplomas from Ohio liberal-arts colleges, it wouldn't fix the problem. The problem that whatever there is, is *all* there is. And it's like a house itself, without an owner to fill it out, just starts to ache, to shiver with all that permanence.

*Wednesday June 16*

Some days, what happens is thinking, and other days it's things. About an hour into this morning's session, I was coming up out of a squat when I felt a sharp twinge in the outside of my bad knee. Twinges are the second cousins of pops—less drama and sound, but just as much certainty that a thing has gone wrong. I must have groaned, and Erik quickly got the rack off my shoulders as I let myself go down to the floor. I sat there for a minute or so, taking stock. This was a very different surface from the grass of six weeks ago, and I don't mean literally, though it is made of rubber. You are allowed an injury, of any severity. Injuries are about the game. But a "setback," if that's what this was—a setback is about you.

It didn't really hurt while I sat there. Just some color lingering around the joint, the way light stays in your eyes after a camera flash. But I knew that getting up could be another story entirely, and I wasn't in a rush to find out how it went. I should mention that when I'm in the main weight room other people are usually around—jockeys who got thrown down in a different Palm Beach, U. of Miami linebackers who come up here to work with the strength trainers. So about five other athletes saw me go down, and while I'm not a big deal here, I am someone they recognize. This is the *SportsCenter* crowd. And as I was parked on the mat I saw their faces take on those focused frowns people get when they realize they're witnessing news. *Go on, send your text messages,* I wanted to say. *I won't hold it against you.*

Jenn actually went and got a wheelchair for me. Not the image anyone wanted, but still the best way to move oneself without walking. I was glad to only have to feel the pain again in passing—there was a faint echo of that same wrong note as they helped me up into the seat. There was a faint echo of lemongrass in the air. And then they just rolled me on out of there, the knee already looking puffy on the offending side.

Jens takes over in moments like these. His office has an exam room off to the side, which I'll wager only gets used when things go wrong with important clients. We got me up on the table and he did some light squeezing around the edges of the joint. I could see the ocean off in the distance, looking hot and white behind the cypresses. I've been learning what the local trees are called. Jens speaks in that strange Norwegian non-accented English where it just seems like the person is American, but in a different mood than they are. "Xandy, Xandy, Xandy," he said under his breath, clucking as though I'd been a naughty boy. I always have trouble hearing my nickname out of the park, it almost literally doesn't work. It's like you go too far into foul territory and it stops being a word, is just the letters, X-A-N-D-Y. You've seen those soccer jerseys where the names are so widely spaced that they're practically initials. And of course, foul territory never stops, not till you arrive at the next line on the next field.

Some further poking and pondering, after which he told me there wasn't much he could tell. He used the term "holding pattern," along with other airline language. As the swelling goes down, they will see what it leaves in its wake, or jetstream or whatever. For the moment, all I can battle is inflammation. I was sent forth with a fresh set of aluminum crutches and an Rx for ice and Advil.

Jenn drove me home in my car, because I had to get home, and couldn't drive there myself. Cheap logistical issues don't go away in moments of personal crisis, even though it feels like they should. We passed Floridian scenery. Jenn lifted her eyebrows at intersections, and I pointed left or right. Yes, the lemongrass was definitely her. Neil Young's "Unknown Legend" came on inside my head, even though we were on a coastal byway. Maybe because Jenn made me think of the line about her long hair blowing in the breeze.

Jenn driving me home also meant that she had to get picked up by her ex. She could have taken a taxi, but I guess when you have an amicable breakup you might as well put it to good use. I wouldn't know. Still, some small errand like that does matter, it does register on the scales between two people. Like I said the other week, I understand as a matter of vocation that there is no such thing as a free-floating fact.

Not that I'm the one to turn to for advice on these matters. When it comes to high romance, a leftfielder is more often wrong than right. One funny thing that happens as a player is, you start to get addicted to your own body. I am an athlete. How am I supposed to go on dates? (*Easily, Xandy. With ease.*) Okay, but every evening at 7:05, I already have a date with myself. And we always get our favorite table.

Anyway, I was just glad the ex showed up quickly, while we were still in the driveway getting my crutches squared away. I wasn't looking for the blips of meaning that would generate if Jenn came into the house, and did or didn't have a glass of orange juice, or use the bathroom, take a seat in this chair, gaze across my personal effects . . .

So now the day ends with me sitting here, back on the patio under a bright sun, holding atop my knee a Ziploc bag of ice cubes wrapped in a blue-checkered dishcloth. I am notoriously bad about doing dishes—the sort of habit that develops when no comes over to share the chicken penne. The sun is turning the ice to slush every 30 minutes or so, at which point I hop across the kitchen for a refill. I mean, you'd think I would at least get some more advanced prescription, being a major leaguer and all. That there is some secret Show remedy they unveil when this happens. *The Coolant*, or something. *Hot-away. FreeZ.*

## Friday June 18

I woke up this morning and stared at my knee, trying to decide if the swelling had gone down. It's strange, when you injure a body part, how it starts to look like something that's not attached to you. I stared at my knee. It was a bird. It was a bicycle.

I lay there for a while, watching the ceiling fan spin above my head. There is central air here, obviously, so I guess the fan is just an ode to hot weather gone by. Or maybe it's to keep the air from getting still. Still air is a longstanding obsession of my mother's, though I've never really seen the big deal. When I was growing up she was a dictator about cross-breezes, flinging open windows in precisely calibrated arrangements, like stops on a church organ. Only my dad had never patched all the screens, and by this time of year we'd be getting lake bugs the size of hummingbirds.

Eventually, I got up. When you can't put any weight on one leg, you are forced to become a good planner. You must leave your crutches within reach of any resting place, and not carelessly toss them aside. I imagine people with poor eyesight make for excellent invalids, because they have learned to be careful with their glasses. I figured this out the hard way in my first couple weeks out of the hospital, before I came down here for therapy, when I was holed up at my season apartment in Raleigh-Durham. I haven't written about those dark days. Like most ballplayers, I keep a place in my team's city, in my case a high-rise downtown, about a mile from the park. It's fine, nothing I'm too invested in personally or fiscally. Fast elevator, swimming pool down on the ninth floor, sweeping views of not much. "It's fine, Xandy, no no, yeah, it's totally fine," is a sentence I have heard several times. Where I differ from most is I don't have a regular off-season place. My first couple years I just crashed at my parents' house, and the last few I got serious about my fitness and rented places near noted trainers' hometowns. I am a drifter making $1.8 million a year.

I might just stick in R-D, guys do that if their team's city is notably nice, but it isn't obvious whether mine is. It is "nice enough, Xandy, yeah, no, it's totally very nice . . ." The Birds franchise was resurrected there a few league expansions back, out of the ashes of a fading Midwestern nine. Research money was flowing into the Carolinas, the metal made in an Iowan city had become obsolete. So go the baseball winds. Research of what. Anyway, when I was there in May, I kept making the mistake of flinging my crutches out of reach. I would then have to hop or crawl after them when it was time once more to move. I guess after all the years of tossing bats toward on-deck circles, my muscle memory just took over. But last night, I wisely kept them propped against the nightstand. I'm not thrilled to be gaining knowledge in this area.

The other thing about crutches is, they prevent you from experiencing your injury. Which is the point, of course, but it also leaves you in a kind of limbo. With a case like mine, where the knee doesn't hurt when you're attaching no weight to it, the problem doesn't "exist," in the traditional sense of the word. Instead it's like there is this event buried deep down in your leg, maybe, just waiting to be let loose. You potentially harbor a truth. So when I got up, eventually, and propelled myself down the hall, there was no drama in front of me, only time, and cereal, and the convenience of an ice dispenser built into the refrigerator door. Given the prevailing wisdom in tropical architecture, there wasn't even a staircase for me to ascend and descend at my peril. But peril could be coming. Tomorrow I go in for an MRI, and Monday I receive the results.

MRIs. In the back of your mind, you think of them as something more elaborate than X-rays, but do you really think about them at all? Do you distinguish between procedures when you come across them, there in 8-point font in section C-9? They all get scheduled, and if everything goes positive they come out negative. I predict you don't dwell on the image of an athlete stuck in a cylinder.

But don't take it from me, take it from Wikipedia. Allow me to quote from the section titled *Claustrophobia and discomfort.* "Due to the construction of some MRI scanners, they can be potentially unpleasant to lie in." Hey no shit! They stick you inside that tube for thirty minutes–plus, like it's your own personal subway tunnel. You practically expect to see Coney Island when you come out, brings me right back to my early days with the Cyclones. I haven't heard of it happening, but I wonder if there's ever been a case of a guy who just couldn't suffer through it. Would his career end, or would he invent some way around it, the medical equivalent of John Madden's fear-of-flying bus? When you're a pro athlete, it's just a given that your personality isn't allowed to get in the way.

I'm not a claustrophobe, and it's probably obvious that I'm not an agoraphobe either, seeing as I make my living in a wide-open space. But I do have other issues with the MRI. The procedure has become so common that you can forget you'll be walking into a giant magnet—a customized war zone, basically, only the weapons come from inside your own body. Once again, Wikipedia: "Pacemakers are generally considered an absolute contraindication toward MRI scanning." A contraindication! They mean the thing would rip right out of your chest, your professionally conditioned torso just collateral damage as it caught a whiff of its attractive opposite. And it doesn't smell like lemongrass, either.

And so today, I had to go through all this security screening, like I was at an airport but the fear was that I'd hijack myself. There were even those Hazmat-type signs everywhere, but they were only in English. They stripped me of my watch, then my clothing—the dimes in my pockets, instant small-arms fire—and we had to have a detailed discussion about my medical history before proceeding. Which kind of freaks you out, obviously. I lay there the whole time paranoid that there was some piece of metal they'd missed. A stray bit of dental work, or a screw from a Little League ankle injury I'd somehow forgotten. Though I guess by then it was already too late.

The other obvious thing an MRI resembles is a coffin, and lying in there kind of feels like a trial run for the end of your athletic life. It's like the test itself is designed to prepare you for what the test results could mean. I tried not to overthink this. I relaxed my form, and let my mind drift to pleasant riddles scattered across my life—a strategy that works well for me when I need to catch a few winks on the team charter. Was Jens actually bald, I pondered, or just cultivating a look? Was it the Intracoastal Waterway, or the Inter-coastal? Para*llel* Atlantic Rehab Center, or Para*lyzed*? The question isn't important, it just needs to capture your attention for a minute. What would Walter Johnson have registered on the radar gun? Shouldn't it have been the Carolinas Bïrds, and could an umlaut stand for bird eyes? Or even the Carolinas Bïrd, like those teams—the Heat of the NBA, the Revolution of MLS—that just name themselves after a theme? This is actually a longstanding gripe of mine, this problem of plurals. I once asked our VP of Marketing about it, and he just stared at me. There in the tube, I decided to avoid thinking about baseball. What was the Assistant GM's brother's handicap? I considered. Can you believe there's an injury *called* the intercostal strain, and that it's so often fixed near the waterway? What was the definition of the word "cruciate," after all, and could you please use it in a sentence? A sentence about me?

*Monday June 21*

The results are in. Wherever you are, you can read all about it. This is a funny thing about life as an injured professional of average skill. No one cares about you when you're in ruddy good health, but tear a CL and suddenly your every move makes the *St. Louis Post-Dispatch*, the *Detroit Free Press*, the *Provo Liberated Mouthpiece* or what-have-you. My first week here, I stopped by the sandwich shop next to PARC, and as I was leaning in line I looked over and saw an elderly man reading a *USA Today* in his booth. And on the front page of the section he had open, there was my last name, and beneath it some short piece about me having just reported to rehab. The irony being, by definition, he *wasn't* learning about me, since it's not like in cartoons where the article on the front is also somehow the one they're reading.

You can probably tell from my tone that said news is good. I went in early this morning. An 8 a.m. Town Car pickup, though I was awake hours before, the usual sleeping tricks not making a dent. Eventually I came and sat out here, feeling that sick pre-heat at the beginning of a day that's just going to blaze. The patio looked strange, because the sun was on the other side.

I'm actually not even sure why we had to do this in person. I guess Jens wants to be present for good news if he has to be for bad, so that the injured professional athlete doesn't go away associating his shining dome with the worst days of his/her life. So we go into his office and he helps me get settled on the sofa and everything. Then he takes his sweet time shuffling some papers around on his desk, as though he really needs to work from notes. Extending his pleasure I guess. Because next thing he's grinning at me and saying, "Xandy, Xandy, Xandy," just like that, and then this cold rush rolls through me from head to foot, I half expect to look down and see a bead of ice water dripping off my big toe. His verdict is full of such melodious phrases as "no structural damage" and "essentially minor"—power-pop hooks to the modern ballplayer. My technical diagnosis is a strain, not severe and not affecting the ligament in question. Jens announced this part like it was the gender of a child. "It's a light strain!" "It's a boy!"

So we have hugely relieving news, the thrill of a crisis averted. Of course, I'd be naïve not to see injury still puffing around the edges of the situation, not unlike the swelling around the knee itself. I now have a body that makes things difficult. Teams notice this, they believe in it as statistical data. Major league front offices are remarkably confident in their ability to pigeonhole your body—what sort of tendencies it has, what attitudes. Sprain a toe one year, then take a pitch to the wrist the next, and suddenly you're "injury-prone." Never mind that the hurler who clipped you was wildness-prone, that detail always slips through the cracks. Whatever happens to you in this game, it's who you are, will be, always have been.

Even your agent is constantly making this sort of calculation. How much rope are you worth giving? I talked to Jeff after my meeting with Jens. Irony of ironies, his agency also represents the kid who's holding my place. I've chosen to assume this wasn't a deliberate hedge on Alexander futures, but I can't help noticing that Dynastic now has the Carolina leftfield market cornered.

Jeff, of course, didn't dwell on this in our conversation. We stuck to good news, and we stuck to numbers. The number of weeks until I can resume my course of therapy: 1.5, they're saying. The number of months until I could likely play in a rehab league game: 3.5, they're projecting. Our theme was that all a setback costs you is time. "A four-series road trip," Jeff said, as though those don't feel five years long. In my head, I kept thinking of other numbers. The number of anti-inflammatories I shouldn't exceed, in the number of hours. The number on the back of my jersey, and whether I'll be able to keep it when I get back. The number of times I hadn't texted someone I liked, because I was watching countless clips of a starter's new cutter. There's a fireballer in AAA who wants it, Jeff mentioned, my #29 that is, and he laughed it off, but the kid throws a hundred, which, while we're on the subject, is another number.

I'm not complaining or anything. It's just that I have this feeling—you know when you see that picture of the earth, and then they zoom out, and the whole planet is just a marble in someone's hand? Well right now I feel like my world is a marble being held by someone standing on the Florida that appears in the marble the guy in the picture is holding. Do you see what I mean? I had just come up with a complete world inside the rehab experience inside baseball, and now I have to come up with a world inside that, and at a certain point there's not a whole lot left to work with.

In a situation like this, I recommend fishing. Now, this is the second time I've talked about casting my line, and I don't want you to get the wrong impression about me as a hobbyist. I'm not one of those bloodthirsty ballplayers, the kind whose entry in the team yearbook lists his four favorite pastimes as "hunting, fishing, sportfishing, and big-game hunting." The forty-head-of-cattle types—gentleman ranchers. But fishing has always seemed to me like an activity you can fall back on when your life empties of everything else. So yesterday afternoon I decided to test my luck in these waters. I went digging around in the garage and found an old spinner jammed in a corner beneath some croquet mallets. I stuck a juicy-looking fly on the hook—some sort of monsters with bright green heads have been collecting on the windowsills. I humped all this out back and set up a lawn chair. I even packed myself a few sandwiches and root beers in a Styrofoam cooler, like it was a real-live expedition.

This was my first time doing that thing where you cast, then just jam the rod in the ground and wait, going about the rest of your business. I had honestly never understood the point of that until yesterday, when it struck me like an inspiration. It is the smallest increment up from doing nothing available on this earth. A guy can't just sit there in a chair, staring off into the middle distance, at least not without attracting stares. So he sets in motion the small possibility of action near his location—then he sits in a chair, gazing off into the middle distance. He is fishing. Brilliant. Sometimes I fantasize about having the baseball equivalent of this: a pitching machine out back that just fires on 80 into a screen, one ball every six seconds, twenty-four hours a day. Whenever I wanted I could just walk over and spray liners. At all times, I could know there were liners available to me.

As it happened, I was only out there about twenty minutes when a woman came out of the house two doors down, holding a Labrador on a leash. "No fishing!" she shouted through the screen door, then emerged waving her hands in a frantic fashion. Labrador descriptions are weirdly inconsistent: black, yellow . . . chocolate. "No *fishing* in the pond!"

I told her with real sincerity that I was sorry, I hadn't seen any signs. *And isn't it more of a lagoon?* I thought but didn't say. I'm sure I was quite a sight, sitting there with rod and reel and picnic and crutches. I offer an ironic mixture of serious athleticism and tragic injury. I still haven't seen anyone else between twenty and forty in this entire neighborhood, and even if I had, he or she would probably feature two operational legs.

"Well, there aren't any *signs*," she said. Her tone softened at this point—I think she'd just seen my embraced knee. "There's just . . . no fishing. Okay?" She had on running shoes, running shorts, running shirt, various concentrations of spandex and cotton, pink and blue. I said that was okay, then gave what I believed to be a rueful smile and commenced bringing in my hook. So that was the end of that idea. I figured there was no use bringing up the fact that I'd once had a twenty-seven-game hitting streak, three years back—tied for second-longest in the history of my franchise. Though that was exactly what popped into my mind at that moment. I even flashed back to the day the streak finally broke, over in Houston, with the Astro rightfielder making a preposterous shoetops grab on the sinking drive I cranked in my last AB. A catch I knew I couldn't have made myself. And I haven't been able to get that image out of my head for the last day. The fact that I got robbed, that by all rights that hit was in the bag. A lesser man might think of it like this: that at the instant that ball jumped off his bat, the probability wheel spinning away, a thing not going his way was so far *against* the odds.

## Thursday June 24

One great way to pass the time when you are homebound, and fishing behind your house is prohibited, is to flip on a ballgame. The Carolina Birds had an afternooner in Philly today, and TBS or somebody carried the broadcast. Maybe you've seen that new kid they have in left. Clemson grad, serious wheels, and just a frozen-rope machine at the plate. Today, he carded a clean 2 for 5, one double off the wall and a skidding single to right, and almost made it three with a sharp lineout to short in the eighth. Got caught stealing, too, but was instantly forgiven by management, who are encouraging him to be aggressive. Even fielded his position, tracking down a tailing screamer that would've given Philly the lead late. The kind of catch that fans don't notice, the player not showing an ounce of uncertainty on his break, but which makes scouts and injured first-stringers sit up straighter in warm parts of the country.

The Birds have risen from third place to second in the almost two months I've been gone. Creeping steadily north from Carolina toward Atlanta, in reverse of the geography. It's not as hard to win a division as it used to be. MLB has gone from two to three to four per league in just a few decades, and of course added wild cards too, so even sub-.500 teams can contend till the last week of the season. It's easier still in the NL South, where no team that could help it wanted to play. I guess when they sliced up the new divisions, it was like all but a few of the South candidates could make an argument for residency elsewhere. Houston, claiming something about a coastline, switched leagues and regions entirely, pulling off a daring escape to the AL West. Then Miami made the ridiculous play for inclusion in the East, even though everyone knew that really meant *North*east, and got it, which is why there aren't more Birds games on here. We ended up claiming Cincy, based apparently on proximity to Kentucky. D.C. was an easier grab—they were just too strapped and talentless to think critically about the Civil War. And of course, if you have even a remote sense of fate and destiny you can say that those extra Reds games, which any mapmaker could tell you never should have taken place, were what landed me here.

It's funny watching your team play, and it's funny watching them play well. I don't put a lot of stock in the whole "band of brothers" thing: bonds of familial strength being forged in the hot ovens of cutoff men and postgame beer showers. Honestly, there's just too much money, at this point, in the majors. Dumping Miller Lite on a guy's head feels kind of like acting when you know he can go home and rinse in a marble shower, then pour himself a glass of Johnnie Walker Purple or whatever. I'm exaggerating, but only a little. It's like deep friendships require a level of desperation that hasn't existed since they got rid of the reserve clause. Men, cut off. *Injured* ballplayers, for example, could take a bullet for each other.

Still, you get to know guys extremely well, in a deep, physical way that is a lot like the way you know your family and lifelong friends. All the nuances of tone and subtle facial tics, without the actual caring. And this makes it kind of surreal to view them on television. Like how if you've ever seen a relative interviewed on the evening news, say your uncle shoveling his front walk after a record-setting snowstorm, all you can think of is things he's said at other times, using that voice, or that breed of furrowed brow, and the broadcast actually makes you forget the snow, if anything.

Watching today, I could see confidence back in my team's bones. The snap of our shortstop's wrist as he brought a ball around the horn. The wiggle our (normally reserved) reserve CF added to his bullhorn signal, baseball's universal gesture for two outs. We do it that way so each finger is visible from a distance, so they don't just blend into one. He was never surprised that the two-out plateau had been reached, I saw right away, and was fully expecting that number three was right around the corner. This is the claim of any two-out signal, but I can tell straightaway if a teammate isn't convinced that the condition is deserved. If he raises his fingers drowsily, with effort, I'll know he is thinking of each out as a terrible burden. The team has been losing, and will continue to lose. Today, two outs was a nicely furnished rest stop en route to bigger and better things.

The game's general lazy ease, the slow windmilling of arms and achy bending of torsos, the stuff that looks like just one steady stream of activity to the newbie—baseball, being played—really has endless variations when you know the guys involved. And today, the aggravation of a day game on the road was no match for the men I saw spread across my screen. They had slept well in their Rittenhouse Square hotel. The rook had gone to see the Liberty Bell the previous afternoon. The pre-game routines had felt meaningful and serious.

Obviously, without teammates of your own, you will not be able to see for yourself all that I'm describing. But I do have a tip for any fan trying to get a read on a player. Look to the five-o'-clock shadow. Practically all of us sport one, with the exception of lefty control pitchers over the age of thirty-six, who are sticklers for a smooth cheek. And I have concluded that a ballplayer's shadow is key to deciphering his mood and station. If it makes a guy look like he's ready for a night at the clubs, he's overeager, probably just up from the minors. If it makes him look pale and wolfish, the squad is riding a losing streak. And if it makes him look flat-out mean, he's a man who knows he is in no danger of losing his job. All the other little indicators of emotion, which a viewer sucks in without knowing it, get filtered through that thicket of whiskers.

Don't believe me? Take the Friday before my setback. I was in the middle of a range-of-motion with Erik, and I glanced over and noticed Jenn using this very trick on me, drinking in the contours of my un-Schicked face. *Ennui*, I wanted to call to her, but I was out of breath. *I know, I know, my stubble screams ennui.* I wonder what I look like right now. I haven't seen the business end of a blade in days. Too bad Jenn's not around to tell me.

When I wrote that baseball friendships don't run deep any-more, I didn't mean to say they *never* do. I was just making the point that you get a weird intimacy with guys you might not even like talking to. My best buddy on the team is our backup catcher, Churchy. His last name is Church. He has a first name, but if I told it to you, you might get the impression that it has been uttered even once in the confines of our clubhouse. Does it surprise you that I'd be friends with a guy I'm not connected to by the layout of the dia-mond? Growing up, I was always shocked when I read some "inside the locker room" report detailing a friendship between a star pitcher and some utility RF. Stars are pals with stars, you think when you're young, and players befriend those adjacent to them on the field. The members of a Gold Glove–winning double-play duo *must* vaca-tion together in the offseason, have wives who trade recipes and are thinking of starting a book club. Tinker to Evers to Fairfield County. But truth be told, talent is much less of a connector than location of guys' high schools. Churchy is from New Hampshire. We are joined by either the coldness of our home states or the lack of serious ball-players they produce, I'm not sure which.

I spoke to him this morning. He checks in periodically, keeps my spirits up, gives me the latest dirt on the team. Apparently a few of the guys haven't been changing their socks during this hot streak, and the bus to the park has been smelling like, well, a minor league bus to the park. We didn't get into the situation in left. He's actually an ideal friend to have in a situation like this, because his grip on his roster spot is as shaky as you'll find. Churchy is a parasite, you see—a merry dung beetle who survives on the team despite a career .220 average because he's the only man who can catch our ace's knuckle-derived out pitch. Not to mention that the guy is a head case and Churchy is a master of the becalming mound visit. He has carved a career out of these intangibles, even as tangibles elude him. But talk about joint destinies. If that hurler suffers an injury like mine, Churchy will either get traded to handle some other team's hothead or have effectively blown out his knee too. He'll go through the same six months away from the game, shadow every high and low, every breakthrough and setback. Rehab as pure goneness from the field, without all the workouts and the Florida.

Here in East Palm, the swelling goes down a little more every day. Like my knee is a balloon with the world's smallest leak. The general dry ache is fading. It's not quite pain, as I've said, but it is something above the swishing white noise of true painlessness. That condition you are physically unable to notice until it's gone. I am a bona fide crutches master now, so the week hasn't been a total loss. For example, when I come out here, instead of sidling up to the door and sliding it with my hand, I stop several feet short, lean on one crutch, and extend the other one toward the edge of the glass, pressing the rubber cap against the handle and drawing it open. I don't really know why I do this, except that mastering tricks of coordination improves my general mood. If my leg were worse, I'd probably be opening beer cans within the month. Lots and lots of beer cans.

*Saturday June 26*

I'm scheduled to go in Monday for a once-over, to make sure I'm still on track for a Thursday return to my course of therapy. We'll be starting with light weights and extension exercises. The modern recovering athlete goes from zero movement to weighted movement within the space of a single workweek. There is no longer time set aside for a leg to just go about its business, trundling around under normal atmospheric conditions. Teams do not trust the atmosphere. It is difficult to determine the atmosphere's agenda.

In any case, it will be interesting to see everyone after our little hiatus. I feel kind of like a starting pitcher who didn't travel with the team for a weekend series because his rotation spot wasn't coming up. The time away wasn't long, but he knows there were pockets of turbulence on the team plane that he will forever have missed. For example, Jenn—she and I had just settled into a little rapport at the time of my incident, finally moving beyond weather and baseball, like PARC was Lexington Avenue and one of us was the doorman. At the moment of my knee twinge, we were in the middle of a conversation about choosing kids' birthday presents. I had been remarking that I guess it's not like anniversaries, where you at least have that guide about materials, tin and wood and the like. And before she could respond, with confusion or a remarkably sweet, musical laugh or whatever, I was going down. I remember this because of what happened to interrupt it, and I'll wager she forgets it for the same reason. It seems certain that we won't ever finish the conversation, which is fine of course, but also somehow sad—terrifically sad, if it is at all. The kind of hard little truth that might not matter in any real way but can just bowl you over for three minutes. She was just going to respond with confusion, I'm pretty sure of it. Though when Jenn laughs, you recall that she has red hair.

So Monday will be another big day, like last Monday, and like selected Tuesdays and Fridays. I always feel like I should do something to prepare for a day like this. It just seems strange to make the step up from eating cereal topped with sliced banana to receiving information valued in the millions of dollars. Strange in terms of altitude gain. You feel a need to acclimatize, like mountain climbers do. For example, I think it would make sense for them to make you not eat for twenty-four hours before a surgery, even if there was no medical reason for it, just so you could get into that place of difference. Not that it's reasonable to do something crazy simply to point out how funny it all feels. In my case, I've noticed I have a tendency to actually exaggerate my normal rituals prior to abnormal days. Maybe it's a ballplayer's fallback. I shower extremely thoroughly. My teeth brushing is excellent. It's like I can't get away from myself, so I become more myself, and then I hand the whole package over to the doctors.

## Sunday June 27

I'm not the *only* person I've dated, of course. Don't let the schedule fool you: there have been 1:05 a.m. starts in the Eastern Time Zone. The tarp has been flung from the field in downtown Raleigh-Durham, and not just after a lengthy delay. In fact, my first season in the league, I very nearly developed "something of a reputation," and I don't mean for my rock-solid baserunning. You see, at the beginning it's perfect, because you don't know what to think of yourself. You don't know if you're a viable long-term prospect. So every date is like a personal tryout with this smooth-skinned scout, you're out there trying to prove that whatever "it" is, you got it.

But then the problem is, you do prove it. And once you're a lineup fixture, once you're penciled in in pen, something changes, the whole deal starts to turn inside out. The game stops being an opportunity to excel in other areas. The game takes you over, takes on wrinkles and textures until it becomes almost too fascinating, all you can see. Other areas become ways to think about the game. And in my experience, you eventually get to have throes of passion or throws, but not both. "You could have anyone," this is said to you on a regular basis, but all that means is you're stuck with yourself.

Well, I'm no longer a leggy blonde. Tearing a CL is kind of like kicking a body addiction cold turkey. Gone are the admirers, the hero-worshipers. All of which are me. It's disconcerting, really. I mean if there is one thing a ballplayer can do, it's admire. We gaze, nearly longingly, at our own feats. In Little League, you will be chastised publicly by another child's father if you dare watch a ball you've hit, but the rule disappears at this level. This is because the things we do are so beautiful. Or always might be—that's what we have to find out. They don't want us to stop creating, it inspires us. And so they let us look. And then the moment we go down in a less than elegant fashion, that disappears, everyone is all "Look away, you don't want to see this, save yourself."

"But ballgirls. What about ballgirls?" I've been asked the question, of course. Is it any different with these fellow stadium dwellers? These pretty young women stationed next to us on folding chairs, like a personal audience for our achievements? Who can appreciate them too, because they also have to field those sharply hit grounders, and usually can't. Does romance ever blossom? Do we ever dramatize a catch, dive when we don't need to, work to score ourselves a date? I'm sure it's happened, but the short answer is no, not really. I think in that case it's just too predictable—it hits too close to home. On their side too, we're really equidistant. Because it's not just that your teammates are like relatives, as I mentioned the other day. After a while the game itself becomes your family. You love it, you hate it, and above all you know everything about it. It would feel like crossing some painted line to start something on the field.

*Monday June 28*

I don't know why they call it a "once-over." How many times would you think they'd go over it? And on the other hand, if it's necessary at all then it's important, so why the need to make it sound rushed? As I've noted before, you have to be careful when they try to trick you with language.

My "once" was about forty minutes long, full of proddings and pokes and halting strolls down hallways. Guys in calf-length shorts and women in bras, watching me through the viewfinders of lifted weight stacks, trying to pretend they weren't interested instead of just not *being* interested. Finally, Jens announced I was good to go. "Xandy, you're good to go," is exactly what he said. *Where?* I thought.

All that dress-rehearsing of the injury, that feeling it, tends to throw a dark cloud across positive news, and the whole morning built up a tension that is only now starting to exit my body. It's actually refreshing to be momentarily directing my world with taps on a keyboard. My powers in this arena, at least, are at 100%. Maybe this has been a draw since the beginning. Who can enjoy writing more than a guy with a leg injury? The whole thing happens with your hands.

It's funny to me how writing feels as a physical activity. Maybe as an athlete I'm just conditioned to look at things that way. I guess for me, writing is sort of like the opposite of soccer: all hands and no feet. And I wonder if the thing that happens to the disabled, where the loss of a sense or limb strengthens everything else, applies to me. Could I be a better writer because my body only has one leg to manage?

Today's news means I'm once again ambulatory, of course. The crutches have been set aside. Do not take this to mean I am "walking." I have adopted a sort of rolling glide for my right half, in which I bend my foot, lean low, and rock through the stride. I am basically trying to pull off a snowshoe function with my right lower leg—to extend the moment of foot-to-ground contact across as much space and time as possible. I guess in a broader sense I'm spreading out the reality of the moment into something paper-thin, so that the step never quite happens.

But hey, at least my crutches are aside. I do mean this literally. They are off to the side, leaning against the mantel in the living room, above the fake fireplace. After I was dropped off at home—still no driving till at least next week—I used them to get to this spot I'd selected for propping them, because carrying them there seemed illogical in deep ways, and then I departed under my own power. What I'm saying is, how is one supposed to approach and exit the place he or she will drop a newly unnecessary piece of medical equipment? And what is one supposed to do with all that gear? This house is slowly turning into a living museum of a leg injury, full of monuments to my ailment discarded where they were last deployed. In the corner of my bedroom, there is a full leg brace with a foot attachment, which I used the first few weeks, and it just stands there—because it is a leg, and what it does is stand—and it looks ridiculously creepy and futuristic at night when there is just enough light in the room to make it and little else visible, but I may need it again, and it's not like it makes more sense to keep it in the kitchen.

*Tuesday June 29*

This morning I took a cab to the beach. I realize this might not even count. Like how if you wear shorts, instead of swim trunks, you only "saw" the beach, regardless of whether you had any intention of going in. Which mindset I fell into this morning. Before I left, I donned my suit subconsciously, carefully sliding the right trunk leg, the built-in underwear, over the knee in question, somehow not thinking big-picture. It didn't strike me until I hit the sand that I wouldn't be taking a dip. Things like that are written into contracts.

Around here you wait for it to cool down, and that is when you go to the beach. And so when I woke up and found the weather descending into the 80s, like some tiring control pitcher, I pulled out the West Palm Beach–Palm Beach–North Palm Beach–Palm Beach Gardens–Boynton Beach–East Palm Beach–Area Yellow Pages and hailed myself a taxi. Despite the title of this municipality, this was my first such trip. A name like that can mislead, though. I like those English, or even sometimes New English towns that have "by-the-sea" or "upon-the-river" tacked on at the end, as though you couldn't glean that information from a rudimentary map. How do they decide which ones get this treatment? Duluth-by-the-lake. Duluth-upon-Superior. Doesn't quite work.

The beach was mostly empty. A few dogwalkers and runners, one large, well-Speedoed German-speaking family looking lost outside of tourist season. Three teenage surfers fought over a frothy little four-foot break. I've always wanted to take surfing lessons, and now would really be the ideal time, if not for the fact that this time has been brought about by the world's least surfing-compatible injury. It occurred to me, as I reclined on the Florida Panthers beach towel I'd found in a hall closet, that I was the only one in attendance without either company, a pet, or a sporting activity, but this didn't especially bother me. I'm figuring out that there is really no way to fight the great quantities of alone-time rehab gives you. Not unless you're the sort of athlete who installs friends in fake jobs. And I am finding myself joining that species of people who know they will be doing most things by themselves. Rather than complaining about it, they eventually start planning for it. The ones you see reading Russian novels in Italian restaurants, while the folks who were simply stood up are left leafing through a brochure they found by the hostess lectern. Baseball teams and loners frequent the same sorts of places—hotel bars, steakhouses—so I have witnessed this often. And the key to not being toppled by despair, it seems to me anyway, is really embracing that planner's attitude: the one basic upside your life now has, which is that you have a pretty clear sense of how any given day will unfold, since you're the only one involved.

So I had packed a liter of water, two turkey-and-provolones on wheat, a little paperback thriller I found in the brother's collection, and no bookmark, because the book was 172 pages long, I read at a steady sixty pages an hour, and I had told the cab to pick me up in three hours. This is what I'm saying. The sunglasses I wore, the SPF 30 I applied before I left. If you had seen me there supine and shirtless, you might have thought I had a familiar face. I would be surprised if my status as an elite athlete entered your mind. A pro ballplayer on the beach isn't even that exciting from a physique standpoint. Any garden-variety personal trainer from Palm Beach Gardens will have better pecs. The only difference between me and some other young man is that if you met me in a less injured state and joined me for a day at water's edge, and we got out the mitts and dog-chewed ball we'd brought in a canvas bag from L.L. Bean, I would throw it harder and farther than you, even as my excellent rotation through the hips made me expend less energy, such that each toss looked effortless. And if we got a game of Wiffleball homerun derby going, and we summoned everyone on that stretch of sand to join us, even if we invited that entire barrier island, I'll be honest with you, I would win.

## Wednesday June 30

A month ends today—the grand old month of June. The longest of my life, someone else always says. And yet it still feels cut off awkwardly soon, just when it was hitting its stride. I've always thought June was a misfit in the thirty-day crowd. September, sure, that makes sense. November I can at least buy. But June is a bright and bighearted month, a month of excess. Jammed with heat, practically spilling over with evening sun. Take it from a guy whose job traverses twilight. If you get into a snappy June pitcher's-duel with a team in the southwestern reaches of its time zone, they may never have to turn on the stadium lights. How are you going to tell me a month like that doesn't go for thirty-one days?

Months matter more to ballplayers than they do to folks in other professions, because they make convenient dividing points for our statistics. I take it you've heard the calendar-based nicknames: a Mr. October is clutch, so of course some wiseacre coined the term Mr. May, for a guy who pads his statistics when no one cares. I don't think you'll be surprised to learn that I'm something of a Mr. July. I'm a career .308 hitter in that month, against .273 overall, though Jeff has never had much luck with this as a selling point in contract negotiations. Not too sexy, though I'd argue a win counts for as much whenever you get it. I can't really explain it myself, this little outlier of mine, but I think other guys just get distracted out there in the middle of the summer, with no beginning or end in sight. My standard plugging away suddenly produces singles past bored shortstops, an increase in hitters' counts on pitchers with mid-season mechanical flaws. I am, for a few sweet weeks, a genuine All-Star, and just when the evening sports programs start thinking about a two-minute profile piece, everyone snaps back out of their enabling funks and I drop back down to where I belong. It's an annual cycle.

Maybe my July luck will carry over into the rehab arena. What's the Para Atlantic Rehabilitation Center equivalent of a thirty-five-point bump in batting average, I wonder? 1.5 fewer groans during a leg bridge? Three extra lunge reps bringing about only pain manageable by something over-the-counter? It's a point worth considering. When you think about it, how is a *baseball* player, that Certified Public Accountant of the sports world, supposed to stay sane in his rehab without any sense of the stats? Imagine trying to wrap your head around Hank Aaron's 755 without ever having heard of Babe Ruth. Sometimes I think everything in my life is pegged to the benchmark of the .300 batting average. I mean, I'd argue everything in *your* life is. That's just America.

But calendars. They get into your head, for better or worse. And I'm finding something refreshing about the fact that tomorrow's return to therapy happens on a 1st. Jens insisted on it, schedule be damned, and I could see why. Sure, right now it looks like a 31st, but as soon as you wake up and hear it isn't, you're already starting to forget what June felt like. It happens every time, in better hotel chains from Washington to D.C. And it's easier to get yourself into that mindset of "fresh starts" and "new beginnings" when the date seems to agree. The best pro athletes have no problem sinking their teeth into all that terminology, but as I have pointed out a number of times, I am not one of them. I need all the help I can get.

# JULY

## Thursday July 1

Iarrived at PARC this morning to find the entire staff assembled in the front hall, split up into two lines, one on either side. A gantlet to be run. As soon as I entered, they all broke out in applause. Nurses and receptionists and professional stretchers, most of whom I'd never even met, all joining in salute to their halfway-famous client. The only thing missing were those "Get Well Soon!" balloons, the ones made out of metal.

Jens stood at the front, clapping hardest and beaming. Which only really made sense if you figured he was proud of himself for masterminding this little show of support, but I didn't mind. "Xandy," he said with a smile, really extending the word, like *Xaaandy*, like I was an old friend, and he gave me an iron handshake and a supplemental pat on the delt. Then he told me they at the Center just want me to know they're with me every step of the way. Thunderous, raging ironies in *that* line.

The whole thing was funny for me. I realized it was the first time I'd been clapped for since my heroic ride off Ohioan grass. They say with stuff like that you don't miss it until it's gone, but that's not really true in my case. You miss it when it returns. I haven't exactly been sitting around this patio longing for a crowd to appear and shower me with applause. But when this morning's friendly group of twenty-five-or-so gave me a hand, even though it had nothing to do with what an assemblage of 22,471 produces for a professional on the field, I had the thought for the first time in my life: *I have been clapped for on many occasions.*

After a few years in the majors, you can tell which city you're in by the way the crowd claps. Or more specifically, you can tell the age of the franchise. Baseball towns of long-standing, like a Boston or a Philly, rarely actually put their hands together. They yell, they gesture, they groan. Their sonic base, a kind of low stadium-wide grumble, is built via the kicking of seatbacks and the beery shoving of co-workers. But in an expansion city—Phoenix, say—they applaud cheerfully in the sitting position, like the impassioned sport on display is some sort of Off Broadway production. They'll even sometimes clap for a particularly agile play by the opposition, which frankly is kind of insulting. It's like they're selling out the whole idea of competition. We might as well walk off the field.

My ovation this morning at the Para Atlantic Rehabiliation Center, though, had no geography to it. It was a generic American clap, rooted in candles blown out at birthday parties, in horrendous violin recitals. Flat and wandering, unrhythmic. And then it was on to my session. Which went fine, in all the technical regards. The knee was stiff, and we were all too focused and nervous to talk much, Jenn especially it seemed, but it had no surprises in store. My pain remained at a level that other people were comfortable with. I went through the motions, and the range-of-motions. But still, there was something dark lodged like a bone-chip in the middle of it all. It's like in some ways the "good" days are the toughest, because you learn just how much relativity you have to throw at the situation for that word to even function, to not just fall right out of the dictionary. It can be exhausting, trucking that much context around on your back.

When I got home, I took about six rolling steps toward the living room, two hops down, then two more to the couch, where I sank into those deep, off-white cushions. And straightaway sank into a deep, off-white sleep. I must have been out cold within forty-five seconds of closing the front door. Or actually the opposite of cold. In a moment of high environmentalism, I'd shut off the central A/C on my way out this morning, and seeing as I didn't have the foresight to flick it back on en route to the living room, I woke up about an hour ago, filmed head to toe in a feverish sweat. The kind that rises out of every long-lost pore and just hovers there. They don't make sweat like that north of the Georgia line.

Sleeping during the day isn't the norm for me, I am just not a napper by disposition. But there are different classes of naps. Take it from a guy whose work forces him to call 7 a.m. bedtime at least once a month. Quick bite at the continental breakfast, then it's good-night. Baseball players in general have a strange relationship to sleep. Or I guess it's that we have a strange relationship to being tired. There is the obvious question, so often asked by non-players: What about a baseball game, exactly, tires you out? The total running for the evening rarely exceeds a third of a mile. It might not even crack the hundred-yard mark if you're a 1B who strikes out often. And this is interrupted by long stretches of sitting, chewing, and drinking electrolyte-laden drinks. It all bears a strong resemblance to what you might do to relax on a Saturday. The visuals are not on our side.

All I can say is that, when a major leaguer's body is playing base-ball, his mind is really playing basketball—making hard cuts and boxing out and rolling off picks. The athletics happen upstairs, with-out the player really noticing it. And after three hours of apparent standing around, he's suddenly just totally wiped and ravenous. SAT takers and ballplayers know what it is to be dead tired when you've barely sweated.

And today, I think what happened was I basically had a dou-ble session. There was the one I went through under watchful eyes. And then, shadowing every lunge, like a pitcher backing up a corner sacker, there was the thought of what I was doing, what it meant. Whether it might fall apart, and what sound would let me know. Deep knee-bends of the brain. And that's not to mention the added psychic gasoline involved in starting once again from zero. Accel-eration of that kind just guzzles fuel. I do my best work once things have been rolling for a while. Like I say, I'm a July hitter.

They actually have a term now for proceeding through the stages of a rehab schedule. They call it "going through the modalities." Can you even get your head around that? Around the heights of modernity this game has attained? A modality for the Babe was orange juice with his vodka. It was two consecutive nights with the woman he'd married. It's like baseball spent so long believing in nothing but dirt and bunts and socks that once they discovered the joys of bloodsucking agents and empty metaphors, they just went buck-wild.

I'm appreciative, of course, of the level of medicine that can come up with this level of language. I know what they are trying to say: no injury, anymore, is unfixable. Every on-field incident is just a title page, a preface to a beautifully orchestrated response. Back in the era of the twi-night doubleheader, there really was a whole different idea of the game. Your career could be finished by one deep divot, then off you were to a life as a mechanic, and a subpar mechanic at that. A CL ripped like mine, even, where it could have been worse, meant curtains. It was understood, and accepted: the end was just a hard slide away. Now a single play *can* instantly end your career, sure, but these are the catastrophes—line drives to the head, fiery crashes into outfield walls. They are by definition glitches in the code, outside the course of the game. A pitcher drafted early enough can have six surgeries on the same elbow before they finally tell him, "You know, maybe throwing objects is no longer your best career option."

Pool work is the king of all modalities. Whatever distrust GMs have in air, they have that much faith in water. As long as you're partially submerged, they'll let you do just about anything. A little while ago I got back in the pool, for a little Friday catch-up session. Like I say, they give you this flotation belt to wear for pool-running, then they have you take these exaggerated high steps as you hoof it at top speed to nowhere. Other than the belt, and the fact that you're alone, in the deep end, and I guess the fact that you're not technically running at all, the whole thing is just like those water races you do with your siblings when you're a kid. Drew routinely beat me in those. In this area, once again, being a ballplayer asks things of you that have nothing to do with playing ball, and which you may or may not be inclined toward vis-à-vis temperament or talent. It means being a frequent flier, a man who takes his vacations in winter but is discouraged from skiing, the face of a city he's probably not from—and it means being a swimmer. Imagine if being an offensive lineman also meant being . . . a squash player.

They do have me do some proper swimming, too, at the end of the sessions, to activate the upper body and extend the cardio workout. Only they don't allow me to kick on my crawl. Apparently it's too harsh a movement for the knee—this directive from Jens, who devised these sessions but only attended the first. My father, who taught me that stroke when I was six years old, focusing specifically on the legs as the source of power, would have cringed to see me in that aquatics center this afternoon—his precious freestyle now lopped off at the waist, my legs trailing uselessly behind, getting a free ride. It just goes against all he values, scientifically as well as politically. Which isn't the right way to think about it, but is true.

The lagoon looks lovely right now. Like a bowl full of juice. If juice was served that way, and occasionally fish leapt from it. It's funny, sitting out here tonight, I've found myself struck by an uncommon thought: pleasure is about to be had in local watering holes, and I will be missing out on it in my essentially homebound state. That notion does sail across my brain from time to time, but not normally because a weekend has arrived. As a ballplayer, you certainly miss having weekends in your life, in a general way, but after the first few months of your career, you no longer miss them on cue, the way a lawyer working late might. You don't hit 5 p.m. on a Friday and start thinking about the nearest happy hour. The happiness of the hour goes unnoticed. At that moment, you are underground, beneath gross tonnage of concrete and steel. You might as well be a submariner, for all the clock of the working world matters to you.

On my way out of the Center today, I overheard the staff making plans for the evening. Some sort of group outing spearheaded by Erik to extract the most possible merriment from the afternoon discounts at the beachfront bars. I pushed out of the doors as he was giving a speech about how the margaritas would be the most frozen, the dollar deals the cheapest he'd yet found—and he had seen some dollar deals. They were going to chill so hard in so much sun, and it was never going to get in his eyes. Did Jenn really go in for these gatherings? Did it matter if she did?

As I limped into the car, stray words from their break room bounced across the asphalt. I listened for Jenn's voice but couldn't make it out. "Happy!" everyone seemed to be shouting, except for her. "Happy, special, *happy!*"

*Saturday July 3*

Experience has shown me that two weeks of inactivity puts you just past that line where you really start to lose your fitness. You can go ten days, and you may technically fall back, but you're not going to suffer when you get back in the metaphorical saddle. But something happens around day fourteen. Deep muscle tissues clue into a trend, and for the first time they start viewing laziness as the rule rather than the exception.

Sure enough, today I woke up in a blaze of warm, healthy pains. All the modern muscles of my upper body—the obliques, the rhomboids, the trapezii of the world, the ones that didn't exist in the '70s—felt tender and sharp, like they had no memory of the thousands of fine swings they've produced on my behalf. I associate this sensation with the holiday season, when I return to a workout program after a brief post-season break. It is my Advent. That's really the only time I will have missed enough days for the soreness pump to prime. My working summer is a minefield of aches and tweaks, of course, but those are the opposite thing, and involve no sweetness at all. The feeling I have today is actually kind of a treat. That sensation of shampooing hair with buzzing, swim-tired arms—any athlete has to love it. Today I had to alternate left and right hands to lather, that's how beat I was, and I'm sure my soaping missed whole stretches of upper-middle back. My calves are wobbly too, especially the underutilized right one, and when I parked myself out here after lunch, I stacked pillows on the ottoman, then had to prop each leg by hand, after which I sat back and marinated in the fine hurt. Pain not indicative of injury: you can about become a connoisseur of it.

This neighborhood is coming alive in advance of the 4th. Grandchildren have been pouring out of minivans all day, and moms in the upper end of my demographic have been passing the house on serious, scowly runs. Those rudimentary drugstore explosives—the mini-tanks, the "snakes"—have been popping off since noon, and I can practically hear from here the black marks they're leaving on front paths. I can tell you from personal experience, those stains will never quite come out.

A funny thing happened about an hour ago. I got recognized, for the first time in weeks. I think you forget about your fame a little bit, when you're not around a group of guys who are in that same boat, all adopting that low-grade suspicion. And I guess I'd dropped some of that armor down here. I honestly didn't remember there was anything to hide, reclining out here this afternoon, and that just invites being spotted.

It's always the same thing with kids, who are among the few who actually know how they know you. They'll form a small group about thirty yards off—you the plate to their third base—then gradually migrate closer, advancing their position in small increments, like they are taking a totally unsafe lead. Does Jenn's son do this too? I should check. At some point, one of them will be pushed out of the huddle, and he/she will stride over with shyness in his aspect. Without making eye contact, the youth will ask if you are who you are, and once this is settled, the others will join and encircle you where you sit. Today the little gaggle formed behind the house to my right, in the backyard of the neighbors who keep the mini Winnebago in the driveway, and pretty soon I found myself surrounded by about eight young aficionados of my sport, all with Little League hats or summer camp T-shirt hems for me to sign. I'd been out of the autographing loop. I had to hobble inside and scour the kitchen drawers for a pen.

These really are funny, rambunctious little events for kids, I've noticed. Youths in the presence of an autographing athlete always seem to start jostling each other, or begin throwing rocks for distance, or commence impromptu jumping contests. Maybe some sociologist can explain this. I don't think they're actually trying to impress you, per se. It's like they just want to express that the physical world in general is something they value. Maybe this is why they're so quick to forgive your bad games. I've had the experience many times, on the walk to the players' lot after a loss, of a kid telling me not to feel bad about some error or botched sacrifice that frankly I *should* feel bad about. They get that the point is just to be out there, taking your speed and strength and power out for a spin, and it's like they sense that you've forgotten.

For the same reason I guess, today's visitors were grave about the knee, submitting me to a whole host of detailed questions, nodding seriously at each response. Kids ask about pain right off the bat. I think I really threw them when I limped that way. It was just so straightforward. And they couldn't stop gawking at the brace. The beautiful athletic equipment of a tragic athletic incident. Hard to wrap your head around, for sure.

Now a bunch of them are setting up sparklers by the edge of the lagoon. They're focusing to a degree that suggests they're creating a pattern, but I can't detect one yet. When I was growing up, the kids on my block used to assemble in our neighbors' yards and arrange sparklers in the shapes of our first initials. This was in the days before I was known as Xandy—that name didn't come to be until High-A, which is where your final handle tends to get forged. The one they'll call you at the 50th reunion buffet. Back then, I was a B, which was unfortunate, because I never had enough sparklers to produce smooth curves. My B's always ended up weird and pointy. And anyway, it's just not a fierce enough letter to look good written in fire.

It always seems to throw off the national sensibility when the 4th of July falls on a Saturday or Sunday. You expect the 4th to extend the weekend, not to be trapped inside it. And then there is a lack of consensus among employers over whether to give their company the Friday or the Monday, and everyone just feels disoriented and vaguely cheated, even though the net vacation days are the same. I know this doesn't apply in my line of work, but trust me, I can feel the different attitude blowing in from the stands, along with the plastic bags and mustard-stained napkins. If I were a working stiff, I'd want my 4ths on Thursdays or Tuesdays, which realistically drag Fridays and Mondays into their vacationy reach. This followed by Fridays and Mondays, with Saturday and Sunday lagging far behind. Wednesday is the worst, of course, there's just nothing you can do with that but wait for next year.

The Birds have a weirdly good record on Independence Days, and now that I mention it, on Labor Days too. It doesn't make sense, but they have it anyway. Memorial Day is a wash. Divvy things up enough and you find all sorts of unbelievable stories happening squarely in the middle of baseball. Guys who have never in their careers had a hit in Mountain Daylight Time, or utilitymen who flat-out *own* first-ballot Hall of Fame locks. Whole suspense novels and rags-to-riches tales getting penned by Anonymous in the heart of the sport, so centered they're invisible to the naked eye.

True to form, yesterday the squad tore up the visiting Nationals, our outfield bats leading the charge, sending their SP to the showers before he actually needed one. A 9–4 win, which for me has always been the line where a blowout begins. A whole exponent higher than your opponent, a different class of scoring. And today they actually do have the day off, just like they're citizens. But only because Monday is MLB's travel day.

I guess I was the only one who had to go into work this morning. The subject wasn't so much as broached. Why no long weekend for the guy on workers' comp? I've been thinking about this, the best way to explain it. It's like time in the majors is managed at a distance. Today doesn't really belong to this week, but to a long stretch of them—whole calendars of Mondays. And that being the case, what kind of sense would it make for me to get a holiday? At certain levels of money, professional sports teams simply stop believing in the present tense. You don't have a meal, you have a diet. You don't have a workout, you have a program. Wealth means time cut in bigger chunks. Among other things.

But if you don't advertise it too much, you can still claim some current events for yourself. And yesterday afternoon, as elsewhere my Birds were swatting the Nats, I determined that the way to feel right about spending the holiday alone was to embrace everything about it. To make it a day on its own terms, I mean. Not sloping toward the ones coming before or after—not connected to any longer streaks or tendencies.

So what I did was, I got into the 4th of July. I invented myself for the day as a patriot—a national, if you will. I took a cab over to the Publix, and when I arrived I gave the driver a twenty to wait while I went in and filled a cart. It's not like Manhattan here, you can't just hail a fresh taxi. Then again, it's not even like Manhattan in Brooklyn, as I found out in my whirlwind summer with the Cyclones. Today, in the Publix sphere, I stocked up on the makings of fresh-squeezed lemonade. I bought ground chuck and ears of corn, pickles and Budweisers and red-white-and-blue bunting, which a short while ago I hung from the gutter, like the patio was Yankee Stadium in 1924. It was convenient, because they had moved all these items into the same part of the store, like they were Staff

Recommendations, and I didn't even use up all the time I'd bought myself. Then, as the sun went down and folks got ready to watch the town fireworks, for which the lagoon area provides a fine and unobstructed view, I prepared myself a feast. And it was downright kingly, just sitting there in the middle of it all, hearing the glee of my countrymen, watching the hot sky beam with color like so much pride. As you get older, you become more practiced at determining what is and what isn't the grand finale, which bursts of firecrackers are frauds and which are possessed of a genuine urgency. And last night I knew exactly when the real one had started.

## Tuesday July 6

I got out of the pool this afternoon to find a message from Churchy on my cell phone. He was calling from Chicago, where the Birds are in town to play a midweek three against the Cubs, sandwiched between weekenders in Carolina and in Milwaukee. One of those geographically convenient series that have that funny touch of the old barnstorm to them. A sort of "Hey, we were just flying by your city and thought you lads might be up for a spot of baseball."

Churchy had a little surprise in store. The All-Star Game is being held in Raleigh-Durham this year, just a week from today in fact. I'd practically forgotten about it. Apparently the league was looking for ways to get some local color involved in the proceedings, and that cagey old catcher pulled some strings to land me, the wounded hometown veteran, a spot sitting in with the broadcasters for an inning. You know those how's-it-healing bull sessions they have sometimes, to show the human side of the game? Well that will be me on Tuesday, top and bottom of the fourth.

Those things are always kind of ridiculous, I know. The athlete is in a funny spot up there, perched on his stool. Perched between the playing world and the world of jeans and button-downs. And then the ex-player in the booth is always eager to win the rapport game. It's like he's proud of himself for being able to chew the fat with a major leaguer still in his prime, but he's gloating a little to see that you too have been forcibly removed from the action. He likes the notion of being on equal footing.

Still, I'll admit that as I stood there dripping, holding my phone a little away from my ear so as not to get it wet, the idea of playing the starting leftfielder role for fifteen to forty nationally televised minutes, depending on the strength and interest of the defense, sounded pretty appealing. I don't want you to think I'm not susceptible to this sort of thing. And I underwent a rush of gratitude toward my buddy, the backup backstop. Catchers do make the best managers, that's a baseball truism of long standing, and it isn't just because they know when to call a pitchout. The best ones essentially have masters' degrees in psychology, and old Churchy read my mind like I was a sore reliever standing sixty feet six inches away, not a blue outfielder 1,300 miles to the south-southeast.

So a little trip is now in the works. He got the team to shell out for a first-class ticket up, naturally—I fly out of West Palm Sunday morning. And I'll be spending the remaining innings of the game in the owners' box, with the various fleshy bigwigs sipping their free Chivas. I'm sure the jaunt will also entail this or that group dinner with whichever players are in the room when someone calls to make a reservation. Some $4K affair where the vets order a five-hundred-dollar bottle of tawny port they won't drink, just so they can stick the tab on the youngest guy on the roster. That was never my world. I wasn't good enough for more than the most basic hazing. Our closer made me carry his bags for half my rookie season. The other OFs hid my glove ten minutes before we took the field for my first big-league start. I mean, really giving it to the kid. No one even stuck around to see how I resolved it.

My point is, my talent isn't exactly uppity. No one feels upstaged when it's in the room. And I always feel slightly like an outsider at those kinds of megastar dinners, even though by the standards of the working world, I'm squarely in the fraternity. An example from today: I was checking that voicemail in a locker room that has hard wooden benches, rather than leather chairs, and features a pretty advanced mildew problem in the shower room. Whereas if I were an All-Star, they would have worked out a membership deal at some private club down here. It would make no sense, this place is just fine, and to my mind a better place to lay down your grunt work, but they would have done it anyway. But on the other hand, as I was standing there in the Five Palms aquatics center, I also knew exactly what it looked like in the locker room Churchy was calling from, which was cut into the foundations of Wrigley Field. I knew what tunnel he must have been standing in, just past the bathrooms off the main players' area. I knew what it smelled like. As it happens, that tunnel smells like piss—but it's Wrigley, so it's vintage piss. Stan Musial's piss. Anyway, it's piss I know about.

*Wednesday July 7*

The big news of the day is automotive, not locomotive. I am back behind the wheel. Keep an eye out for the twentysomething male rolling around in sensible Swedish engineering—he's hard to miss. It occurred to me this afternoon: a Volvo may be the only car you'll truly never see a major league ballplayer drive. I guess Volkswagens are also pretty rare. But actually that's not really true, because at any given moment the league will always include at least one vintage Beetle aficionado, even if the last of the Microbus-favoring Deadheads faded back into the minors sometime in the late '80s. He's a sidearm relief man, you can bank on that, with a candy-apple paint job he buffs on his Mondays off.

No, ballplayers opt for the extremes. That can mean extremely fancy cars, obviously—your Maybachs, your Bentleys. But plenty of times, it's the opposite: the Ford F-250s. Cars that are, I guess you'd say, extremely American. It's important to understand that this is 100% a choice. Even a guy making the league minimum could afford anything BMW might manufacture, and just above that we're already in Ferrari territory. So what car a player drives ends up being a pretty uncut look at his personality, the way he sees himself in the world. And it's like those guys with the pickups—pickups with $10K after-market sound systems, mind you—have figured out that the farthest extreme you can reach is back near the bottom. The very vehicle you'd be driving if you'd blown your arm in high school, then stuck around your town and found work as a subcontractor. Only here it's the conscious selection of a man making $4M per. A very different automobile.

What would you guess I drive, when I'm on my home turf? Would a black Dodge Viper, $88K base, strike you right? V-10, 600hp, more valves than you'd believe, 8.4 liters of oxygen getting displaced to somewhere other than here? Here is my own extreme: the fastest car Detroit makes. I want buckets of speed, but pegging myself to the Michigan state line makes the purchase feel more personal, not to mention saving me a hundred grand. I used to have a Corvette, which comes close, but then you're a little like the truck guys. They're nice cars, sure, but realistically there's a slumming component there that's just pointless. Like the occasional player who drives an old beat-up Taurus because he's "salt of the earth." Now *that's* showy. Imagine if I did that. What would I have to say to Jenn when she showed up with her son in her certified pre-owned Mercury Sable? Seriously, I'd like to know: What could we talk about then?

One thing that's true of vehicles nationwide is if you don't drive them, they won't start. Though show me one person other than my father who thinks of this before it's too late—who actually pops by the garage on a biweekly basis to give the engine a stir. I climbed into the Volvo at 8:15 this morning, congratulating myself on a speedy morning routine. The knee slows everything, but I've introduced some key new edits, and I'm really getting my times down. And as I put the key in the ignition I suddenly knew exactly what was going to happen next: nothing. A few dying flickers on the speedometer and tachy, but not even one cough under the hood. So I called up the first jump guy I found in the phonebook, and I called the Center to tell them I'd be late. ("Oh I think she'll wait, Mr. Alexander," the receptionist assured me.) And while I was killing time I called up my pops, too, knowing he'd get a good long chuckle out of it. Ever since I made the majors, I've had this urge to keep him informed of my lapses in common sense. As if he'd think that because I'm in the Show I'm at risk of becoming perfect.

The mechanic who gave me the start turned out to be a Birds fan, so he knew who I was. He even had a sense of humor about it. "Guess I don't need to ask for your autograph," he said with a particular dryness when I signed the credit card receipt. I told him he should just keep the third carbon, I can never figure out who gets that one anyway. They say it's a stereotype to assume that guys like mechanics and tree surgeons will always know sports, but I think it's also a stereotype to think they shouldn't. It's like you can't ask a guy in a blue-collar profession his opinion on the Series anymore without it somehow meaning something.

I did feel bad about holding up the whole rehab show. I ended up pulling into my glistening parking space a full fifty minutes behind schedule. When you're the valued client it's almost worse, if you have any moral compass at all, because you know everyone's obligated to forgive you. And Jenn had her kid there today and everything, and as we know, the young man doesn't even enjoy baseball. I've noticed Jenn is the only one at the Center who calls me Blake, which for some reason I appreciate. Erik seems to think if he says "Xandy" enough I'll cave and start calling him Erik-y.

The good news is that the knee is moving forward. This morning was the first in which I honestly thought the setback was in the rearview mirror. For the first time in a while, I had a vision of not just being OK, but being impressive. I didn't simply want to play, I wanted to defeat opponents! I can't think of the last time wins and losses even entered my mind.

## Thursday July 8

More progress with my little All-Star Game cameo. This morning I spoke to an intern from the league office, an enthusiastic young woman named Nicole. She left a message on the house phone while I was in the shower, and when I played it back and heard a female speaker, in the seconds before she said "from MLB," I became very curious. And how like a phone of mine to dissolve a promising voice into pine tar and resin.

Nicole told me when I'd need to be where, in preparation for going on-air. I am to head over from my box to an area behind the press booth during the top of the third, where I'll wait for the game to pace me in. They call it a booth—it's really more of a balcony. I wanted to ask her which top of the third. Ballplayers don't think of innings like laymen. Each out condition—none, one, or two—really amounts to its own sub-inning. How could it not? Everything about how you'll play, about the game's balance of power, is tied up in those outs. It would be like rounding off time in a football game at the 5's. So that top of the third is itself divided into the thirds, if you want to be authentic about it. But I didn't get into that during our call. I will show up when there are no outs, because that is how I was raised.

They're setting me up in the players' hotel, a plush new place a mile from the park. I always forget what it's called, and sure enough, I'm forgetting right now. It's named after a letter. I know what you're thinking: Why would they have me stay in a hotel in downtown Raleigh-Durham, a city in which I own an apartment with richly textured furniture? All I can say is, MLB culture is built around the idea of the hotel, the very philosophy of it. No one works where they're from, no one lives where they work, no one's child attends school within a thousand miles of her dad's office. It's really a madhouse of legal residency and personal identity and Republican absentee-ballot voting. And there are owned properties in the middle of the chaos, but these are confusing and unpredictable, and the only thing to do with them, half the time, is ignore them. Strange, I know, but try thinking of it this way: the four-star hotel is really the player's apartment, only it's spread out across many cities. He is essentially the owner of a thirty-two-bedroom flat. His apartment, on the other hand, is sort of like his favorite hotel.

Also, I demanded the hotel room, because I couldn't stand the sight of that sad, empty bedroom.

Anyway, my car would be dead, down there in the bowels of my building. We've covered this. So there I'll be, rooming amid the guys who do what I do much, much better, and the old-timers who once did. Don't think the class system ends after retirement. The ones not there by luck or timing or even—with a few exceptions—hard work. We'll see how it goes. But I do feel like being injured connects me to that crowd, in a way. It can happen to anybody, to tear a CL. It's not like stronger skills equal stronger ligaments, though you could almost see that being true. The long-form DL is baseball's great democracy: everyone can show the same aptitude at being absent from a twenty-five-man roster.

*Saturday July 10*

I am an expert packer. You could probably have guessed as much. Packing is another one of those things that the game asks you to get good at, even though they never scouted your raw skill. That's not to say everyone learns. In fact some elements of on-field talent make guys worse when it comes to prepping luggage. For example, the wide shoulders and broad back of a prototypical line-drive hitter also make carrying a duffel bag *too* easy—guys lose their incentive to run a tight ship. So they overpack wildly, bringing entire video game systems, three "going out" shirts for one night. I wish my teammates could see that a well-packed bag is its own reward.

I had a packing epiphany around my second year in the league. It really isn't all that different from what I do out in left. I'm surprised more outfielders don't realize this. In both cases, the key is making your choices ahead of time. You can't cover the entire field in one play, and you can't wear every shirt in your wardrobe in one night. You stake a claim—X number of paces toward the line, French cuffs or buttons—and you live and die by it. So I force myself not to bring more pairs of boxers than there are nights out of town. I maintain a strict two-belt limit, no matter how long the road trip. I think it keeps me sharp.

Today, as I filled my favorite short-trip duffel for the first time in months, I had to figure out what look I wanted to present to the baseball world. This is more important than usual. If I'm playing, it doesn't really matter if I dress like a slacker, but if I'm rehabbing, I need to dress like I can seriously play. I figured nothing says "total five-tool package" like an untucked spread-collar dress shirt with alternating yellow and blue stripes. I'll be wearing my baggiest jeans, whether that's the fashion or not, because they're the only ones that fit over my brace.

While we're on the subject of traveling to Carolina, I should give an update on the Birds. Both the team and the rook have cooled off since my last report. I do check the box scores every day, by the way, even if I'm not watching all the games. You need to digest that information daily to really get a sense of the storyline. Processing a week all at once won't get you into the ebb and flow. So I can tell you that Atlanta's current lead isn't just a number, 4, but something more solid, already starting to etch itself in stone. You wouldn't know this if you just glanced at today's standings. It's not insurmountable, but it will require serious work to surmount—there are seven-game leads flimsier than this four. I can also tell you that *someone* has been leaving men on base with two outs, and has a nasty little caught-stealing streak going, but his name is also looking less and less glaring in the lineup. A surprising name will jump out right away, give you a little prick in the eye, but you expect to see his there now. Like it's a puzzle piece dropped into its right place.

## Monday July 12

I am sitting in my room in the attractive new hotel in downtown Raleigh-Durham, finally getting some time to write a few things down. Let's just call the place the Letter—I can't imagine you need to know which one. It's late right now, almost midnight, and instead of looking at water I'm beholding a bank. Talk about messing with a routine. We're actually only about five blocks from my place. This is the bank where I bank when I'm in town, but I haven't been by. You will notice that the apartments players own and the hotels they stay in are often just a few blocks apart.

The Letter is one of those elegant brick-and-marble jobs they've started building again in city centers—the kind every town of fine standing once had. You see this all over now, but really it's kind of a trick. Because just when you think your city's urban core is genuinely being revitalized, that the various moving and shaking downtown has sprouted a fine hotel of its own accord, you spot a centimeter of pale text toward the bottom of the lobby literature that says, "A So-And-So Hotels Production." Like you're on a set showing you what your city could be like, in the future.

It's been strange being back amidst the game. You reenter this world gradually, over the course of several hours, just as you leave it. I walked, well, stutter-stepped out of my front door in East Palm at 11 yesterday morning, and as I proceeded like some palindrome from limo to airport to plane to airport to limo, I became more and more noticed, and attached to something, and by the time I got to the Letter lobby I was flat-out famous.

As expected, I got an invite to a big players' feast last night. My room is next to a certain Philly pitcher with a taste for the nightlife—I won't name names—and he immediately enlisted me as his advisor on the best R-D dining. Since then I've been like a personal Zagat's guide for the class of the National League. Where to get the best porterhouse. Or to mix it up, where to find the finest filet.

So we all got pretty blitzed at the restaurant, even some of the guys who were involved in tonight's Home Run Derby. None of whom ended up as finalists, it bears pointing out. I hate to burst your bubble, but a player isn't going to put an exhibition over a night out, I don't care how competitive he is. And you know those guys who come in leading the league in slugging percentage, then can't get it past the Little Leaguers in the outfield, even though they're handpicking every pitch? Well, guess who was ordering the jeroboams of Domaine Somebody the night prior? The imperials of Chateau X-and-Y? Baseball is never as arbitrary as it seems. Everything that happens has eight reasons, a whole pedigree of cause stacked behind it.

Still, the Derby is fun to watch. There's nothing better than horsing around inside the set pieces of your sport when you have professional-grade skills, and those guys really get into it. Just like with the three-point contest at the NBA game, or the part where hockey players do stuff with cones. No pressure, just the pleasure of your talent. Tonight I watched in my street clothes, from the bench in the NL dugout—*our* dugout. I sat there and separated no seeds from their shells with my tongue. At one point they showed me up on the JumboTron. I got a polite little hand from the crowd. Most of the fans at these things aren't local, they're recipients of corporate perks, and I saw a lot of "who's that?" getting mouthed. Two words you get used to, living my life. But I didn't mind, it's not their fault they're good at marketing or sales.

It was weird going through our locker room, though. The All-Stars set up shop in the home guys' lockers for these things, obviously, only normally you're not there to see it, and the equipment managers do a great job with the cleanup after. They *are* the best in the business, after all, this is the Show of their industry too. But as

I've detailed, ballplayers are a superstitious lot. And I hustled right through that clubhouse, that suite of rooms where I've spent more time than any other in the last seven years, without letting myself look at the absence of a "B. Alexander #29" nameplate over the fifth locker in from the right.

## Wednesday July 14

I am back lagoonside. Back on schedule. Sweating on east patio. I like to keep my chair in the shade, as I've said, but when I came out a little while ago, after four days away, and stretched my legs out on the ottoman in my customary fashion, I noticed my knees were starting to fall into shadow. I hadn't moved the furniture—the angle of the sun must have changed by a kneecap while I was gone. You see, when you stick tight to a routine, it's just easier to see things going on around you. So I've moved the chair forward, and my joints are once again fully lit, like I like them.

I got back this morning. An uneventful hour-and-a-half flight. What does that mean, "uneventful?" No crash? But I say it, same as everyone else. Domestic first-class on flights of less than ninety minutes is a funny idea. Are there really people who are paying full fare for that ticket, just for the glass of champagne, the exclusive use of the forward lavatory? Half the time these days the seats aren't even made of leather. And yet a ballplayer almost feels obligated by income to fly first-class on those occasions he does go commercial. Here's what it is: you're *not* buying a coach ticket more than you're buying something else. And today, of course, someone else was paying, and with my brace I actually made use of every inch of that legroom. I drank the champagne, too. I was seated next to a petite elderly woman in a bright purple pantsuit. She stared out the window the entire flight, and poked me to announce cities she recognized. "Young man— Charleston! Young man—Jacksonville!" Like that.

My stint on national TV went pretty well, I think. They're mailing me a recording of the telecast. The broadcast duo consisted of one of those velvet-voiced pros and an old second baseman from the '70s. These former players really are an interesting species of American, especially the ones who could really play. Who were good enough that their skill was going to define them after they left the game. They weren't just going to buy some carwashes, though of course they'd do that too. These guys express their jock status in middle age through iron handshakes, powerful cologne, out-of-date moustaches and gold-link bracelets. I believe I've figured this one out. It's not like ballplayers were ever tastemakers to begin with, but there's something else to it too. They want to keep making the plays of baseball—the uppercut swings and takeout slides—but all they have to work with are the tools of society. And so they just gravitate toward anything of size, of strength, of hideous color—anything sharp and forceful. They're literally *still trying to play the game*.

The guys in the booth wanted to talk about the knee, of course. They asked about the progress, inquired gently about the setback. I attempted a casual charm that was at once realistic and upbeat. The ex-player in particular was full of questions about my rehab, what exercises I was doing and so forth. "So they got you doing those range-of-motions?" he asked, during a break in his scent. "Doing those squat series and them?" I told him yup, all the modalities. If it's a modality, you can bet I'm doing it.

What else of three days in Raleigh-Durham? Oh right, the game. The American League won, 8–3. A snoozer from a strategy standpoint, heavy on solo home runs. The American League always wins, they started rattling off ridiculous nine-year win streaks around five years ago. They say the AL is the hitter's league, that whenever an NL hurler goes over there he's bound to get lit up. But this doesn't really make sense. Obviously it must then be a pitcher's league too, otherwise *those* guys would be getting shelled. And if it's a better hitter's league and a better pitcher's league, then it's just a better league, and maybe they should stop holding these contests.

The knee. Sometimes it disappoints me that there is skin on the outside, that its important functions are hidden from view. I look at my knee on an afternoon like this and daydream science-fictionally. I imagine it is translucent. I could hold it up to the light and check in on the repairs. Like those see-through insects and minor amphibians, the ones that have all their major organs on display. They get to be clear, but they don't even have the brainpower to appreciate it. Such a waste.

The tear of a ligament is not exactly like the tear in a sheet of paper, though. You don't look at it and think *Hey, big rip there, better get out some Scotch tape.* Ligament tears and their ilk, once you've seen them on enough medical images, start to seem soft-edged, more like frays, or crumbles even. The injury does not appear organized.

My own has taken on a new dimension. "Stiffness" doesn't quite capture it. There's no pain involved. I can only describe it as a certain toughness. Like it's been stewed too long in a pot. The real point about hurting your knee, I'm starting to think, is not that it feels any certain way. Most sensations drift away as fast as they came, and aren't cause for alarm. No, the point is the change itself—on its own terms, I mean. What you start to expect is things being . . . different. It turns out bodies aren't just made up of rights and wrongs, like everyone leads you to believe. They're just as often a matter of some newness you can't explain, of things feeling not worse or better but simply not like they've ever felt before.

New neighbors have moved into the house to my left, on the near side of the "no-fishing" lady, who still can't decide whether to smile or glare at me when she takes her dog on runs. The woman looks to be in her late fifties, petite and in good shape, dark hair, crisp features. He could be a decade older—burly and sunburned and old-guy strong. I've seen him three times, and each one he's been wearing one of those navy blue U.S.S. Something hats. As a professional hat-wearer myself, I've never quite gotten the gist of those, which you see all the time around here. I mean I understand the serviceman's pride, just not the ball cap format. He is not a *fan* of the Navy, nor is he currently on the ship. I have never, not once in my entire career, worn or seen a player wear his team cap past the outer circumference of a stadium, not even in the parking lot. I wonder if Navy guys think, "What's the deal with ballplayers, going around with nothing on their heads?"

Anyway, he stopped by this morning to introduce himself. It was in fact the first time I've been properly introduced to a neighbor. Gave his name as Bill, described himself as "semi-retired." We don't have that category in my line of work. Not since the days of player-managers. Bill wore a Hawaiian shirt, steel-framed glasses, and a handshake to shame Mike Schmidt's, I mean an absolute crusher, the next time I'm in an imaging machine I'm going to have them take a look. He seemed keen on the fact that he had a ballplayer living two doors down. But not in a fan way at all, it was something else I think. It was like a certain mutual understanding came into his face when I told him. There are strange, complicated overlaps between the armed forces and the major leagues, things that run deep and far back in time. We are both involved in standing for things—national things. And there's a problematic aspect, too, on the baseball end, in that we are battling for wild cards while they're battling Charlie or whomever. And we're the ones getting paid millions.

Actually on some level I think that shame filters down through everything we do in the game. That burden of being a symbol of the country, repping its great metropoli, while only taking up the weapons of sport. Have you noticed that some TV stations have started listing our time in the league as "MLB Service: [X] Years"? That's no accident of terminology. They're trying to defend our whole enterprise to suspicious viewers. "We know, we know," they're saying, "what you're watching *looks* like play, and there's a war on. But you must try to see these infielders as, in their own way, infantrymen."

*Friday July 16*

Jenn was out sick this morning. Erik was flying solo. "Flying solo today, X man," said Erik, articulating a tricep. He is cut in that way of people who spend full days around high-end fitness equipment, with hours to gaze across specialized machines and consider what mixing and matching will produce beautiful human shapes. I think bodybuilding is really a mental exercise as much as anything. Once someone tells you which weights to lift, you just lift them, but drawing up a program is like landscape architecture.

As usual, Erik was eager to talk baseball. He filled me in a bit more on his own history in the sport. "Actually played a few years of college ball myself," he mentioned as he slid the squat rack off my shoulders. ("Oh yeah?") "Yeah, third base. I could hit a little bit, too. I mean, not like you or anything . . ." I've had this exchange in various forms throughout my career. At least half the time it ends like that—with the guy, usually encountered in an autograph line or bar & grille, assuring me that I shouldn't be threatened by his athletic exploits, his talent does not in fact exceed my own.

"That's pretty chill," I said.

"You know what? That's exactly what it was."

Something about the morning left me feeling off. Something was missing. The knee actually had a solid session, well above average, but my mind itched. There's an exercise Jenn usually has me do at the end, just a little limbering thing, actually it kind of tickles the way she does it. But you know the way these things can build without you really noticing. You come to count on them, and to my surprise I felt like the session just wasn't complete without it. And I decided that rather than going straight home, I'd take a good, head-clearing drive. So I picked up two tuna sandwiches at the sandwich chain, selected some Skynyrd from the console, and off I went in a southerly direction. An advantage with Skynyrd is they all died before they could start writing bad songs. Though they still tour.

People don't seem to "drive the coast" here the way they do in California, or Maine, or in all the Great Lakes states. The motion is point to point, small city to small city—there's not that whole vertical sensibility, that sense of logging a distance. This isn't a coast story, but one routine I developed back in high school, when I was starting to see I was actually going to be good enough to get drafted—a realization that came around the same time as my driver's license—and every AB began to count in the context of the next twenty years, was to every now and then climb into my GTO and make the drive over the Canadian border. This would be on a Saturday, after some scout-attended 1 for 4, when I couldn't sleep right. Canada isn't that far from Duluth. It's less than a three-hour drive to the border at International Falls, which you've probably heard of because of how cold it gets. But still, it had that exotic ring to it, which was all I needed. Driving to Canada. Doesn't it sound a little impossible, if you say it quickly? Like driving to England? Like kayaking to the moon?

Of course, then you'd get to Canada, and there wouldn't really be anything to do, or anything different. You'd just be . . . in Canada. And I always ended up feeling stupid, the three or four times I did it, but I couldn't really admit that to myself. I'd walk around some Canadian bookstore for a half-hour or so, trying to figure out how long I reasonably had to stay. I started going to bookstores all over in that period, when it became clear I was too talented to get into college, was going to have to educate myself. I boned up on history and philosophy, found fiction that spoke to me. Naturally I devoured all of Malamud. Novels seemed more expensive across the border, but when you did the math, they were pretty much the same.

This area gets a bad rap—that was my thought as I cruised today, those big blue rock songs blaring. Skynyrd were actually from Florida, but the northern part, where the state's part of the South. I guess it's almost like it gives itself a bad rap. These beach towns are naturally beautiful, but they don't seem to trust that fact. They try to argue for their beauty, to frame it, building fifty buildings in a row with beautiful views of the ocean, but also of each other. It's like they were designed by a lawyer.

Like I said though, I wasn't really going in hopes of fantastic sights. All you want in a good car trip, a Saturday drive on a Friday, is to move your mind a little. I got as far south as North Miami. It seemed to me that if I went all the way to Miami, then it would have just been the time I went to Miami. You can't have a popular destination, if you want the driving to be the point. I got as far south as North Miami, and I pulled off the road and into a parking lot near the sand, and I got out to stretch my legs, carefully in my case, and then I just turned around and drove back.

It's just a cold, Erik assured me. What Jenn has.

## Sunday July 18

So far, I haven't had weekend work—nothing more than the sporadic urgent test. This isn't because they want to give me days off, I can promise you. It's only that, in the first couple months after an injury as authentic as mine, there aren't seven days a week of work to be done. You'd hit diminishing returns. There are approximately five days. And if 5/7 is the fraction we're working with, they might as well put me on market hours, imply the weekend's there because it's the weekend. By unspoken agreement, Wednesdays are usually a little lighter too, like at the boarding school Churchy went to.

But this schedule is about to change. I am entering a transitional period, wherein I go from having an "injured" knee to a "weak," "compromised," downright "pathetic" one. From the best of the bad knees to the worst of the fine. We basically shift from healing mode to improvement mode—the protectionist stance comes to an end, we turn into a bunch of Woodrow Wilsons. There will soon be things I can do with my leg on Saturdays, and will be expected to.

The real shift in thinking is that the knee stops living alone. Right now it is the bachelor of my body. Sectional couches, subwoofer, the works—shades of my season apartment. (Overheard in downtown Raleigh-Durham: "You really need to get some shades in this apartment . . .") Soon it returns to the larger operation—we welcome it back into the fold, revisiting larger motions of which it is a key part. For example, and the non-player may not even think of this, but a solid knee is essential to the proper swing of a bat. In its way, it is more important than arms and hands, and a guy can rupture all sorts of things taking a hack too soon. I haven't so much as touched a length of lathed white ash since the half-inning before I went down, the top portion of the same sixth, when I skied a tall fly-out to first off a fastball up and away. A ball that might have gone into the stands at a cozy park like Fenway, but Cincinnati's got farm-able acres of foul ground. Now I'm slated to be back with a bat in less than two weeks. And this is the sort of thing I'll be doing on week-ends, for example, as opposed to just sitting here, like I am right now, watching Bill mow his lawn for the third time this week.

The first sets of swings they have you take are without a ball, that's the other reason I can do them out here. They call these "dry swings," if you can believe that. I mean, what's a swing if not a swing, right? I guess you have to think of it like bartending. If you're at a bar, it's a virgin margarita, whereas in your kitchen it's just a lime-ade. Same goes for pro baseball: situation is everything. If a bat is always used for hitting balls, then when you swing one at nothing you must be going "dry."

And get how organized the modern game is about the whole thing: they actually have you take those first cuts at air with a fungo bat, before you proceed to a real one. They developed this policy for guys with upper-body injuries, shoulder dislocations and the like, where the bat swing is the big activity you return to, the triumph. I guess they just can't get their minds past the minute differences in weight distribution and what-have-you. And now they even put a guy like me with leg problems on the fungo-first program, because if there is ever an opportunity to divvy it up one more time, to make the slope of the process just one degree more gradual, which is really the same as adding milestones they can say you've passed, you better bet they'll take it.

*Monday July 19*

I haven't been able to get bats off my mind. The cool feel of a good Louisville. The way it fills every hollow of your grip, almost like a liquid poured there. You don't really know your own hands till you've held a custom bat with them. Any player will say the same. To get my fix, I just placed an order for a dozen of my favorite sticks: Louisville Slugger ash, 33 ½" long and 31 oz. heavy, 2 ½" in diameter at the widest point. This is one of the true joys of being a major leaguer, I'll come right out and say it. You get to just . . . place shipments. Your little preferences—for this bagginess of pant, that shade of wood varnish—not only get acknowledged, as I've commented. They get replicated, and many times over. Your desires, showing up shining in a box. And no one will say a thing, go ahead and abuse the privilege all you want, teams practically beg you to spend the extra dollars. The game is viewed as such a psychological mess that an owner will jump at anything that can actually be touched, bought, ordered by the pallet-load. It gives everyone something to do.

I settled on this particular model two seasons ago, after a little dance with the maples that are all the rage now, the way the open stance was in the '90s. As bats go, mine would be called a conservative choice. Start with the color: an old-style natural ash, as opposed to the ebony and deep cherry models some guys use. I'll admit those look great. For me, though, they look *too* great. I ordered some reds once, my second or third year, and I could stare at them all day, but I always felt like I was carrying a statue with me to the batter's box. Something already finished, completed, rather than a tool I'd use to bring about events. Baseball happens too fast for you to be able to afford that kind of thinking. Sure, you can get over it, work it through your mind, but by that time the ball's already past you.

Some guys swear it's just a numbers game, picking your sticks. You're selecting an ideal ratio, bat speed working inversely to bat weight, and optimum power happening where they meet. But that's complicated by the fact that *you* are a ratio, too—a blend of strength and agility and heavy muscle that must be tweaked piecemeal for optimum performance. So the notion of the "right" bat has to be tailored toward the type of player you are and wish to be: an all-or-nothing bomber, a better-than-average average hitter, a roper of drives. Picking your bat involves all sorts of introspection, it's really like picking your self. In my dotage, I've settled on a midsize model that can guarantee me a steady sixteen dingers a year, rather than a twenty-four-upside battleaxe that carries the risk of ten.

I placed my order through our team equipment manager, Sam, who deals directly with the companies. I know what you're thinking: Do you really need a dozen bats right now, if you're just going to be taking dry swings, with an eventual progression into live pitching, followed by an if-all-goes-well rehab assignment in a Sun Belt state's fall league? No, but you do need your bat to have come from a larger dozen, and that's really the only way I can explain it. To have lived among its peers for a time. Sam, an original Birds employee who like most EMs is bald and ribald both, and fish-belly pale from too much time underground, didn't bat an eye (I could tell over the phone). He just asked me how I was feeling and told me to call if I need any more—and we both knew that need would express itself in multiples of twelve. He believes what everyone else in baseball believes: quantity is the magic elixir.

They'll be here by Friday—Christmas in July. Sam's expressing a couple team-approved fungoes, too, he doesn't want to be responsible for me swinging the real jobs too soon. The best part about getting new bats is rotating the handle until you spot your own emblazoned name. The people in Kentucky burn it on there for you, from a handwriting sample you provide. And it's a thrill every time, still, and you're still never 100% sure it will be there. And sometimes you'll pick it up such that the name is 240 degrees away from where you start, so you have to do a lot of turning before you spot it, and you think that this is finally the time they forgot, and you make peace with it in those sad few seconds. But it's always there.

Honestly a whole book could be written about the idea of a name branded with a searing hot iron into the particular bat specified by that named man. Though actually, Rawlings gloves are even more interesting, because they don't use your actual signature. They have some in-house author write everyone's in his or her own hand, the player's name looped customly up the heel, just a hair crooked so you know it was done bespoke. And I've wondered on many occasions: Whose handwriting is that? And how did he get the job? Was it his H's that set him apart, or his F's or J's? Was he thinking about me when he sewed my B?

J was back at PARC today. "I don't want to touch you!" she chirped, holding up a stop sign and backing away as I approached.

"Why not?" I asked, wounded. She gave me a little look, right on the edge of a grin.

"Because I have a cold, Blake."

There's really so much luck involved in being a pro ballplayer. I don't mean luck in the way you usually think of it—of making it to the bigs, of a timely injury in leftfield, of an uncommonly high Batting Average on Balls in Play (BABIP) in the era before they clued in to that stat. I mean luck in a bigger sense: that this strange game became a major American athletic test, and you popped from the womb with just the right skills for it. I was thinking about this today as I was swimming. A local junior water polo team has started practicing on Tuesdays, which means I must now do my laps horizontally, against the grain of the pool. On Thursdays, too, because they don't move the line. Swimming, it occurred to me, is highly *un*random, it ranks behind only running as an inevitable sport. Running and maybe biathlon. To be good at swimming is to be an athlete in the least arguable sense, which is to say you excel at something involving traits valuable for being a human. But baseball? Baseball not only made up sports ideas—swinging a piece of wood, throwing wrapped twine—it mixed them in a way that rewarded freak bodies and crazily specific skill sets. Take a look at Gaylord Perry and tell me he didn't absolutely *luck out* that this was the talent mix they started paying for. The guy actually rode his salivary glands to the Hall of Fame—what made him pudgy gave him his spitball.

The situation is more extreme for some guys. Baseball has gotten more fitness-focused, so these days you do have plenty of players who are centerfielders in the same way they were All-American quarterbacks. But witness the percentage of jowls in any team photo and you'll see that this sport is still much more about being good at this sport than about being good at sports. I should know. I played a little hockey in high school, why not, but I wasn't even on my team's first line. No, I'm here because when objects are hurled at me, I can make decisions quickly, and I can torque my above-average form in a way that makes my decisions matter. And one weekend in the mid-nineteenth century, a few guys started valuing that.

My All-Star appearance DVD came in the mail this afternoon. Things like this are never quite what you remember. I've done the local sports shows on a few occasions, so I have some experience. Your good jokes seem bad, your bad jokes seem fine. I'm more used to seeing myself televised than most, which just means I'm braced for that shudder of strangeness when you see how you actually look in the world. But it's definitely different when you're in street clothes. Watching yourself in a game, your viewing is wrapped up in things going statistically right or wrong. Success or failure is the point of each play, so that's what you notice, and you don't have much time to worry about your haircut, though of course you'd rather it not tuft out to the sides below your hat. When you're up there in jeans, though, your hair literally becomes an obsession, it's all you can see, it creeps you out. Some of this is easily explained, of course: You're used to seeing the part on the other side, in the mirror. Since I realized that, I've relaxed a bit.

Anyway, the image that really stood out, as I watched an hour ago on the brother's plasma screen, was the former player. Sitting there gleaming in dark royal double-breasted, tie the color of warning track, moustache tapered down past a reasonable southern boundary. I didn't notice this when I was in the booth, but he was wearing these massive gold cuff links, which were revealed every time he illustrated the correct form for blocking a short-hop. And at one point one of them must have gotten stuck in a reflective angle with a camera light, and for about twenty seconds it glowed unreasonably big and bright in the middle of the screen, like some holy grail.

I don't know. With a guy like that, even on TV the cologne is so strong that you can almost see it through the screen, hovering over his person. You can hear it, permeating his 643rd diatribe against the Designated Hitter. No Midsummer Classic is complete without that speech, by now it's as sacred as the .097-hitting pitcher once was. By now it is the midsummer classic. And it's not that I think pitchers should get out of hitting, I mean that's a ridiculous rule and everyone knows it. It's just that as I was lying there, with my head on the fulcrum of the sofa and my leg propped up on an arm, elevate when possible, I got to wondering if there's any way for me to avoid being an ex-ballplayer when I'm an ex-ballplayer.

*Thursday July 22*

I must have been thinking less about the knee the last couple days. I didn't realize this until today, because you can't think about not thinking about something. I mentioned it to Jenn—some half-baked line about all I hadn't been thinking. See above. To my surprise, she caught my drift (and my barbell, too—a forty-five-pounder was slipping). She nodded slowly and said that's the secret to making strong motions, not to work harder but to forget you're there—to up and leave your personal Florida. I said I bet she tells that secret to all the boys. "I don't," she said, with the strange gravity of a catcher whispering to his pitcher that his curve is shot. I was glad there wasn't a mitt covering her mouth. "I really don't."

The Birds have a big series starting today. A four-gamer versus Atlanta, in Atlanta—four being the same number as the Bravos' division advantage. Their lead has hemmed and hawed, but in the end hasn't budged one inch. You'll see this happen sometimes: two teams getting stuck on a particular gap, gravitating back to it again and again, like certain warm objects. Like certain warm people. It's as if they've worn a physical groove in the standings. And of course, each day that lead stays the same is a day it's actually bigger.

These four-gamers are tough, they're just massively consequential. The difference in available outcomes is huge. You can tie a four-game series, which is weird for guys weaned on rubber matches. But it's even weirder if you do anything *but* tie, because then it's 3–1 or 4–0, and those ratios are so top-heavy. The whole divisional picture changes wildly, and suddenly you're either pretty well cooked or right back in the hunt. It's all very American, the feast or famine of a four-gamer. But it's emotionally exhausting.

I'd been weighing whether to watch the games. ESPN is carrying the Sunday broadcast, and that's the matchup that will decide if the series is a catastrophe for one side, so I'll definitely watch that one. But I wasn't really sure I needed to see all four of them, piled one on top of the other like that. That's a lot of cordwood to carry on just one good leg. Then this morning I figured out what I believe is a perfect compromise: radio. I'm not talking about crowding around the family wireless drinking whole milk. They have it now so you can sign up to get all the local broadcasts online, through the league website. And that really seemed kind of perfect, as far as total data received. All the information, the drama, buckets of ebb and flow, but no added visuals of budding rookie-of-the-year candidates. Reducing the senses involved—a clever plan, if I may say so.

Sometime after I finished entering my credit card information into the subscription form, and checking the box "NO," I did not wish to receive promotional e-mails from MLB, my agent called. These calls have reduced in frequency, to about two per week. You'll remember how I said they felt overplanned? Well you could argue the opposite has become true. Jeff now seems to be calling in between calls, if that makes any sense.

The best word to describe this morning's discussion wouldn't be "good" or "bad" but "medical." It's funny, or maybe it isn't. Jeff and I used to talk mostly about baseball. Now the Birds hardly come up, but he can fill a whole call with obscure facts about regenerative tissue. With words like *trochanteric, debridement,* the kind that will just fight off the rest of a sentence. "No one will work harder for you," he said when he convinced me to come over to Dynastic three years back, and I guess that's technically been true. Today he embarked on a spirited six-minute discourse on cartilage theory before ending our call, probably to take a call. A lesser man would wonder what he talks about with the budding ROY candidate, and open a bottle of something brown instead of the audio plug-ins page in his Web browser.

"What do you know about the term *debridement*?" I asked Jenn later.

"Plenty," she said.

I just got it.

Bats! Bats. My handsome dozen arrived an hour ago via FedEx, 4 p.m. local time, beaten by two hours by the fungoes, which came UPS. Sam did his job. Neither deliveryman seemed to have any idea who I was, or what he was bringing, which is especially funny when you think about the relevance of the cargo to my fame. What a strange job that would be, don't you think? Portaging around goods all day without knowing what they are? After the FedEx guy slid the box of twelve signature models up to the screen door, he had me confirm my name, like they always do, then sign with that portable electric pen that never works. The letters you could read ended up almost producing my nickname.

As things stand, I start swinging the fungoes on Wednesday. I'll take my first cuts at the Center, under the supervision of the hitting coach from the Homestead Cane, the Birds' Low-A affiliate. Baseball used to have B-, C-, even D-class ball, but now they just subdivide the A. I've never been sure if it's Cane as in the sugar or the tropical depression.

He'll be there to make sure I'm not favoring anything I shouldn't be. I feel like he should just ask Jenn that question. But I enjoy this term, "favoring"—one of those English-sounding expressions that shouldn't have lasted a week in this country. I mean you'd think it would have died out on a clipper ship in Boston Harbor, one last limping bo'sun, then poof! I can never remember whether the leg you're favoring is the one you're using or the one you aren't. And that's what I mean, we Americans aren't used to inside-out terms like that.

Our men of Carolina, who are mostly from California, dropped game one last night, the final score a sour-tasting 8–4. All the scoring was done by the fifth. Relievers on the winning squad hate four-run leads, they have zero upside. The meaningful relief stats—saves, "holds"—are built around preserving leads of three or less, but a four-run game is still very losable. You almost want to see your seventh-inning guy cough up a run for the team, just so the hurlers of the eighth and ninth aren't doing their work in a vacuum. That would be a steak dinner for him, right there.

None of this applied to the Birds last night. Our final four innings were split by two so-called "long men." This is a truly thankless job, the very bottom of the baseball ladder: the guy who eats innings when you're way behind. Four runs is one thing, but sometimes it's seven, ten, and they don't call the mercy rule in the pros. Someone has to see things through. Pitching turns into pure passage of time, the tossing of arrow-straight strikes in the hope hit balls won't land where they ain't. It's a stat-killer too, and there's no point taking you out and burning another arm, so if you happen not to have your usual velocity, your ERA is just out of luck. You'll get a steak dinner, though.

Young Roy, as I'm now calling my replacement, had the night off. Teams will commonly do this on a Thursday or Monday, since those are the travel days, and when games *are* scheduled then, managers like to take things into their own hands. They really fancy themselves sleep scientists, the skips of pro ball. Masters of the circadian rhythm. The other day it occurred to me that I get the itch to write just about as often as I would have played—say an average of 5.2 times a week, with the occasional eleven in a row. Only now I take my rest days whenever I please.

Subbing for Roy was our third-and-now-second-stringer, a career minor leaguer named Scales. In a pretty amazing turn of events, no one calls him Scaly. Scales shows up in the Show for eighty ABs every year or two, amiable and mediocre as you please. Where you really see if a guy's got big-league staying power is in his speed. Not his sprinting ability, but the pace of the game as it appears against the backdrop of his person. Does he look like he's been dropped into one of those quick old movies, but he's stuck at a modern pace? Then he'll only ever be what we call a Quad-A guy. Too good for the minors, not good enough for the bigs. And that's Scales.

I could see it right away last night. Of course, I couldn't *see* anything, listening through my laptop. But I'm so trained in reading the sound of a park, in doing that whole taxonomy on the different species of bat cracks and bleacher groans, that I actually find myself forgetting it isn't all there in front of me. Those radio guys do a good job, too, they really know what to leave in and what to gloss over, what to tell and what to arch their eyebrows in the direction of. For example, last night, instead of saying "a liner to left, and Scales is running as fast as he can, but the ball continues to tail away from him at a rate I doubt he can counter," they'd say, "a liner to left . . . (crowd noise) . . . Scales giving . . . (pregnant pause) . . . *chase*." And you'd get the whole picture, as clear and finely pixeled as HD, from the way they perched his name on the edge of a cliff.

The other entertaining part of these radio broadcasts is that they feature all the funny local ads, the ones you don't even remember remembering. As soon as I clicked into the feed, I was hearing the jingles for Dodge of Chapel Hill, Chevy of Cary, Mercury of Zebulon, and it practically knocked me out with nostalgia for the drive home from the park. As a ballplayer, you build up a serious repertoire of these, from across the country. There's a great one in San Francisco that goes, "In the hearrrt of the ciiity, San Francisco Ford, Lincoln, Mercuryyyy!" I had no idea I even knew it until we were in SoMA last summer, and someone in the clubhouse described our hotel as being "in the heart of the city," and boom—I suddenly realized I'd had that jingle stuck in my head, at varying strengths, for approximately six years.

## Saturday July 24

It's weird how complete a ball game is—how truly it is the beginning, middle, and end of its own world. Thursday's game finished 8–4, and you could get sucked into seeing this as the start of a pattern. It feels like the next contest should also end in even numbers, or in a 2–1 ratio, or at a four-run spread. At least *some* numerical logic that allows the viewer to see how Game B proceeded from Game A. But it never works that way, even in doubleheaders played an hour apart. Error-ridden slugfests begin almost the moment elegant pitchers' duels wrap. A shortstop's oh-fer follows his three-fer. Each game is like a little planet floating around, and some have rings and some are red and some support carbon-based life.

Sure enough, after Thursday's crew-cut numbers, last night turned in a non sequitur of primes: 5–3. Doesn't that score just look sleazy, like it didn't wash behind the ears? You'd rather win with ragged numbers than lose clean, though, and the squad took the second of the series, behind seven two-run innings from our SP3. I do love a good seven and two, speaking of numbers. It's a long enough and good enough outing that a team will always take it, but it's not so good that you can't reasonably shoot for it next time out. A fourteen-foot birdie putt instead of a chip-in for eagle. The modern game considers six innings and three runs the prototype solid performance from an SP, and they actually have a name for it: the Quality Start. This is a technical term now, a stat they keep. But there's no name for the seven and two, and I think there should be. The Sparkling Start, or the Marvelous Start—something highly complimentary that still leaves room for true gems.

Roy was back in the lineup last night. Back in the two-slot he now occupies like it's deeded real estate. I'd be misleading the reader if I didn't present him as the star of the contest. In the top of the first he logged a single, a steal, and the game's first run. Then, when the Braves grabbed the lead with two in the bottom of the second, he responded as if to a personal affront, belting a two-run no-doubter in the third that put us in front for good. The lack of doubt in a no-doubter is easier to sense over the radio than on TV. You can hear the play-by-play man struggling not to call it gone before it actually is, because after all his duty is to report, not speculate. But there's no stopping the momentum in his pipes once that first note of awe has been struck.

What I really heard, as I listened to Roy cut a path through Atlanta pitching, was the game becoming personalized for him. A matter of demeanor. In those games where everything's truly clicking, of which God grants me about five a year, this funny sensation takes over. You actually start desiring things to occur, rather than thinking about the actions you need to execute en route. You forget the middleman that is your body. I suspect stars feel that way about one game a week, and for superstars it's every night, that's just what playing baseball is. It can be hard to discuss the game with a true superstar, because he doesn't think about at-bats, per se, with balls being pitched to him. He's moved on, to considering where he'll issue those balls as they sail outward from his bat. The actual striking of one is just a step, an errand. And last night, that was our Roy. A vet can spot the symptoms a mile off.

## Sunday July 25

I have arrayed my twelve fresh bats across the double bed in the lagoon-facing extra bedroom. Their fine ashen color stands out handsomely against the royal blue of the comforter, and the whole room smells woody and resiny and delicious in deep ways that go beyond smell. Here is where I write that this brings me back to my childhood—that's what scents like this seem engineered for. But of course that's not true at all. We ballplayers now use odorless aluminum bats at every level of the sport until the pros. Only when you're at the top do you finally immerse yourself in Louisville Slugger nostalgia for a youth you never had.

I wonder if the brother's kid plays. My bats are in the room he uses when they're here. I've gathered as much by comparing color schemes and poster content. He has one of those names that end in -den. Okayden, who I'm putting at about nine, judging by the most advanced photos in the house, is clearly a basketball fan. Magazine pull-outs of Love and Lin decorate his east wall, and there's a massive poster of Dwyane Wade next to the bed. It might even be life-size, though Wade is a guard, so that's less impressive than it could be. These days baseball fights an uphill battle against basketball, which does a great job convincing kids that it's instant and brainless and giddy—pure athletic candy. What's funny is that basketball is actually a more strategic game than even its top practitioners give it credit for. Think about it: correctly played, it's really about making a spreadsheet with all the percent-likelihoods—eighteen-foot jump shot, seven-foot skyhook, pressure free throw—then placing the best bets. But it doesn't look like that on a poster. Jenn's been asking me more questions about baseball, including whether I'd share a few thoughts on the game with her uninterested son. Careful what you wish for. But maybe I'll share my spreadsheet theory with the little

LeBron fan. Basketball as explained by Xandy—what do you think of your precious hoops *now*?

I am trying to be a good caretaker of the house. The front screen door started acting up the other week. I'm staying true to my dad's terms here. Other things in our house could break, but the screen door always misbehaved. In this case, the hydraulic that prevents it from slamming was being *too* preventive, not releasing the door from its regularly scheduled pause with enough leftover force to engage the clasp. The thing wouldn't close. So this morning I headed to the hardware store, which is located in a little strip mall five minutes away. It stands conjoined with a pet-shampooing place and a tanning salon. Speaking of smell. Today I registered once again the cologne of any hardware store—that scent that somehow cobbles itself together identically in shops with greatly varying exteriors. What in their stock produces that? Sniff a hammer, or a sealed can of paint, and you get no hints, the absence of odor. But it's like together all those individual unpungent items cancel each other out. A smell that is the naturally occurring byproduct of nothing.

The hydraulic I bought is an aggressive modern job, big and steely and hissing with seriousness of purpose. None of that yo-yoing door motion of the old-style models—this thing is clinical. The fix was basic but harder than I expected, owing to the knee. A person doing home improvements likes to really embrace the problem, getting down on all fours and throwing his or her form into it. There are echoes of a pitcher squaring for a sacrifice bunt. But I was forced to bend at the waist like a repair rookie. I think knowing the knee is on the upswing has made me more careful with it. It's like before I didn't really *worry* about a wrong motion, as discomfort and stiffness would wave me off if I was starting down a bad path. But now I could make the mistake of moving like a healed man, and then I'd be in trouble.

Looking at those basketball posters got me thinking again about nicknames. Superstars get a whole different class of them, beyond the basic "y" addition. Shaq, for example, used to be known as the

"Shaq Attack." I say "known." It's not like anyone was addressing him that way. "Hey, Attack!" This is the strange thing about traditional nicknames: they aren't actually things people call those stars. Try to picture the young stickballers in the Bronx shouting "C'mon, Yankee Clipper!" at DiMaggio. It doesn't work.

All this has changed in the last decade, though—that's what I was thinking about today. Now all the hotshots have that thing where the first name's initial and the last name's first syllable get mashed up, as in D-Wade. In baseball it started with A-Rod. And now we have K-Rod and L-Rod and M-Rod. With some guys this is obviously impossible from a language standpoint, but they'll push the envelope of syllables and sense further the better you are. B-Boy and A-Woo and C-You. But an average LF named B-Al? I mean, what do you think?

*Monday July 26*

I'm realizing I didn't report Saturday's score in yesterday's entry. Maybe I had a hunch as to how things were going to play out. Maybe I realized I'm not ESPN. Because now that I'm getting to it, it doesn't matter. We lost on Saturday night, 3–1. We won last night, 4–1. Which means the series ended up tied, the Braves are still up four, and everyone could have just taken a four-day weekend—postponed the battles till a later date. That may not sound like a lot of time, but at our income level, you can experience a remarkable amount of pleasure in four days. There are fourteen tarpon still alive because they played those games. Thirty-one bottles of vintage Kristal continue chilling in wine cellars. Cubic inches of the years 1982 and 1988 and 1993 remain.

Last night's game was on TV, so my little radio experiment came to an end. It was like 1952 on steroids—I suddenly went from tinny voices to bright, booming athletes. A touch of a button and there they were, wowing me with prowess. A picture is worth a thousand words, naturally the phrase popped into my head. It's really a more interesting expression than it gets credit for. I always thought it was kind of misunderstood. You hear it and you think at first they're saying that pictures are infinitely more valuable than words. But a thousand words isn't actually that many. They didn't say a picture is worth *five* thousand words. And when you get down to it, one thousand is pretty much exactly how many words it takes to give a good depiction of a given still frame. Whoever came up with that wasn't just picking numbers out of a hat. He or she was providing an exact equation.

I was reminded watching the rook how he really is just about the exact opposite of me. I mean that literally: his oppositeness is exact. The symmetry of it is almost comical. For example, we're both better OPS than average guys. OPS meaning OBP + SLG—it's one of

the favorite stats of the modernists. I weigh in around .810 for my
career, and he's at .814 for the year. But he gets there via the slugging percentage, whereas I take the walks. In the outfield, I've always
counted on a quick break to get to the ball. He seems to have about
the same range, but he reacts late and makes up for it with speed. I
wonder if anyone else has picked up on this. I mean he practically
has my same mole on the other side of his face.

Watching the team without me on it is an excellent motivator.
I woke up today ready to work. I woke up ready to hit the weights.
This was a new thing for me. I don't mean the motivation, I mean
the setting. I didn't just want to go to the Center—I wanted to go to
the gym. And it must have come across, because I noticed Jenn kept
delivering glances to Erik, which I judged to be meaningful glances.
Like I was a stock outperforming on the quarter. In Texas now they
have a rehab facility called TMI. This is true.

After a workout like that, you want to get your nutrients back.
It's like you've cleared bodily space and you have about an hour to
refill it with the right stuff before what you already have sloshes in.
So after I got home, I grilled myself the majority of a lone grouper,
and mixed up a protein shake, too. They tell you now to eat fish, for
your body and mind both, and they tell you to down protein powders packed with fish oils. Once baseball gets an idea in its head. In
five years the postgame spread is just going to be one big tuna and
a bunch of forks. Guys will hit eighty home runs and never make
baserunning mistakes.

*Tuesday July 27*

Last night I had a dream about my old Little League team. I was pitching, as I did back then. Only when I'd deliver the ball to the plate, it would turn out I was also batting. Then when I would rope my own hanging curveball into play, no matter where I hit it, I would be the one fielding that position. And all of that's probably standard self-absorbed stuff for someone who's spending too much time alone. But get this: I was umpiring, too. And when my dream panned to the stands, there was my face, the age-twelve version, stuck on the heads of all the assembled dads, even though they kept their normal bodies. I know this for sure because I spotted my own dad's arm. He was wearing the gold digital watch that for a while was something of a trademark. I guess he bought it in the early '80s, when it seemed like a gold digital watch was going to be the next big thing. You actually can't fault that logic. My dream was diligent about the details.

It got me thinking this afternoon about my real Little League team. I was indeed known as a pitcher in those days. This is true of 95% of major leaguers, even the ones who are famous as professionals for their terrible arms. And with the other 5%, it's just that they grew up in Orange County, and weren't even the only future pros on their clubs. I was a pitcher and a cleanup hitter and an all-around feared performer, and kids from the southern and western parts of town would actually lean back against the outfield fence when I came up to the plate, just hoping to spear a liner on its way out, and like everyone else in the Show, I batted approximately .792. That includes AL pitchers who now swing like cricket batsmen.

I think it's important to remember, when you're watching a major league baseball game, that all of the players out there, even average guys like me, have wild success in their rearview mirrors. You know this objectively, but stop to consider what it means, because it really is strange from a psychological standpoint. They have a history of joy. This isn't something a lot of successful people can say, even CEOs and the like. But you are acquainted with these players in their major league careers, which are more complicated. When you're watching a middle reliever get shelled, just as he has for the last four years, you see him as a terrible pitcher. And you're right: he is a terrible pitcher. His early success was aimed at letting him rise and be judged at this level, that was its whole point. But he's also an incredible pitcher. That past was real, and long. So you're left with a league of schizophrenics. And it's just something to keep in mind. That sad sack on the hill has been blissfully happy in 98% of the innings he's ever pitched.

*Wednesday July 28*

I don't know how I've managed to write about fungo bats all these times without discussing the term "fungo"—that must be some kind of record. It's a word that begs you to challenge it in a game of Scrabble. You get used to saying it in baseball, but still, in all my years around the game, I've never met someone who knows what mother tongue it hails from. And in the world of the layman, there are those who remain unconvinced. For example, the word processor I'm writing on right now doesn't recognize it. I can't say I blame it.

"So, why do they call them that?" Jens asked today, his accent so thin I could barely understand him. We were in his office, reviewing next steps.

"'Cause when a coach gets them out, there the fun goes!"

Outside his open door, a melodious giggle bounced off the tile. I poked my head out and saw a swoosh of red hair disappear around the corner.

The actual bats do their name justice. They're long and skinny and light, and the weight inside them seems to be juggled up all wrong, like they're lined with sand or something. They're not, but something about them is suspicious. They're built that way so aging coaches can send forth liners with precision. At least they were, before the off-label rehab use upped sales 200%. And they're useful enough at this task. Still, it's weirdly unsettling to look at a fungo, more unsettling than it should be. They're always kind of shocking and alien the first week back in spring training. And ten weeks of not seeing one reminded me of this, when I opened up my box last night and they seemed like they were kidding. I think it's that we've all absorbed the shaping of a proper baseball bat, somewhere deep in our system. I'll even include non-fans in this. A bat should begin

to swell right here, and by this much. Comparisons have been made
to Marilyn Monroe's hips, in terms of engrained American rates of
curve. I guess when she and Joe were together they were practically
working for the Bureau of Standards.

I took my first swings in eighty-six days at 8:45 this morning,
in the side room off the main room at the Center. I'm not saying
they should embed a small brass plaque at the site. But how could I
tell you it felt anything other than great? It seemed like my strokes
should be leaving bright red vapor trails in the air-conditioned air.
I swung easy and slow, because I was supposed to, but also because
I was on a strict count and I wanted to taste every drop—every fine
morsel of muscle memory.

Our man in Homestead was up to monitor me. He was only
about five years my senior, it turned out, a fit and serious guy. You
know the type: a thirtysomething to a tee. But through the stern
expression I caught him enjoying himself as much as I was. We were
in a similar boat, when you think about it. His morning was also all
about professional progress. Just to be the one standing there, issu-
ing that small bit of impact northward toward the majors. "Goood,"
he kept saying. He'd brought one of those count tickers the gate guys
have at ballparks, which gave him something to do. I mean, what
was he really going to tell me about swinging a bat? He was there
to hold the ticker. He was there because it would feel irresponsible
not to have had a witness if I went down. "Goooood," he'd say, every
three cuts or so. And there may have been even more o's than that. I
could have given the guy a hug.

What else needs to be said about today? I mean, swinging bats is
a thing they do in baseball games. I'll admit it now—I'd been thinking pretty consciously about the knee the last couple days. By any
objective measure, it was coming along fine. But you start to get that
hypersensitivity when the stakes increase. You just *feel* the appendage all the time, even when you're sitting still. It's like all the nerve

endings in your leg have traveled to that one spot, and you notice every shade of everything around you. I don't want to say anything to Jenn, not yet. I don't want her to see me without my upside. But the best way I can describe it is that the knee feels fluish: always a little hot or a little cold, but never quite at room temperature.

## Friday July 30

A heat wave has come to South Florida. I about laughed out loud when I saw the Weather Channel folks forecasting it two nights ago. East Palm in July is so hot already that you just can't figure out where they'd *put* any more degrees. I think for a non-native, living here is kind of like being stuck endlessly in some other region's once-a-summer event. If not for the lizards, you could believe every day is a horrible day in Virginia.

But sure enough: 94 has given way to 102, with humidity of about the same, and the difference is appreciable. For starters, it's pushed me inside today, to the sanctuary of the air-conditioned living room. The closed windows in here have taken on that emergency look of the ones on an airplane—you stare at them wondering if they could fail. I've been thinking more about degrees Fahrenheit, how they really are so similar to their mph counterpart. 94 is the definition of heat—of a baking sun, of a whistling four-seamer. 102, though: That has the scent of death to it. On the field, when a guy is throwing that hard, you almost stop thinking about the game. It's not that you're scared of being hit, though sure, you'd rather the ball get you somewhere fleshy. It's more that everyone becomes aware that this level of force isn't sustainable, and nerves jangle. Apocalypse enters the stadium.

And in the real world too, 102 makes whole systems strain at the seams. The house—it's almost like the house starts to sweat. When I got back from the Center around noon, the freshly fixed screen door wouldn't budge. In the four hours I'd been gone, it had swelled itself into its frame. Then the metal in the handle practically gave me a second-degree burn on my first attempt. A fine way to ruin my rehab that would be. Right up there with the pitchers who punch walls with their pitching hands and the guys who get carpal tunnel from too much video-game baseball. It's always their own character they've been playing, too. These games have become extremely realistic— with the exception that the guy in the game never goes on the DL from playing himself in a video game. In the end, I had to put on a batting glove to pry it open. It's a good thing that I'm swinging bats again and had one in my pocket. I don't know what a non-player would have done.

I progressed to fifty hacks today. My second and last supervised session, at least until the swings get wet. Until I take a fine, refreshing plunge in the swimming pool of a pitched baseball. Actually, there will be a half-step in a couple weeks: hitting off a tee. Just like in first grade, except they won't put anyone's dad on the mound and have him pretend to pitch. I suppose you'd call hitting off the tee dipping my toes from a seat on the diving board, as far as swing saturation is concerned.

The swings felt different today. They felt *thicker*, somehow, even with the skinny fungo. Like I was cutting a broader path through the air. I think it's that I was trusting my legs more, was really getting down into the stance. I thought I was doing it on Wednesday, but I now see with the benefit of hindsight that I was still babying the knee. Good as they felt, my cuts were not truly driving the invisible ball over the imagined fence. I was flying out to center, reaching the warning track at best.

It really is all about the legs, whether or not you want to admit it partway through a torn knee. Every sport is all about the legs, and the funny thing is that everyone knows it too. I guarantee that there is not a game you've tried where you haven't been instructed via this phrase. I mean, ping-pong is all about the legs. Horseshoes is all about the legs. So why aren't we all playing sports better? Because this goes against our instincts, when we're young. And I think the ones who go on to become serious athletes are the ones who surrender at an early age to this seemingly insane advice. The kids who can take that leap of faith. "It's really about taking that leap of faith," I'd tell Jenn if she asked, about her son. There is a period of using your body theoretically.

Really, once you get to the high level of baseball and look around, you see that arms are pretty meaningless. They're an afterthought, about as important as fingertips, just a distant extension of your grip on the ball. When they say a guy has a good arm, they're really saying he has great legs. I don't think I'm boasting when I remind you they've historically said this about me.

When crisis hits paradise: the power is out. It blew about three hours ago. I was halfway through a ham and Swiss, watching the 1 p.m. *SportsCenter*. They were in the middle of the Dodgers-Astros highlights, and the last thing I saw was the Houston catcher hit a grounder to third. It seemed like a one-hopper, but I never found out for sure whether there was a second hop, because right then the TV and the rest of the house clunked out. These new screens don't collapse in from the corners like the old ones, they just suddenly become off. The central A/C does make a sound when it goes—not that shudder of a wall unit, but a kind of homewide gasp. Which actually struck me as a pretty apt noise, when I heard it and realized what it meant. The idea of air-conditioning turning off in South Florida is not the same as elsewhere. Here it feels almost like ethics. The Palm Beaches are gluttons for refrigerated air, it pours like hospitality out of every building you enter. And now there has been overindulgence, and the sound of the shutdown seems to contain the entire range of accusation and repentance, the whole history of the technology and the state.

Anyway, the heat in the house started rising noticeably about nine minutes later, and it's now officially fierce. Frying the power grid is very different in summer than in winter. Winter may be more alarming, but your response is uncomplicated. You just go around and tighten things, and seal up other things, and put on more layers, and generally execute a more rigorous version of the plan you'd already been following. When you lose power in an air-conditioned house surrounded on all sides by hundred-degree heat, you have a dilemma. You first do the same sealing and tightening, in a desperate attempt to imprison the cold air. But you can feel the heat start to silently encroach. It worms its way around hinges, transmits itself through glass. And of course, your whole image of cold air as something you can trap is wrong anyway, it's all the same air, it's happy to change teams. It is a highly unrestricted free agent. And so you're faced with a critical decision: when to throw it in reverse, to unseal and aerate and make peace with the outside. The sweat starts to bead, and you stand there frowning at the windows, and you just think *I am 100% sure this is a metaphor for something*.

I caved about thirty minutes ago. I could tell the house had become a fake island. The thing you eventually realize is that the outside is already in—there is nothing left to preserve. So I went around and flung open every window I could find, even the little one behind the toilet in the third-string bathroom. About eight dead flies dropped off the bottom when I raised it. They were so dry that you could hear them when they fell onto the sill. More heat oozed in. I ended up just coming back out to the patio to write, because it's now pushing fastball numbers *in*side. Greg Maddux's fastball, but still.

And now the neighborhood waits in sweaty limbo. It could be more than the neighborhood—I can't exactly turn on the TV to find out. I can never keep straight which things work in a power outage. Telephones were always the confusing ones. I remember that like it's history. I pay for two landlines in Raleigh-Durham and use neither of them. I guess I overestimated the number of calls I'd receive, or underestimated technology. Anyway, I seem to recall that either cordless or corded work, but not both. Answering machines of course go haywire. I'll have to go investigate in the kitchen when I'm done out here.

My cell phone is still operable, though, and luckily I had just topped off a charge when the power went. So after I finished my sandwich in the last of the true cold air, I decided to give Churchy a call to get caught up on the highlights I missed. They hadn't gotten to the Birds recap when the screen cut out. I reached him on his way to the park. Churchy drives a navy Jaguar—it fits him like a padded glove. Backup catchers always drive the most tasteful autos.

They have earned their money through intelligence, and know their wealth is significant but fleeting. So they select the same vehicles as architects, and without fail have Pat Metheny in the dash.

Over the shimmering chords of "This Is Not America," Churchy told me the team has pulled to within two games. I knew this from reading the box scores, but it sounds different coming from someone who helped produce the news. "It's a real two," he said. The highlights I missed included his own alert eighth-inning pickoff throw to first, and the ones they wouldn't have shown involved crisp hitting of cutoff men and general *esprit de corps*. They have D.C. to beat up on this weekend, too, so there is hope in the clubhouse that August will be breached in a tie for the divisional lead. My friend spoke with the confidence of a backstop whose designated pitcher is in ruddy good health.

I cut things off there, like a shortstop who knows the man is going to score behind him. I wanted to preserve some power on my phone. One never knows how long something like this will last. How much time do power outages generally take? It's something you forget the minute they're over. How many hours or days that dark period actually was. Speaking of which, I should probably end here and keep a little juice on my laptop. And actually, just as I write that, I am hearing someone ring the front doorbell. This house has one of those doorbells that are recorded—that play the recorded sound of a doorbell. I am looking through the sliding doors up the hall and seeing Bill's wife, whose name I forget. Neighbors always check in with each other during power outages, even though there's rarely anything they'd need to go over. "So, the power's out." "Yes, yes it is." It's like we all can't accept that we can't fix the problem by sheer force of group agreement. She's ringing again—a two-tone electric toll of someone else's chime. It's going to take me a minute to get to you, neighbor. My knee and all.

# AUGUST

The power must have come back in the middle of the night. I'd gone to sleep on top of the covers, which is something I hate more than most. I've learned to conk out just about anywhere, in any position—the buses of the California League will teach you that. The overnighters to High Desert, to Inland Empire. Those are real baseball towns, by the way, I'm not just making a dramatic point. I determined around High-A that the ability to nod off in strange circumstances would be at least as important to my career advancement as the ability to poke a sac fly. And I believe that's been true. My lone requirement is that I have something covering my person. It can be the slimmest fabric imaginable, I mean Saran Wrap would be fine. There's just got to be *some* material draped across me.

Anyway, I'd tossed and turned into something resembling sleep, which occurred to me as I drifted off could be kind of dangerous when your leg is on the mend. There is a level of hazard too pathetic to be mentioned in professional settings. These you must spot on your own. I'd carefully tossed and turned, and when I opened my eyes next I saw the ceiling fan moving again, and heard voices jawing in the living room. Too amiable to be burglars: television. Over several seconds I became aware that the house once again had that smell of sound. You know: that sound of light.

So I went down the hall to turn everything off, and what do you know, *SportsCenter* was on again. *SportsCenter* is always on, with an unclear mixture of live and taped components. It strikes me as a masterpiece of management, of tweaks done on the fly. They used to have an ad campaign in which pro athletes announced not that they watched it—a given—but *which one* they watched. The 6 p.m., the 7 p.m., the 8—they progressed through the whole day, each airing had a famous devotee. Instead of the NL versus the AL in the All-Star

Game, maybe they could just pit the morning ESPN watchers against the nights.

I was up at that point, so after I went around and resealed the house bubble, I perched on the couch to catch the highlights. The West Coast games had just finished. Those West Coast games are funny, when you're Back East: they seem to be coming from about the moon. Beaming in at 1:30 a.m. with their palm courts and micro-brew beers and dreamy fans. And I say this as a guy who's played in them. The late games mattered to me in this case because the Braves are out playing the Giants, who have embraced their role as the summer's pests—not good enough to contend for a wild card, but eager to spoil the opportunities of others. When they smell the chance to ruin something, they're suddenly a bunch of McCoveys and Mayses and Marichals. And last night they tore up the jet-lagged Atlantans, 8–3, as much of a midsummer slugfest as you can have in that kind of fog.

I guarantee you my teammates were watching closely, over Miller Lites and rubdowns in our clubhouse. Ballplayers opt for cheap beer the way they opt for trucks. They'd just done their part—a taut 3–1 home victory, our relief men tying off the win with ten consecutive outs. A tourniquet of retired batters, the sort of win that will make a manager sleep for fifteen downy hours, and a wounded starter for three. The division lead now stands at one. The needle has officially jumped the standings groove. Churchy told me yesterday that they're all going to start growing some sort of weird facial hair if and when they pull even. They haven't decided what kind yet, or what would make them eventually shave. They don't want to jinx anything.

The heat has finally eased a bit this afternoon, which is to say it's about 91 degrees in the shade, and I'm about to grab the fungoes and take some swings. I've been thinking again about months. When June ended, I mentioned how it always gets cut off too soon. The medieval mathematicians didn't properly consider its spirit. They couldn't ask the ballplayer, history's greatest aficionado of summer. July, though, is everything it appears, the truest of the thirty-one-day months. It gets called long, and it even looks long when you see it on the semicircle of a baseball calendar—towering over the other months as it spans the apex of the arc. That great July bend: it always makes me think of the curvature of the earth. Maybe that's why I always hit well then. The month feels so vast that the pressure to perform just drops away, there will always be more opportunities, this is never it. And now August has commenced, and it's something else again. The first month you want to be a Mr. of, the one where all the issued flavors finally start to combine, to leave a particular taste. A month stewed in juices. Looking at August, I always see it as marinated, as cured.

*Monday August 2*

I overslept this morning. Not the way you want to start a day, a week, a treatment month, making staff wait for you. But in this case it genuinely wasn't my fault. The outage reset all the clocks to 12:00, and some of them stayed flashing on that number, but I guess the bedroom clock just treated the moment the power returned as a fresh midnight, which some clocks will do. So it never caught my eye as being wrong. But it must have established 12:00 at approximately 2 a.m., and when I woke up and ambled down the hall leisurely, thinking it was 7:45, the stove informed me it was actually 9:48. Before the power went, the microwave and stove had been perfectly in sync. They're on opposite sides of the kitchen, so you couldn't actually watch them change numbers simultaneously, but they were even enough that you could never catch one out in the time it took your head to swivel. Today I reset them twice, but I couldn't get them that close. There's a little hiccup now.

The PARC team didn't look thrilled when I appeared, but I couldn't tell if it was because I was late, or because I hadn't been late often *enough*. When you're a pro athlete, people assume you have other important things to be doing. They can't believe that the thing you're scheduled to do with them is actually all you've got on your calendar. And I've gotten used to the look you receive when you were supposed to be famous, and then you arrived at the restaurant at 7 sharp. There's always a startled little "*Oh* . . ." emitted by the host, who had been told to set aside a fine table, and you can see the wheels turning in his head, he's now wondering whether to give it to someone else. It frankly embarrasses people when a celebrity arrives on time.

"I tried to call you," Jenn said quietly, when I finally turned up. She did seem embarrassed, but not in the way I've gotten used to.

"Yeah, *sorry . . .*" I quickly slipped under a metric ton of iron and prepared to move it in two-inch increments. Then I thought of something. "That's weird though, my phone should have been working again." Phones in outages, would there ever be clarity?

"No, I mean I tried to call you yesterday."

"Huh. And it rang? I'm trying to remember which phones ring."

"What kind of phone is it?"

"Cordless." I let out a grunt as I moved a small Fiat half a centimeter.

"Battery-powered handset?"

"Think so." *Argggh.* "Uniden." *Blunngh.* "Matte gray."

"That should work."

"Wait." *UNGGGH.* My sounds were becoming embarrassing. "Why were you calling on a Sunday?"

"Uniden kind of sounds like one of those 'den' names kids get now, don't you think?"

"*Uh-HUHHH!!*" I screamed on an exhale.

"My ex was into those for a little while."

"What'd—*blunnghh*—you go with?"

"John."

I winced beneath the weight. Should have remembered that. But before I could apologize, Jens was next to us, blathering merrily about tissue loss, his spirits revived by my big delay.

Of course a whole different code goes into tardiness with the team. A ballplayer is faced with an endlessly updated series of bus times and wheels-up times and BP times, so he has plenty of things to be late or punctual for, and it's important for him to weigh his options. Being timely is not always to your advantage. Do it too dependably, and you're reminding the squad that you're something less than a star. They won't forget when it comes time to negotiate a contract. But arriving late if you're not good enough to carry it off with swagger—that's a sure way to get yourself designated for assignment. So it's really a poker game. I gave up daring to oversleep on a team bus years ago, I know I'm not holding aces. I'm not above the perfectly timed missed meeting, though, if I feel my stock needs a push.

But that's league politics—hardly something I'd inflict on the people caring for my leg. This is a big week, too: the week I return to real bats. Wednesday is the day. I'll admit that I've been stopping by the blue bedroom several times daily just to weigh them in my hands, to test out the preliminary motions of my celebrated singles stroke. I've been behaving myself, though. I haven't seen a swing through. Any first base umpire would rule I was checking it. Only the surliest of catchers would even appeal.

In updates from the out-of-town scoreboard, the Birds crack the new month still a game out in the division. They won, but the Braves did too. Maybe that's what Jenn wanted to talk about, calling on a Sunday. Well, the Fu Manchus will have to wait. The Chester A. Arthurs. Somewhere our Roy is silently celebrating his luck. Those beard confections always look the worst on rooks—their peach fuzz has nowhere to hide. Me? I can handle all facial hair requests. My lone whisker weakness lies in width of cheek coverage, but that very rarely comes into play.

*Tuesday August 3*

I became aware of something, as I was sitting out here with a Louisville this morning, spinning it in my palms and counting down the hours until I could reasonably leave for the pool. My cursive name wheeling into view approximately 2.5 times per second, like those cherries on a slot machine. Forget bats, I realized, sitting right here. I haven't picked up a *baseball* since May 3rd. And not since an inning earlier, too, when I returned a sharp Reds single to the infielders before a K sent us all back to the dugout. Tossed it in with that slow, resigned loop of the arm: whatever has gone wrong, the ball is still needed back on the mound. A life lesson. And that would turn out to be it, for me and the old horsehide. I had to go take a piss after my AB in the sixth, and by the time I arrived in left for the bottom of the inning, the warm-up balls had all been thrown in and I was getting a glare from Billy.

I think I've figured out what made me think of this. Bill has installed a birdhouse behind his residence, one of those freestanding pole-top models, set about ten feet back from the water. I'm sure he could discourse at length about local warblers and such. The thing about this birdhouse is, it's dead white and trimmed in red. And as I was sitting and perceiving it in a general way, I realized I was squeezing the bat tighter, and rocking back and forth in my chair. I looked down and watched my grip getting into an athletic lather, without any directive from me. And crazy as it sounds, I'm convinced that what happened was my mind saw those colors and thought: *a baseball.* And then it went: *sweet lord, I haven't held one of those in months.*

Where would I even get a ball right now, I wonder? And is there any reason to have one around? Some do believe in the importance of simple proximity. There's a color commentator on one of the West

Coast teams, I can't remember which, who always keeps a ball by his desk while he's doing the broadcast—he just tosses it back and forth from hand to hand. This is classic ex-ballplayer stuff, but I see his point. Anyway, I don't think I've actually purchased one since I was about seventeen. Since then, they've always just been in front of me at the moment I've required them. What would it be like to go buy a baseball in ten minutes? And what would it be like to be a cashier at an East Palm Beach sporting goods store when a major leaguer fished three hardballs out of the bulk bin and plunked them down on the checkout counter, guarding them with his still-substantial forearm so they didn't roll away?

But that birdhouse, which a little brown lizard is now sticking his head into. It's gotten me thinking more about colors—a critical aspect of American baseball, in my opinion. An aspect that goes tragically unmentioned. There is really a whole storyline happening in the pigments of the game. Start with that white of the ball. It is the most famous white in the land, only Hanes T-shirts and chalkboard chalk are even in the same sentence. But even all baseball white isn't created equal. The balls get whiter and whiter as you rise through the leagues, but by the time you reach MLB they've outdone themselves, and the umps have to dull them back down—which they accomplish with a specific brown mud from the Delaware River in New Jersey. Its color recalls that deeper chocolate you only see when you see chocolate actively being made. There's no need for the farm teams to import this. A minor league baseball is covered in plenty of mud from its own state.

Then there is the color of the MLB ballfield: a green greener than you can believe, so green that when you come upon it—after the russet smog of Orange County, the brick brownstones of Queens—you always gasp a little. Don't think this isn't the point. Have you ever noticed how nothing near a pro diamond is green at all? Ballparks are never next to . . . parks. Ebbets Field was, and look what they did to it. It's like they want to make you forget this color even exists, then boom, own your view. And this is why I think the whole natural grass debate of recent years has missed the point. You notice we are the only country to get hung up on this. Baseball gets played on the artificial stuff in Canada, Korea, Japan. Smart nations. They know you could play a game on emerald-painted cement and still hit 98% of spectating sweet spots.

By now you're probably waving your hands in protest, giving me the old third base coach stop sign. "But the smell of the grass, Xandy, the smell of the grass!" Well, I'm going to run through you here, because I think I can score. Think back to the last game you attended. Your company got a block of "View" level seats. Not until you arrived did you realize this was code for the highest deck. Nice in apartment buildings, less so in stadiums. During the course of the game, you smelled beer, peanuts, cross-trainers, urinal cakes. But I promise that one thing you never smelled was grass. There is a pushing and pulling at work in my league, a tug-of-war between ideas and sensations. At a Japanese game, you drink Suntory whiskey to the tune of symmetrical AstroTurf and leave feeling good about your life.

I have a hitch in my swing, it's not a secret around the league. It happens as I begin to unfold my hands in earnest, when the bat is about a foot gone from my rear shoulder. Just as the head passes the catcher's eyes, it floats ever so briefly above the swing's invisible surface, like a pebble skipping off a pond. I've watched it umpteen times in super-slow-motion video. I know my hitch like the birthmark above my left ankle. I guess you could say the arc my bat describes becomes a little wordy.

Needless to mention, they tried to iron this out in Double-A. I had swing coaches drop all kinds of analogies on me. I was told to picture my bat as a skiff plowing through a calm sea. As a hammer being swung in an ancient Olympics. None of it worked. No one found the right symbol. And eventually it became clear that we could risk the skills I did have trying to make me into a star, or we could accept that cut fastballs from top-tier righties were going to shame me, and just hope that pitch didn't become fashionable. It turned out to be a stroke of career-saving luck that those Braves pitchers had all that success with the circle change, back in the '90s. Suddenly everyone wanted to learn that pitch instead of the hard breakers. I've always been an excellent changeup hitter, which is unusual for a guy who can handle fastballs. Honestly I've never seen why guys make such a big fuss about the pitch. Here's the trick: you have to imagine, in those nanoseconds after you realize you've started your stroke too soon, that your whole body has just been soaking in an ice bath. Literally, keep an image of an old clawfoot tub on reserve in your mental files, fill it to the brim with cubes. Your limbs are stiff and slow, they are sapped of strength. The point is, you have to convince yourself not that you don't *want* to bring your arms and legs around quickly, but that you physically *can't*. And once you do that, your motion self-corrects, the timing falls back into place, and you find yourself pulling a double down the line.

I'm pretty certain I've found the hitmaker among my stash of Kentucky lumber. As soon as I got back from the Center this morning—my knee still wrapped in one of the special ice packs that Jenn has started making for me, she chips the ice down so it's not so uncomfortable, they're great—I brought all dozen bats out to the little grass plain between the patio and the lappy edge of the lagoon, where I would be taking my first authentic cuts, and I spread them out to be surveyed at my God-given remove of six feet, one inch. I'm sure it made an entertaining sight for the neighbors, but understand that this was essential. A relationship forms with any bat you swing, and I needed to properly examine them all before I got attached to a stick with no prospects.

What sets a bat apart, from a visual perspective? This is one of the game's enduring mysteries, but for starters, I think a bat needs to not look too woody. That is, you don't want to go to the plate remembering that you're holding a piece of a tree—it's just unhelpful. So any bat with those implications is out, and today I could disqualify three right away. Then of the remaining nine, two more struck me as less than perfectly shaped. A professionally crafted bat will always be even enough that you can't actually "see" a shaping error, but you can sense it. You have to look a few inches away, and then let your peripheral vision do the ascertaining. It's like so many things, you can't see it clearly when you're looking right at it. That left me with seven, and at that point I started picking them up, but not yet in a baseball-related way—just hefting them like any household object, or maybe a pool cue at a bar. Another two failed that test: one seemed weirdly end-heavy, and the other struck me as fragile. The last thing was to pick them up with my grip intact, and there was immediately one more I just got a bad vibe from. I then decided I was wrong, but at that point I'd already doubted it too much, and it had to go anyway. A player can poison a perfectly good bat, and once contracted, the disease has no cure. This left me with four worth keeping around, and at that stage I went inside for some lunch. But the time away gave me fresh eyes, and after I came back outside, I felt I could see a certain deadness in the second stick from the right. And so this was how I decided which three I'd take to the swinging stage. A typical selection process for a major leaguer, I think you'd find.

Of course, all that's just the beginning. You don't learn the soul of a bat until you take it on its appointed rounds. Even a grip can be misleading. A grip can sway you with the romance of feel—it's cagey like that. Because a delicious handle might make you think that the best bat feels like the best bat, when really the best bat is the one that makes you feel like the best swinger. The one that accepts your hitch, partners with it, doesn't view it as a personal failing. Loves you for who you are. And the first two bats I swung were solid, and of course I was downright giddy to be whirling them in baseball circles. They will travel with me to my next destination. But the third was in that special category. And the way I knew it was that white ash beaut made my right knee feel like it was positively bolted to the ground.

That knee of mine. Things have been suspiciously quiet down in my leg of late. No mystery twinges or tinges or twangs. No squeaks or clicks or shifts. It makes a guy antsy. He feels like something is being planned behind his back. Like while I'm staring off at the water, a calamity is being plotted, only when I glance back down to catch it out, everyone quick, clams up. Maybe on one level an injured athlete just never gets over the fact that nothing was exactly what he heard right before the whole symphony of disaster. He loses his trust in that silence.

But I am taking my knee at its word. This week I have begun venturing out on long walks around the neighborhood. This on the doctor's orders. "So now we'll have you . . . take a walk!" was how Jens put it to me on Monday. The sentence was as sudden as it looks. It sounded like Jens was surprised, but I think he was just ebullient.

I'm sure taking a walk seemed like a simple enough instruction to a rangy Scandinavian born with Vibram rubber on his feet, but I've been having some trouble finding my rhythm. The issue is, there are so many kinds of walks, once you start thinking about it, and I have had a hard time deciding which applies to me. On Monday afternoon, I went out in jeans and a T-shirt, and I just felt confused out there. I kept itching for a destination. I'd brought a Birds-issue water bottle, which felt stupid in my hand. So then on Tuesday, I changed up my equation. I went out after dinner, with a bottle of spring water, thinking this was the walk Jens had in mind. The so-called post-prandial stroll. The lagoon would be my Seine, my Danube. Back home in my kitchen there would be unpasteurized cheese, and I would not refrigerate it. But I realized two blocks from the house that I'd jumbled it up again, by wearing workout clothes. And maybe also by not having a lover by my side.

So it sounds like a crazy problem to have, because what's more natural than ambling, but it's like being a ballplayer at this moment in history kind of messes up your instincts. Motions that are athletic but also part of a lifestyle—when are they which? You exist in a sort of Los Angeles of the mind, in which you lose sight of how and when to use your body as a source of horsepower. Only those Manhattan athletes seem to keep it together. They stroll to the bagel shop on Saturday morning. They jog around the scenic Central Park reservoir, even if they do have a Town Car drop them off. They are New Yorkers of a certain standing whose job happens to be baseball. I seriously feel that if I were on the Mets, I wouldn't be giving this a second thought.

Today, though, on my fourth walk, I finally started to get the hang of it. What I did was hedge my bets. Confuse my system. I went out in the early morning, for exercise or fresh air. I brought with me an organic peach: workout fuel or picnic food. I sat back and let the situation define itself for me, which is how you're taught to hit a knuckleball. And I must have found my stride, because before I knew it, it was forty minutes later and I was all the way around on the opposite shore of the lagoon, looking back at the patio. It's not too far as the crow flies, but the shoreline is heavily inleted. I imagine there is a local fun fact about how long it would be if stretched straight, and everyone "oohs" when they hear it. While I was out there I ate my provision and threw the pit satisfyingly far back toward my origin, watching it plunk into the water. Like I say, it is pleasant to deploy your skills.

One thing I was still having trouble deciding, though, as I strolled home with the latest version of my gait, which still cops to some nerves on the right, almost like I am testing the thickness of pond ice, was whether it made sense to explore the cul-de-sacs, or stick to roads with outlets. This seemed significant to me, in terms of the bigger picture. And at first I just did it both ways, but they are so common here, you really need to have some sort of policy.

*Saturday August 7*

Well, they've done it—the guys have pulled divisionally even. The boys in Carolina blue-ish. What is our team color, anyway? I've never been able to decide. Pale midnight? Slate cyan? It's like a Miles Davis album on our bench. You'll find this a lot these days, especially among newer clubs: uniforms that reference eight hues without ever settling on one. For the Birds' first five years, their color scheme actually referenced a bird—or a future bird, at least. Hats and jersey trim were a pale robin's-egg blue. But then a new ownership group came, and I guess they got scared that the blue was too certain, or something, was too definitely the color it was. Opinions could be had. And so they came up with this one, which no one has ever argued about, because it makes you forget you have feelings.

The game last night went into extras. The Birds are over in Houston this weekend, in the Central Time Zone, and by the time they hit the seventh the EDT Braves had already coughed up their half of the one-game edge. Not prettily, either. Their leftfielder dropped a routine fly in the top of the ninth to let a man score from first, snapping a tie they couldn't recreate in their turn. I was listening as it all went down up in Georgia, so I knew it was a legit error. There is a particular tone in an announcer's voice, a whole attitude, called "routine fly." I have decided that a good alternative, on nights when the live feed from my own team sounds too clear, just seems to have a rawness I'd need to soften with some censor's delay, is to listen to the other games that matter, that relate tangentially to our fate. Other than the Braves, I've also been dipping into the wild card happenings in the East and West and middle. The wild card is our backup plan, of course, although the teams in the NL South are all bloodying each other so much and so evenly that it's unlikely we'll be a division that sends one. Division title or bust—there's something vintage about this.

So the Braves lost their draw in the ninth, and the Birds basically did the opposite an inning of time later, in the top of the eighth. I was listening at this point. With Roy on first, our rightfielder crushed a 3–1 pitch about halfway to the Gulf of Mexico, and 5–3 became 5–5, and we were suddenly coasting down that bunny slope toward extras. In San Francisco you can actually do that now, hit homers into the ocean, it's not just hyperbole anymore. And that makes sense out there. But who knows what makes sense in Houston? As a baseball town, it can't decide if it's a tropical city or a Southern one or a Midwestern one or a Texan one. This is reflected in its field. I don't have a big problem with turf, as I've said. They say it kills knees, but clearly fresh grass doesn't save them. And there was a certain sweetness to the old Astrodome. The way, when you thought about it, looking up at the ceiling from the dugout, you were all just in one really big room. But that new indoor/outdoor park they have now, where it's real grass but there's a roof they can deploy for rain or heat, depending on what kind of city they are—that place I cannot stand. Because the people there are never like "Yes, this summer day in Southeast Texas is pleasant enough that we don't want you to turn on the A/C." The retractable roof never gets retracted. The Astrodome was honest about human nature.

They did get into extras, and at that point I went and fetched a fresh beer and resettled myself on the other end of the sofa. My one real problem with listening to games on the radio is that I don't know where to look. If I'm listening to a day game, no problem—I just sit out here, and the lagoon offers the perfect ambient noise for my eyes. But inside at night it's just walls and golf. And kind of ironically, I find I end up looking at the blank TV. It's just the most neutral surface. And that's where I was looking when we walked in a run in the top of the eleventh, and again when our closer preserved that lead in the bottom. If you had peeked in through the back window, you would have sworn I had the comprehensive cable package. The away team gets to save its closer in extras, because they know if they have a lead to protect. A hole in the game. There are still a few.

Who the big win really affects, of course, is Gillette. The stubble on the guys' upper lips doesn't know it yet, but it is now being collected and collated. Stored for eventual deployment. A whole new talent sort will become visible on television, separate from the hitting and throwing: who can grow and who can't. Without exception, it is a weenie utility second baseman who suddenly distinguishes himself. He's 5'9 and averages 5.9 home runs a year, but his beard is major-league loamy.

I ran into Jenn at the Publix this morning. Apparently she is not a churchgoer either. It was my first time seeing her outside the confines of PARC, or considering that a slim white sundress is something she might own in addition to yoga pants. That can give you quite a jolt—running into someone at the supermarket. I think in part because the items in your cart suddenly feel very exposing. In an alternate version of our society, this would be kept confidential, like prescriptions. Like how in an alternate version of baseball, there would be no ground-rule doubles, the fielder would just have to go get the ball. Jenn was pushing about eleven containers of soy milk, along with a half-dozen pint-sized carrot juices and several boxes of some sort of fiber cereal that looked, in the picture on the front, like a writhing mass of worms. Those three items only, even though she was clearly on her way to the checkout when we crossed paths.

I actually find it impressive when someone has a cart like that. They know so perfectly their own tastes and needs. *Now there's someone who knows what she wants*, I thought approvingly. One would not get this impression looking at my cart. I've tried, but I've never been able to approach the supermarket with that kind of focus, that drive. I meander, am swayed by colors and slogans and snags of childhood memory, and without variation I walk out with a case of some root beer I drank once when I was sixteen. They say you divide your brain, drifting when it's OK so you can focus when you need to. And I wonder if my grocery store wandering is what allows me to stare down the barrel of a fastball with a mind as clean as an empty steel pail. Though lately I've also been wondering what happens when your mind doesn't have *enough* time to wander, just deciphers too many net curves. Your eyes get worn out from all those reads on all that spin. I'm missing things, I'm sure of that, but that's the same as not knowing what they are.

Jenn was gazing at me expectantly, and I felt a sudden urge to say all this to her. Tell her all about the root beer and the curveballs and how humbled I was by her cool, decisive cart. Explain how baseball gave me vision but also infected my brain sometimes, made it hard for me to get a read on events outside the lines.

What I said instead was, "Soy milk—mmm."

We both looked at the floor mournfully. She said she guessed she'd better check out now. I said yes, she probably should.

It's been a quiet afternoon around here. Quieter even than usual. You learn to distinguish between levels of quiet in this development, just like you do with heat. Every region has its own subdivisions. In San Francisco, the temperature changes by five degrees all year, but they still have hot days and cold days and warm ones. In Seattle, it always rains, so they carve sunny days out of the lighter drizzle.

The issue now I guess is that it's August, and everyone leaves. The runner is in street clothes somewhere. The Winnebago is gone, off touring this or that national monument. They never really seem like monuments. It's true all over the world, the August exodus, except in the places those people are going. It's interesting, because July is hotter, but I guess in August you're more tired of the heat. My family tried a July vacation exactly once: nine days in Sandusky, when I was around ten. A week and a half of funnel cake and vomit. No one got what they needed, even I could tell. There was too much hope left in the summer, not enough longing. Of course, if you leave it till August's fourth week then the sadness is upon you, you might as well not go. This, right now, the second week of the eighth month, is literally twice as good a vacation time as any other. I guess it's just one more example of a ballplayer traveling in an opposite direction.

Remember those tee balls we all used to play with, back in Tee Ball? The cushioned ones with the satiny surface that made no sound when you hit them? They even had that raised red line to suggest "stitches," only two fabrics had not actually been joined at that place—it was more like a pipe cleaner had been glued on. Then after those, we spent that one year playing with the balls that look exactly like hardballs, but give shockingly when you squeeze them. When I was in high school, one of those accidentally got into a game for two pitches, before our catcher hit a grounder from the dead-ball era and we all realized something was up. I guess some youth-league team had left it on the grass, and someone thought *Hey, what a beautiful white ball.* You have to be careful. No game imitates itself better than mine.

I'll be doing my tee hitting at another junior college, presumably with genuine hardballs. This area is teeming with JCs, and each seems to have a professional-grade facility in one sport, but not several. I guess the term junior college has been falling out of fashion—"area" colleges, they are now called. These have long been the schools of choice for top baseball prospects. I have no idea why. Rising stars go to D-level two-year schools three states away from where they're from, there's no logic to it. Only a few four-year universities around the country, like the one Roy went to, have any kind of baseball reputation at all. This seems to happen arbitrarily: which sports' high amateur levels end up being associated with high academic colleges. And it makes sense to plan ahead. If I had an ounce of foresight, I would have gone into lacrosse instead.

But here I am. I have reached the period of rehab that everyone longs for, uses as the great benchmark—the return to "baseball activities." What is a baseball activity? It is a motion exclusive to the execution of a baseball task. Simple enough, it seems: taking BP, hitting cutoff men, these obviously qualify. But, for example, running is not a baseball activity, because you could run for many reasons, even though if you're like most ballplayers you probably only *would* if a game were being played, and possibly only a game with playoff implications. However, running on manicured grass if a ball has been thrown nearby—that counts. But if it's just a ball a friend has thrown to you for fun, or if you're not wearing a mitt, then once again it is not a baseball activity. It's a slippery concept.

Running is probably a bad example, in my case, because I of course am not allowed to do it, baseball version or otherwise. But the key to baseball activities is that you only need to cover one to qualify—to give your agent and GM something to crow about to the press. Jeff lives for this stuff, he believes it is an entirely helpful way of assessing progress. And like a lot of agents, he's eager to push the line. I mean, he'd call my walk to the patio a baseball activity if he could, because of the echo of a base on balls. He'd call me tying my cross-trainers a baseball activity, because of a guy lacing up his cleats.

I talked to him this afternoon. He needed a good quote for the latest press release. I think he would issue a new press release to announce that a ball I'd hit, which had looked foul off the bat, now appeared to be curling fair. But that's the system now, and you have to pick your battles. I told him I was taking it day by day. "That's *great*, Xandy!" he shouted at my ear, and I could practically hear him squirming with delight, his Mercedes winding dangerously through this canyon or that. "Exactly what you should be doing!"

The water polo team has been slowly encroaching on my end of the pool. I wasn't sure of it at first. Like I said, they have one of those lane dividers, the kind constructed of many plastic discs, which you assume are made by the same company behind gutter cushions for beginner bowling. And I thought I was crazy, because things like that you just think of as permanent, once they're in place. Like the pool was born with them. But I started counting the number of tiles between the line and the wall, and sure enough, it's dropped each of the last two weeks. I can picture how this must have gone. "You guys need to make room," they were told. "There's a major leaguer in the water." But then they saw me, and I didn't jibe with the picture they'd had in their minds. And so they started chopping off a few inches each time, and now I just have a little country lane left to myself, and they have been hurling booming yellow passes within inches of my head. Would they dare do this if I were known as a 20/20 man? The problem is, my numbers don't translate. I am a 16/6 man. That doesn't sound like baseball. It sounds like carpentry. It sounds like welding.

On my way back from the pool, I stopped by the self-service car wash. There's one just before the causeway, stuck on the end of a larger complex that includes a driving range and a batting cage. It seems they never know where to put self-service car washes, because they aren't really structures in their own right. They are superstructures, regions to pass through. And I guess this developer just decided to put all the coin-operated things together, that was his organizing principle. It made sense to me. I'm always glad to see a batting cage placed with something serious, as opposed to a go-kart track or mini-golf course. You'll see it treated both ways: the cage as a game, or the cage as heavy machinery. And I believe in the latter. Selecting 90 should be like selecting a high-pressure foaming brush with extended reach. Time running out on pitches should be like time running out with soap still on the hood.

I hadn't washed the Volvo all summer, and the regional grime had gotten pretty thick: a skin of mosquitoes and flies stuck to the hood, two months of receipts piled up like leaves on the passenger side floor. I don't like to get so behind, but I was worried about contorting my knee while running the carpet vacuum, and I'm adamant about doing my own car. Only in the last week has this task started to seem reasonable. It started seeming reasonable on Friday. But it was great, because I had a summer's worth of quarters in the console, and I could use the full arsenal of cleaning options—the special tire cleaner, the buffing wax. I knew I could always go back for another rinse if something went wrong. That's what holds everyone back. And I recommend this as a treat. Go to a self-service car wash with *extra* change. It will alter your whole perspective.

I had so many quarters, in fact, that after I'd washed and waxed and vacuumed, I was struck by the urge to go drop some on the cages. It wasn't like there was a Laundromat I needed to save it for. Laundry is a great perk of the bigs, by the way. Technically you're only supposed to give game wear to the equipment managers, not street clothes, but no EM builds any kind of career taking this rule literally. Many are the polo shirts I've snuck in with the away grays. "Just keep 'em taupe, that's all I ask," Sam has sighed. The "gray" load of laundry exists in my world alone.

Taking cuts at some untested batting cage was strictly forbidden, of course, not to mention slumming it. But I figured if I didn't actually swing at any balls, I wasn't hurting anything. So I just grabbed a beat-up helmet and one of those eight-cent aluminum bats, and I turned the machine as high as it would go, which was 90, and I got in there and let them whiz deliciously past me, showing my best "take" stance. A good take is when you act like you really wanted to swing, but decided *shoot*, you just couldn't. Except everyone knows that, so it's also the biggest giveaway. One after another, I took, my bat twitching with discipline on my right shoulder. You've done this before, I imagine. Adjusted your helmet and your nerve and put it on 90, to see what 90 looks like. You do this because it looks exotic. But I was in there for the opposite reason. I know what 90 looks like. It's not even an average fastball in my league, if a guy threw like that pitching machine, he wouldn't get past AA. 90 to me looks like a golden retriever. It looks like a home-cooked meal. And I stayed in the cage just licking my chops, considering seams and spins and laundry. "Poor Jenn—no *thwack!*—doesn't even have a Sam—lack of *thwock!*—to keep her sundress—almost took a rip!—colorfast." I could have gladly stayed there not swinging all day, but at last my quarters ran out, the teenage attendant in the flat-brimmed Marlins hat giving me a glare that could have pierced an ump's chest protector.

You know what the real thing of it is? Soy milk isn't even tasty.

High-definition *Baseball Tonight* on a fifty-inch screen confirms it: something beyond stubble is now darkening the faces of the Birds. Your first impression is that they just look exhausted. But they're playing at home, so there wouldn't be any jet lag. And they've been blazing through their double-play turns and legging out doubles and generally making hay of the sluggish Padres. It doesn't add up. All of this processing takes about 2.8 seconds, and then you remember, *Oh yeah, they're just highly successful.* It's a good thing raw speed isn't important in baseball, that body hair doesn't hold you back. Water polo players would have no way of celebrating a division lead. Those guys get rid of hair you don't even remember you have. They shave the tops of their hands. They pluck their big toes. I've seen it.

The crowds at our park have been swelling with this run. You can sense it in the highlights. They don't look bigger, per se, they just sound more electric. In other new-market cities, you'll also see the waving of small towels at this stage, when a fanbase has been inspired. These are always called "terrible towels," or "horrible hankies." "Satanic washcloths," something vicious like that. They're never even 100% cotton. The Birds don't do anything like this, I think because everyone knows it would have to be plastic beaks strapped to foreheads with rubber bands, and no one wants to deal with that.

We do get good fans at our field, even when the team is running cold. They're a positive group, without being ignorant. I didn't get into this when I was there for the All-Stars, but our park is actually called People's Park. It's not what you'd think, though. People's is actually a bank in the Southeast. Of course, this is confusing to many, who read community spirit into the title. And I know there are certain Carolina Republicans who don't like it—who would feel much more comfortable if the stadium were named something less socialist, more recognizably pro-business. Something good and anonymous and initial-heavy, PZNML Field or what-have-you, that they could change in the event of a merger without anyone noticing. A ballpark that could be an office park.

Those poor Padres. It was almost hard to watch the clips: we tore them to pieces in two out of three, and the Tuesday contest they were lucky to eke out. Teams hate to lose big and win close. Road games for that team are horrendously surprising. They play in such an extreme pitchers' park that their hurlers can approach the game with an entirely different strategy at home, just disdainful fastballs down the heart of the plate. Only they never know what they have until they travel. They can't judge their own organization's talent. In their worst years, the Padres practically inspire sympathy from the other teams in the league. They even have the kindliest nickname in sports: "the Dads." The Birds don't have a nickname. They used to call teams like the Cardinals and Orioles "the Birds," until we came along and stole the generalization. We would have to be nicknamed something more specific, and it doesn't work that way.

The team now has today off, a travel day, even though they're still at home this weekend. By now I think you see what I mean: Mondays and Thursdays are about identity, not transportation from city to city. I, however, was on the clock, finally hitting the tees this morning. An anti-climactic thing, as it turned out. You think the weird part is going to be that no ball is being pitched, but what actually throws you is that you don't know where you should hit the ball *to*. All that time away to ponder it, and I found myself having no idea where to deposit a baseball when one was finally propped up for me. The college had deployed a few JV guys to shag, and I couldn't decide whether I should specifically aim toward or away from them. But I got some good swings in. The knee supported my cause. Our man in Homestead was back to watch. He voiced no complaints.

In other news, I have now once again touched a baseball. After I was done hitting, I decided to throw some long-toss with one of the college guys. I hadn't thought to bring a glove, though I do have one at the house, so I borrowed someone's—it must have been the first time in years I'd worn a mitt without my own name on the heel. Instead, it had Cal Ripken's on the palm. It was an infielder's glove, too: stubby, for better ball control, and with a closed web, because IFs don't need to peek through for fly balls. As though OFs catch them that way. Catch was neither a part of my program nor not part of my program. I guess when it's your leg that's hurt, rather than your arm, they just figure that the day there's a reason to be around balls hitting-wise, that's the same day you're allowed to toss one. And so I did. I can report that it felt about as I remembered.

One of Jens' favorite games is to try to pin down exactly how my knee feels on a given day. This is his job, as the one supervising my therapy, but he takes it further than seems strictly necessary. He is obsessed with coming up with the perfect image, the most evocative turn of phrase. Usually these involve fruit. I'll supply basic sensations, and he converts these to a multiple choice of verse. I might remark that it's feeling sound, but with some tightness around the edges. "So would you say, a beautiful cantaloupe picked just a bit too soon? Or the final grapefruit of the season?"

This morning, he came over as I was finishing some step-ups. To his credit, he is willing to get his suits dangerously close to my perspiring form. I mentioned that I felt good about the stability, but the knee was still missing some bounce. We concluded that it was like an expensive mattress that yet needed breaking in.

Seeing Jenn at the supermarket has really gotten me thinking more—about diet. It's an amazing thing, in pro baseball. With all the attention the bigwigs pay to every little detail of your life, they are just now, like in the last six months out of a hundred-odd-year history, starting to notice what we eat, and how this just might have some impact on our performance. And even this has happened in reverse: it took protein powders to make them think more about food. It's like they just discovered fish last year, swimming in the waterfall at Kauffman Stadium. Baseball is still fundamentally a lifestyle game, same as it was in the 1880s. The first rule is that you're only expected to do as well as six-packs, tobacco, and fries will allow.

What eventually saves most guys who last is a realization we come to about wealth. For me this happened about two seasons ago. I finally clued in to the fact that instead of jumping in on the room-service orders of fried chicken and chicken-fried steak, of chicken rigatoni (to mix things up), our older vets would get out of the hotel and go somewhere nice. And not only steakhouses, either, but places where you could get poached halibut or wild-caught salmon. Something floating in something other than ranch dressing, all washed down with a triple-digit Pinot Blanc. You see that, and it's kind of an *aha!* moment. You realize that the only way to enjoy your salary is to become a more adventurous diner, and so you start to educate yourself about food. You find yourself skipping the breaded stuff, the food-service cream sauces—or at least having a *reason* to imbibe, like if there's a nice béchamel. And you start to feel better, physically as well as emotionally. So I'm by no means perfect, and I still have my ballplayer's weakness for whole washbasins of cereal. But I want to shout at some of these second-year guys: "You're not a jock anymore—you're a rich guy! Now act like one!"

My point being, for the last few days I've been trying to think of a good casual remark to make to Jenn about our run-in at Publix. "Made any good smoothies lately?" No. "Linen-cotton, eh? I wish they'd make *our* uniforms out of that blend . . ." But I didn't want her to know I'd let her sundress brush my calf when she'd walked past. Stood my ground like she was an inside fastball I didn't want to get out of the way of. I made a pact with myself while I was watching Roy excel the other night, a few IPAs deep: no more diving out of the way of fastballs, I don't care how much they'll hurt. I mean, my leg hurts. Everything hurts. And getting on base is just worth it, you know? I saw this with clarity, as though for the first time. Getting on base is always worth it, is everything.

So finally, today, I was getting a little desperate. It had been five days since Publix and time was running out to make a mindless, passing comment. So as she fixed her hair in that loose bun she favors, I began, "So, I was just thinking, you know?" Only I hadn't thought this part through. She looked at me expectantly again. I'm beginning to expect that look. A single long lock fell across her eyes, a reminder that it could all come tumbling down thrillingly at any second, that this bun was just a choice. "Your hair," I blurted. "It's like ..." What was it like? It was reminding me of something, something I couldn't quite place. "It's like . . . the red on a Cincinnati home jersey."

A gator turned up at the lagoon this afternoon, about two hours ago. This has been about a biweekly occurrence. But this guy was big, at least Jenn's height long, and kind of disconcertingly close. I was sitting here, going through the game write-ups in *USA Today*. One thing you learn, as a ballplayer who is also a hotel regular, is that there's really no beating *USA Today*'s MLB coverage. I say this in all seriousness, and realize it's surprising. It's like they're holding on to some deeper notions about duty to the national pastime, America's paper representing America's game. Like every couple years, the topic of cutting the baseball budget arises, and some longtime editor steps up at the meeting and thunders, "Gentlemen, I implore you! Are we not this nation's paper?" There's something touching about it. Anyway, I was sitting here, sifting and gleaning my way through the sports section, and I looked up and there it was, just parked stock-still at the edge of the water. It had that gator way of throwing time: there it was, and by appearances always had been. A crazy thing, that we just accept this fact, hardly even discuss it—these cartoon carnivores living in our midst. I returned cautiously to the paper, and got absorbed in a short feature on the American League West. And then a little while later, I looked up and it was gone.

I should have just asked if she'd made any good smoothies lately.

*Saturday August 14*

Did you know that when baseball started, pitching was just an afterthought? I don't think most people are aware of this. It's not like you'd think to ask. In the early edition of the sport, the pitcher was only supposed to set up the action between hitters and fielders, not to try to get guys out. He was a stiff, a patsy, only a pawn in their game. This is an amazing thing, when you think about it—this idea that you should not do your best to help your team win. It required a degree of sportsmanship that is hard to fathom today. And from a logistical standpoint, it would be tough to even pull off. They weren't telling you to lob it. You were expected to throw a pitch hard enough and serious enough that the game wouldn't be a joke. Batting skill had to be brought into play. I guess your obligation was really to the quality of the contest as a whole, instead of to your teammates. But how do you get the level of compromise right? That was where talent came in.

Of course, this couldn't last. One guy noticed another sneakily trying to pitch well, so he started doing it too, and then it continued back and forth, an arms race in every sense. And after a few years, the game's human-nature flaw self-corrected. Baseball became what it hadn't known it was always supposed to be.

Home runs were never meant to be important, either. They were seen as accidents back in the game's adolescence, when it was played with raggedy balls, and on fields where a fence—if there even was one—was just that: a fence. Not some great boundary of the soul, but a way of marking property. Which is funny, because these "home runs" were obviously such *good* accidents. But that was a different time, and players did not automatically try to replicate the good things that happened. They had a different attitude toward fate. And they had been told that playing the game meant one thing, and home runs fit an entirely different image. So guys laughed when they occurred, shrugging their shoulders and not really noticing that they'd accomplished the entire goal of an at-bat. They still thought of themselves as playing on an essentially endless field. Balls went out of reach, but did not become "gone." It took time for them to adjust to the truth forming in front of their eyes.

Now we are in the "modern era." We've been in it for who knows how many years. We'll realize we're out of it twenty years too late. My knee *is* still missing some bounce, by the way. I notice it in some of the Center's more abstract exercises, and also when I'm walking anywhere at all. I am trying not to overthink this. But of course, the better the rest of it gets, the stability and ache and flex, without that raw juice coming along too, the more I wonder if I might have left a little something on the field in Cincinnati. Not a lot, but something. The thing is, when would I even know? An injury is like when you spill a liquid: you can't see if there's a stain when it's still wet, because all wet things look the same. It's drying out now, but with plenty of dampness remaining. I think it's a little darker than clear water would be, but I can't say for sure.

The good news for me is, I was never counted on for bouncy knees. This is where it helps not to have superstar skills—there's less to lose. If I do come back with half a step gone, I'm really the only guy who will know it for sure. Our pitchers will just appear to give up a couple more hits to left. I'll continue not to beat out infield singles I didn't beat out before. A small cloud of change will swirl over the field, but no one will be able to pin it on me.

It's interesting, though. Injured ballplayers and their agents talk all the time about percentages: "He's still at 70%, but he's ready to help off the bench." "I'm at 85%, but I'll be all there in a month." Yet the reality is, unless everyone heals perfectly from every injury, and doesn't age a day in the process, there's no way to know where that 100% line now stands. Two years later, after whole seasons of thinking he's still just at 92%, a guy may have to face up to the facts: this, now, is the whole thing. 100% moved.

The Birds are migrating south this week. It's time for their annual three in Miami, that "eastern" city. What MLB should really do, from a division perspective, is add teams in Jacksonville and Orlando, move the Rays across leagues, and just add a fifth division: the "NL Florida." The guys will be flying out of R-D tomorrow night, racing to the charter after an afternooner with the Cubs. Baseball teams always spend their off hours in the arrival city, not the departure one. They are in a perpetual, unreasonable travel rush, starting each road trip as soon as possible, even if it means lost time with hometown loved ones. Of course, they're all going to be giddy about an off night and day in South Beach. Miami is a perfect storm of what ballplayers who aren't me, Churchy, married, or forty, love. Fake tans in a land of sun, fake margaritas in a state built on citrus. In the '30s, it was the king of apostrophe 's' places, but the nightclub punctuation has changed. Me, I've got work on Monday. I am planning to go down for a game or two, though. I mean, who doesn't want to watch a winner?

*Sunday August 15*

The Winnebago is an alligator. I had this thought this morning, as I stood in front of the house in my Four Seasons Pittsburgh bathrobe, sipping a ballplayer-sized glass of orange juice. Surveying my lands. There it was, sitting silently in the driveway ninety feet to my left. Like it had never moved an inch. The shades of the house were down, no signs of life anywhere. The only difference was, when I took a few steps closer, I noticed a very fine layer of beige dust coating the entire surface. I recognized that dust—it was desert dust. Dust that's a naturally occurring byproduct of the phrase, "But it's a dry heat." You can't find it east of Fort Stockton, Texas. Trust the guy who spent his last two months as an illegal drinker slugging Lone Stars in Corpus. Slugging .519 in Corpus. Could they possibly have driven that far? Where have they been? There seems to exist a kind of deep geriatric cover, American grandparents traveling unseen in the dark cracks of the day. Just like American ballclubs, actually. I've been on the night charters. But like I say, you turn on a TV and they're just there, at 7:05.

It may be a dry heat, but I'm about to douse my swings. Tuesday is the day. All these hours spent hacking at nothing, followed by the fool's gold of the tee—it's like I've been standing in the on-deck circle for three weeks. I feel like I'll stamp the knob of my bat on the ground and about nineteen donut weights will fall off. The Homestead pitching coach will be the one throwing to me—this message relayed from somewhere decisive by the Homestead hitting coach. I decided not to request that the team import my favorite BP hurler, Burkey Burke, who is the bench coach at Arkadelphia, one of our Double-A affiliates. We all fight to get Burkey at spring training, because he was born throwing 69-mph fastballs as straight as I-70, I mean he can make a Johnny Bench of the lowliest "good-with-pitchers" catcher. Which is huge, because all eyes are on you then. Spring training is the time they set aside for analyzing skill—displays of talent at other times do not mean the same thing. They're just, you know, interesting. To be taken under advisement. We'll watch out for more of that during next year's spring training.

So I didn't play the prima donna card and summon old Burkey from whatever word-jumble flyspeck he's spitting in this week. Texarkana. Tennebama. Missilou. But those juicy fastballs bring up a beef I've had for years with the prevailing BP wisdom. I've long been of the mind that batting practice should be made harder—that it's too much about confidence boosting and not enough about truth. Pro ball doesn't understand real practice, because we play too many games to have time for it. And you see this in the stupidity of BP. Where is the breaking stuff? Whenceforth the bat-cracking cutter? How does this get us ready for the game?

The thought crosses my mind sometimes: half a decade in the majors and all I feel is underprepared. Overstuffed with batting practice that's nothing like batting.

One pitch you'll truly never see outside of a game situation is a slider. Baseball still hasn't worked through its relationship with this pitch. Our game is at its core conservative, downright right-wing, and everything about the slider reeks of revolt. Start with the disorienting grip. You probably know that a fastball is held with four seams—by which they mean a pitcher extends middle and index across the horseshoe in the stitches. A classic cross-hatched pattern, looking like that symbol that means start a new paragraph now.

It's the opposite for a curve. The pitcher now works in parallel, cozying his fingers hard along the seam, which will give him purchase for spin. So far so dignified, everything on a nice ninety-degree axis, sportsmanship fills the air. But the slider: here he goes rogue, draping his digits *at an angle* across all that is sewn and sacred.

This shocks the purists. They look at that grip and think lefty, guerrilla, social unrest. All of which seems confirmed by how the pitch behaves. Coming in fast, then darting sneakily—it sneers at the gentlemanly loop of the old 12–6 curve. They call sliders nasty, but they also mean nasty. As in, mean-spirited. Teams encourage the pitch, because they want to win, but they have trouble looking at themselves in the mirror.

Roy can hit a slider. He'll screw himself into the dirt on a changeup, his celebrated quadriceps going to jelly, his vaunted ankles corkscrewing toward nowhere. I watch him and think, *He does not know about the bathtub full of ice.* But as a four-year college boy, he had a baseball education that was more technical and less moral, and he was taught to hit the pitches there were, not the pitches there ought to be. He had years of actual practice, was drilled by educators chewing nothing more toxic than Double Bubble. And so he knows when a righty is likely to throw him that pitch, and how he should adjust his swing, going inside out with the bat head and taking it to the opposite field. Playing it as it lays. No surprise, then, that he did it twice this afternoon. First a sweet grass-court slice in the third, which went for a single. And then, because they hadn't learned their lesson, a seventh-inning RBI double that rolled all the way to the wall—a two-on, two-out two-bagger that turned out to be the difference in the contest. Which gave the team a two-game divisional lead. The Cubs catcher was calling pitches based on his age, not his university background. Forget watching film. Alma mater should be the first note in your binder.

All this happened just about four hours ago, but now the guys are already south of me. And at least one margarita deep. Another thing about baseball travel: sometimes the game feels like something you do to kill time before a flight. I just left a message for our AGM about getting tickets to the contests. All teams have dedicated ticket assistants at this point in the history of perks, but I can't find the phone number of ours. It is not a service I've employed often. I doubt it will be a tough get. When you see the Marlins' stadium on TV, the outfield stands can be so empty it's actually confusing. The guys seem to be playing in a vacuum, like no one called and told them the game had been called off. I could buy my own ticket, of course, but I'm not looking to creep folks out.

## Monday August 16

Some private progress today: I am allowed to drive with one leg again. I guess you could call it a return to Xandy activities. Of course I was supposed to be doing this a month ago, after the All-Stars did battle, but then a twinge twang, or whatever they do. This has to be one of the few areas in which doing something with only one limb means progress. This and waterskiing. And it was strange—you do have a sense of being overloaded at first, like too much activity has been concentrated in one part of your body. For the first ten intersections, I felt like I was performing a maneuver. I felt like *Look at me, I just dropped the ski.* "Drop the ski!" they always shout from the launch, they are obsessed with this. And then after that you're just driving again, and you can hardly remember that feeling you just had.

I was looking for ways to extend my driving time, so after I got back from PARC, instead of pulling into the driveway, I continued on. Just cruised past, like it was first base rather than second. I figured I'd use the car to scout more places I could walk. And I ended up making an interesting discovery. Get this: it turns out there is a whole development *inside* this development, cozied hard against a far southern inlet of the lagoon, which I can't see from here. It's gated and everything—they had a little guardhouse with a guard in it, sitting on one of those guard stools that makes tall men look short. This kind of blew my mind, when I stumbled upon it. That this guard had just been sitting there the whole time. I wanted to ask him about it, what that was like, but as I started to pull up to his little hut, stuck right there in the middle of suburbia like those photographs of phonebooths in the middle of the desert, I realized there was no way he'd be able to answer a question like that, because what whole time? So I just gave an apologetic little wave and did a three-point turn out of there. Which in retrospect, must have seemed weirder than if I had just said something. From a small plane, the rows of shore houses must look like fingers gripping a curve.

I know a lot of players swear by gated communities, and of course I've been to plenty of parties behind guarded hedgerows. Some of the guys are probably within such walls right now, sixty miles down the road. But they've always kind of weirded me out. I think I just don't like to commit to being in that exact place, and nowhere else. "Do you know what I mean?" I asked Jenn this morning, and she nodded intently and said she did. She knew exactly what I meant about exact places.

Because that's really what that gate does: it tells you you're nowhere but in a neighborhood full of dermatologists. I like the possibility that the spot I'm in is a little bigger, fuzzier around the edges. And let's be honest, I've spent enough of my twenties walled inside fields whose dimensions are painted for all to see. Yellow 330s and 324s and 361s burned into my brain. It's a rare treat playing in Toronto, because the number is given in meters, or metres I guess, and you don't see the paler "feet" conversion right away, and for a delicious moment you're a little lost, a little more free.

The field in Miami is so big that you do a double-take when you first see the numbers. It's no wonder those upper decks are empty. A scary place to get nosebleed seats. As soon as our AGM gets back to me, I'm going to make dead-certain he's not sticking me somewhere in Broward County. The Marlins called their old field Pro Player Stadium—another name that sounds more connected to the games than it actually is. Think about that: Pro Player. It would be the most apt ballpark in history, if it weren't named after a sporting goods company.

*Wednesday August 18*

There's something in the air. I can't quite put my finger on it. But when I lick said finger and raise it to the breeze, I can feel it, coming from the north-northwest at eighteen mph. I can smell it: a top note in the gusts, like the tang of smoke at Chavez Ravine when the Santa Anas are blowing. Those weird nights when the wind that carries home runs is the same threatening the real estate of the fans cheering them over the Dodger Stadium fence, and everything seems to fall into itself.

Our AGM didn't get back to me about the tickets till ten on Monday night. Not so late, in and of itself, and it wasn't exactly an urgent matter. I mean, never in history have Marlins tickets been an urgent matter. But it seemed to just cross that invisible line, where a small switch has been flipped, and a silence has gone on slightly too long. Fifteen minutes earlier and I wouldn't have given it a second thought. But now I was officially thinking. And you know how even when that kind of call comes, and you feel that relief, the fact of the previous delay hangs over the conversation, and the person sounds physically farther away.

So we started in that halfway hollow place. And then everything in the conversation just seemed to wobble in the air, nothing had any support struts beneath it. We talked about the knee, but we talked about it wrong. There was too much . . . curiosity, I guess, in my Assistant General Manager's tone. You would have thought that we hadn't been talking about my knee all summer, that it wasn't the whole point. And then when we got to the tickets, the type of favor he was doing seemed to be a fan favor, not a player favor. I don't know. An outfielder runs on instincts. And I was just sensing too much total quiet, too much space that wasn't being filled in. And now I feel like I'm noticing it on all sides, wherever I look. It's like that spooky silence in my knee has slipped the borders of my leg and bled out into the larger situation.

The good news is that I spent yesterday morning ripping baseballs like it was my job. Which, of course, it was. I raked seeing-eye singles and humpback doubles and fluke triples. Gappers and wall-bangers, headhunters and moonshots, Texas Leaguers and other leaguers. They told me not to overdo it out there, but they didn't say I couldn't treat myself to the whole roster of hit types, and I stood in the box with the intention of hitting as many nameable balls as I could. Duck snorts and dying quails, every bird we've got. One fine thing about this sport of baseball, I thought as I swung away, is how much meaning you can create without even taking a step. Without even having anyone out in the field. It's like writing, in a way. I swung and I swung. I swear at one point I even dropped a bloop single between the second baseman and rightfielder, who didn't exist.

I used my number two bat. I didn't feel I could risk the hit machine. It's an irony that affects all ballplayers—the truly perfect bat is the one you can never use. You must save it for a situation more important than the one you are in, no matter what one you are in. I guess you could use it in the ninth inning of a World Series clincher. But then what if the game went to extras? The coach they brought in threw straight and steady but by appearances actually *couldn't* throw hard, which was probably why I was able to explore my full hitter's palette. I should tell the guys about him, or I guess I shouldn't. There'd be a mad scramble. Burkey would be out of a gig.

In the end, on Monday night, I just asked our AGM for tickets to tomorrow's game, Thursday's that is, which is why I'm sitting here right now, about to go in and watch on TV. They dropped last night's—a surprise, given that our ace was on the hill, going against their four. I'll never understand why managers aren't more strategic about these matchups. Say their ace is much better than yours:

Wouldn't it make sense to burn your weakest arm against him, bite the bullet, then have a leg up the rest of the series? Tennis teams do it too, there's too much pride. I told him I wanted the best normal seat he could give me. I'll be down among the fans, not on the field but in the Field Level. Who knows, maybe I'll catch a foul ball.

The cameras found me in the stands in the bottom of the third inning. I was just sitting there like you might, fifteen rows back on the first base side, taking a sip of lemonade and looking up at the board to see where they'd clocked our hurler's last heater—94, using himself up too early, Churchy looking antsy over on the bench. Most of the seats in my row were empty. This can happen when one corporate concern has too much control. For a brief moment it did look like the two next to me might get filled. On Monday at PARC, I had the thought that maybe Jenn and her kid would like to see a game. I had the line lined up and everything. "So, I was just wondering if you and *Johnaden* wanted to catch the Fish . . ."

"That's hilarious! You mean go to a Marlins game with you?" she would have said.

"Yeah. I know they're not the best team, but it's the Birds . . ."

"No no, they're great. I love an underdog."

"You do?"

"I sincerely do!"

"Okay, cool. Wow, this is going so great."

It didn't really sound like her, I had to admit, but I wasn't complaining. And so I was gearing up to begin my line. But then the second I opened my mouth I remembered, dammit: little Johnny doesn't like baseball. The last thing I needed was to make her think I'd been tuning out again. Did I know anyone in the basketball field?

"Blake? Were you going to ask me something?"

"Oh, just . . . The Miami Heat. So true, right?"

She frowned. I really need to start paying more attention to details.

And so I was just sitting there in the stands, contemplating the game and that particular dumb idea. And the next thing I knew, there I was on another JumboTron. I gave a little wave and a grin, but the camera always stays on you too long in that situation, so you just try to go back to what you were doing before, only this time it looks fake. Of course our reserves in the dugout just about lost it, watching this little performance. All bench players are All-Star razzers.

I was surprised the camera guys spotted me in a visiting park. I'm not sure what gave it away—the famous face or the famous brace. Jeans would have covered it, but it was furnace hot here yesterday, so I'd decided to risk cargo shorts, which left about four inches of blue neoprene showing when I sat. I no longer require the serious robo-brace, but support is still advisable, so the other week they gave me this slimmer job. A sport model, for performance. But it kind of undoes all the clever little moves a ballplayer at a ballpark can pull to hide his identity. There are a few tricks I've learned. Like any celebrity, the ballplayer may find sunglasses quite helpful, but they can't in any way recall sunglasses he might wear on the field. Movie stars do not have this history of flip-down shades to contend with. I own a pair of Ray-Ban Wayfarers that has served me well. The tortoiseshell really throws them off the scent.

The hat, of course, is crucial. An actor who doesn't want to be seen will always wear a cap, but a ballplayer has to do the opposite: we have to take the cap off, misleading folks with the rarely seen haircut. Though truth be told, wearing my team hat would not be as fatal as it would be if I was, say, a Yankee or a White Sock. The Carolina cap is weirdly minor league in appearance. Our bird doesn't look intense enough, is the thing. He just looks pleasantly surprised, like we've walked in on him mulling some vegetarian feed. Minor league teams can be named things like the Mudhens or Sparrows or Flickers, and often their cap icon will feature some abundant species doing something mundane. Building the nest, instructing the fledglings, prepping to migrate. But this is not appropriate in MLB. The Birds represent entire states—*two* states, themed into one. Our image should be, you know, stately. And then there are his eyes, so close to an umlaut.

There is so much you see in person, at a ballgame, that you miss on TV. Which is an obvious point, but I also mean it sort of literally. There is so much you see *in the persons*—the players, they really look different when you're right there. You forget this, as a guy who knows them as people. But now that I've been away, I have some fresh perspective. I think when you watch on TV, you're overly influenced by the face. If a guy looks like a quiet sort, a polite young man, he instantly appears smaller. You shave inches off his height and waistline. The opposite is also true. The lightest-hitting catcher in all MLB, a guy who once went something like nine hundred ABs without an HR, has a lumberjack chin with a cleft like a ravine. Stubble goes in and is never heard from again. And watching at home, you view him as a slugger. But then you take your seat in the Field Level, and he is highly slight. With a different face, he could be the batboy.

It was hard to believe, but last night was the first time I'd actually seen my replacement in person. Right away, there the lad was, right in front of me. Opening the game in the on-deck circle, as the two-hitter for the away team, taking silken lefty swings. All college guys have true two-handed swings, the mechanically better way to hit a baseball—they don't pull off at the end, like those of us who at nineteen were trying to mash our way through the minors. They enjoyed several years of not seeking a promotion. And as I watched Roy stand there taking cuts, left hand glued to the bat even past the far reaches of his right shoulder, I realized my assessment of us as mirror images may have overstated things. On a screen, he gives off an average quality, but you realize up close that he just has a bland face. Sizing him up after your eyes have grazed across a hundred gnawing Americans, you see a guy who is about six foot three and ripped. He is—as they say these days, without saying "of" what—a specimen.

He actually didn't have much of a game. A clean slate in the field but a blank slate at the plate, though he did maximize a fourth-inning walk with an attentive follow-up steal. But only someone new to the sport would have seen the lapse as real information. A ballplayer knows the difference between a bad night and a night when you just don't feature in the plot. The long, hard-to-follow narrative of a baseball season means there are games when it just isn't your turn. And last night our 3B was the dramatic lead, the guy who shocked everyone with an error in the fifth, then redeemed himself with a go-ahead triple two innings later. He was running that hard because of the guilt he felt. Every night a separate story inside the story.

Right now I'm wearing the same shorts I wore to the game, and they're making me think of another reason I might have been spotted. Besides my empty row, that is. When I planned my get-up, I was forgetting how all out-of-uniform ballplayers love cargo shorts. They're a dead giveaway—I was playing my own part perfectly. I think it's because we develop a reliance on pockets. What sport but mine features pockets in its game uniform? Rugby, I guess, but they don't seem to use them. Tennis, but many items would fall out. Ballplayers have a tradition of carrying all sorts of objects onto the field, from batting gloves to snuff. They demand to have everything at hand. And I can just picture how this went before the modern era, when the line between uniforms and clothes was grayer. Guys carried house keys out there. They tucked away hip flasks to sip on second, legged out bunts packing daguerreotypes of their sweethearts. A century-plus of spoiled sportsmen.

*Saturday August 21*

The word "setback" has been rolling around my head for the last three nights. I'll be lying in bed, and I'll suddenly catch myself hunting for anagrams. BASCKET. CABSTEK. I didn't say I found any. But it's like wherever I look, those seven toxic letters just appear. Gazing over the lagoon, I watch a Cessna spell them out. Skywriting gone wrong. Looking down at the page my saga's written on, I see them hovering on top like a watermark. Pick your image. You remember those old Alpha-Bits ads, where the letters float into words on the milk? It's that too.

More people who left the neighborhood have been coming back to the neighborhood. They left when it was time to leave, and they are returning now that it is that time. How very baseball it all looks, when you can sit back and watch it work as a circle. Our endless fanatical trips to the home plate where we started.

In my mind, everyone who drives his or her car to a weekly August rental is going to Cape Cod. You could be the wife of a Seattle Mariner, living in a "smart house" on the piney shores of Lake Washington, and I would still picture you driving your towheaded brood 2.5 hours to Chatham. Growing up, I thought all the cars were headed up the shore of the lake. Which I guess they all were. But I think once you've spent time on Cape Cod, that becomes forever the destination you picture for the station wagons you also picture, because of course they're not station wagons anymore.

Bill and his wife have been among the few to stay put, which hasn't surprised me. They strike me as the sort who will either travel somewhere incredibly close or incredibly far, but either way, do it in the offseason. They'll rent a cabin by the Everglades in June or suck down Mai Tais in the rain in Phuket, and everything in between they won't bother with. Their trip will be based on the notion that other people are just too fussy about the weather, and are missing out on all the incredible deals. They strike me as that sort, but I'll never know. By the time other places' offseasons arrive, I'll be gone.

I suddenly have only four weeks left in this state. September 20th is the day, barring, et cetera. A leap month of therapy remaining, plus a few leap hours. A February. Pitchers and catchers come to spring training in February, before everyone else. They refer to this early arrival by name, as "Pitchers and Catchers." Baseball. Try to understand the language it speaks. SETBACK buried in the keyboard I type on. S E T B A C K popping from the Nutrition Facts on a carton of juice. *Set Back* scripted on two halves of a jersey that buttons up the middle.

Baseball games are normally in the afternoon on Sundays, but every week ESPN swipes one contest to televise nationally in the evening, broadcast special by its most cologned crew. Their goal is to pick that day's most entertaining game. But they have to choose it a few weeks in advance, so to figure out which games will fascinate, they have to get predictive. To scout lineup strength and bullpen depth, endurance of rooks and trustworthiness of a star who says he's at 90%. They must become baseball men, to save their jobs as television people.

As a backup plan, you'll see them turn to geography. Tonight's broadcast features the Pirates versus the Phillies, and they'd have you believe it's some kind of Keystone Klassic. I just popped a Yuengling to celebrate. Both teams are technically in it for the wild card, but only because they haven't had the chance to lose enough games. Talent assessment gone awry. Setup men lying about tendonitis. No state is the subject of more mistaken "rivalries" than Pennsylvania. The two sports cities, Philadelphia and Pittsburgh, barely made it into the eastern and western borders, and in truth they're way farther apart than that. A real map would show Philly on an island somewhere off the Jersey Shore, near a barge dumping medical waste. Pittsburgh is in Wisconsin.

Over in the real Midwest, the Birds have a little losing jag going. A nasty U-turn after a solid 2 for 3 in Miami. Did I mention that the game I saw was a rubber match? Could you sense its rubbery quality? But now, before you can even turn your head, they've been swept in St. Louis. Shown up in the Show-Me State. St. Louis is famous for having "great fans," by which they mean they know the game but don't boo. New York, Boston, Philly, Chicago—they know it but they use that knowledge against their own players. You show up in St.

Louis and the Cardinals are just bobbing in a birdbath of local love. I know what it can feel like, walking into that. Our guys were the visiting team to the extent that they actually became tourists. They hit in the extreme tops of innings. Somewhere in the middle of the weekend, Roy walked from the hotel to the river and finally understood how they fit an elevator in the Gateway Arch. In postcards it looks flimsy, like a giant bracelet stuck in the ground, but up close it's surprisingly thick.

The thing about the Birds' losing streak is, it's all right, because the Braves have been cobbling together one of their own. Over in Cincy for three, they've been pitching like they're in a hitters' park but hitting like they're in a pitchers' park. You need consensus on that point to have a chance. And so the possibly catastrophic Cards series, guys wandering lost around the Anheuser-Busch factory—it actually doesn't mean a thing. Just melts like ice on the schedule, leaving no trace. It's crazy, isn't it, how slippery the standings are? Your failures don't matter if the other guy is failing. Same with your successes. The wild card race keeps you honest, because so many teams are vying, and they can't *all* lose. Some are playing each other. But all truth is relative when it comes to a division title. And a team will feel no different about getting there either way. No one ever remembers whether a playoff berth was earned by winning or losing. I've always kind of thought they should.

Can your own body part impress you? I'm feeling proud of my knee. My knee makes me stick out my chin. It's a hard thing to explain. I guess it's a little like what a captain must feel for his ship. The sort of fondness and faith that expresses itself in calling an "it" a "she." You just—you see how far she's come, you know? You see how she's persevered in the face of heavy metals. How she's put up with all manner of untoward prodding. A player wants her to know she's done right by him.

There's a new MLBer at PARC this week. I was about halfway through an especially heroic Monday lunge set when I saw Jens blow by in his white coat. I should add that white to the list of baseball whites. Right next to foul-line white and parking-space white and home whites and white lies and the white of the plate after an ump has swept it with his little black brush. Jenn filled me in. The guy's a shortstop on the Mets, about five years my junior. Apparently he got taken out by a particularly hard takeout slide as he was planting to turn two, and something gave in his labrum. A particularly accurate takeout slide, I guess. I'm not clear on whether it was the labrum in the shoulder or the one in the hip. There are both, which seems like an amazing confusion for them to let persist. Something "giving" is less severe than something doing what mine did, but it's still not good. He wouldn't have been out for the season if this was May, but as an August injury it gets the brutal four words: Out. For. The. Season. So young.

The two labrums. An honest-sounding injury, when you tear one of those. People don't even need to know which one, they just believe you. Not all injury titles are created equal. Some over- and some under-sell. Mine, for example, always seems to convince people, and I'm pretty sure it's because "cruciate" sounds like "crucial," and no one bothers to tell the two apart, the science and the seriousness just mesh in their minds. But if, for example, you hurt another ligament in the same knee, the medial collateral, think about how different that would be: medial collateral damage. Like it isn't even the central issue. Then there's the "itis" family, which just sounds too pesky, too chronic, to take seriously. Anything "sac" is confusingly liquid. And finally you have the simple fact of size. The smaller the wounded appendage, the more demeaned the player. An injured hand sounds lesser than an injured arm, a finger is nothing next to a hand, and on it goes, right down to the fact that the index and thumb put a pinky to shame. The least desirable injury in all of sports is "turf toe," which sounds downright adorable but actually involves horrific, debilitating pain. It too can be an OFTS, depending of course on the month, and it was just guys' bad luck that those two T's mixed so well. Do you know what turf toe is technically called? Metatarsalphalangeal joint sprain. Doesn't have the same ring.

What I'm saying is, the Met can at least be glad his wound has that ancient Latin feel. That you could see it in a sentence about a discus. I wonder if any of the others feel proud of my knee. I wonder if my body part has impressed them. It must be a strange thing about being in medicine. The way you deal with small pieces of people. Just the stray nuts and bolts. A rounded edge of something here, a tail end of something there. I mean, it must make people look kind of funny to you, all that painting by numbers, that beating around the bush. That working on connectors of things, but not the things.

After I'd cleaned up, I went back out to the floor. I was excited to share this theory with Jenn, thought she might be able to clarify things. But as I entered, I saw she was in there alone with the new guy, massaging high up his arm. Which gave me a strange unsteady sensation, and it wasn't my knee. I wheeled around as quickly as I could wheel. It's the labrum in the shoulder, must be.

More stuff in the air. More Scrabble in the sky. I can't get through to my agent. I have a call in to Dynastic's secretarial moat. A "call in," just nesting there somewhere in the atrium ferns. I hate that term, and what it indicates. I should clarify that it's only been a few hours. You couldn't hold an AL East game in the time it's been. But here is the thing you have to understand about agents: you can always get through to them. They operate a revolving door on a PDA that seems to have about six lines. There is no longer such a thing as an agent being busy in a meeting, or relieving his bowels, or actually turning off his mobile device on a commercial airliner. In other words, anything normal is abnormal. In Chavez Ravine, if the fires are close enough, at a certain point you go from smelling smoke to actually seeing little flecks of ash, trees and houses all turned into the same stuff, the same color as your visiting pants. Los Angeles snow. As though the smell itself has become touchable, can land on the ground.

AL East games are longer not just because there's more hitting, but because they're more important. Does this make sense? How can significance translate into time? Well I've mentioned that one key to baseball is the fact that there's a limited amount of sacrifice guys are willing to make. And most don't want to spend extra time at work, even if it means rushing things. Managers especially, because they are older and tire easily, in body as well as spirit. You would never see a football team rush. There aren't enough games for them to be OK with a loss. They try onside kicks down twenty-one points, laterals and Hail Marys, whatever it takes. But having 162 games, ballplayers are sort of fine with losing one. There, someone said it. Me. A baseball loss is like a football loss on downs. It's like the loss of a quarter in a vending machine.

So even though baseball teams have nothing forcing them to speed, are in fact playing the only sport with unlimited timeouts and no clock, they motor ahead, don't do all they could with strategy, generally let a game decide its own fate. Except in the playoffs or the late playoff hunt—or in the AL East. The math of it is, Boston and New York are the only two teams that would rather beat each other than sleep. So they actually use all the tools at their disposal, calling endless timeouts and putting specialist relievers in for 1.5 pitches and visiting the mound like it's Mount Rushmore. They do this most furiously head-to-head, but they hate each other enough that they'll play other teams that way too, out of spite. And the contests take forever. Though really, they just take as long as all baseball should. No one wants to admit this. They're the only ones making the most of the rules.

This is the time of year a ballplayer starts wondering why they even have 162 games. "Really?" we say to ourselves, under our breaths, in the fourth inning of a blowout, as a guy drifts off second, halfheartedly stealing signs. "*162?*" It's the way the number isn't just massive, but also random. The trouble is, it *is* physically possible to play baseball every day, and someone confused this with meaning we should. Actually it used to make more sense to play a lot of games, because the travel was slower, so they crammed in as many as possible once you finally arrived. Making the most of your train ticket. But now, instead of a doubleheader and an off day, which would be preferable, because hey, once you're already at the park, the schedule just drones on, day after day.

Jeff still hasn't called. I know what you're thinking: "You already wrote that." But it's different now than when I first typed the words, a little while ago. It's information again. Even in the AL East, guys would be toweled off, climbing into street clothes. Ready to be back on streets. Just one time, in one career, I would like a guy to change at home, to wear his uniform to the park like a Little Leaguer, pilot his Ferrari Enzo in metal spikes. You think that writing happens in a sort of suspended instant, a little gold nugget of time in the world. But this isn't true. It's kind of like a rehab assignment. It looks like an object you can't get inside, but actually it plays out, unspools, sees change, runs clock. It's kind of like getting injured. Tobacco juice descending from lip to soul patch.

Jeff called last night at 9:58. I know the exact time because the call came during that little briar patch of baseball evening when all the East Coast games have ended and the West Coast games have yet to start. It only appears once in a blue moon, and never for more than ten minutes. Pitchers' duels in Atlanta, Boston, the Bronx, folks forced to flip to Royals–Twins, try to gin up interest in a prairie battle. It's a great time for an agent to take a piss.

Actually, last night the Birds were playing in one of the flyover games, which I was listening to when he called. A mile-high matchup with the Rockies. The worst team name in baseball, because it makes no sense: the players are not a bunch of Rockies. Each guy isn't a Rocky. This was a game with playoff implications on our side, but not an ESPN-caliber broadcast. ESPN also carries a weekly Wednesday night game, in addition to the Sunday but less excitedly. *Wednesday Night Baseball*, is the title they've given it. You wonder why they had to title it anything at all, why they couldn't just put it on. The advantage of the Wednesday version is they don't move the schedule, so they can pick the game last-minute. They are always showing the most perfect, most thrilling game.

Ours wasn't one for the aficionados, but it was action-packed. Home runs flying in all directions, even eight-hole guys jacking them out. This was Roy's first visit to Denver's hitter-happy environs, and he seemed to find them to his liking. That will tend to happen. Baseball has never really known what to make of the place. When a Denver ballclub was being planned, and physics experts said, "Hey careful, the ball is just going to fly out in that thin air, and curveballs won't really curve and sliders will more like stumble," all the baseball men laughed, thought this was a real hoot and a holler. "*Thin air.*" Baseball men like to refer to any experts as "so-called experts." They distrust expertise itself, except for their own. But then of course, the physics guys were proved right, and after a year or two of fly balls flying like a Neil Armstrong tee shot, they not only believed in the altitude, you couldn't convince them there was anything it *didn't* explain. The Coors Field fences eventually got moved back, the effect was reduced. They even got a humidor to keep the balls moist and dead. A lesson some owner learned from his Cohiba. But to this day, anyone hitting well in Colorado is immediately viewed with suspicion. You're best off there just plugging away in the 50th percentile, not drawing added scrutiny. My stats would be perfect in Denver. They really have that "no artificial help" quality.

I didn't feel like listening to the end of the game, because what Jeff said in the call, which came just as HR number five whistled out to right, my phone starting to buzz its way across the coffee table like a windup toy as our play-by-play man gave his salute ("Oh, *doctor!*"), was that they've set up a little call. They meaning him and our AGM, who apparently have been having an easier time reaching each other than I have either one of them. This will be on Monday afternoon. Just to, you know, talk as a group about where we're at. Are we at somewhere? In my experience, and I have a few years, you never want to be at anywhere other than where you are.

## Friday August 27

It was the labrum in the shoulder. The Mets' shortstop, I mean. I walked past him today, lying facedown on a mat, Erik working the wound. "Yeah, I get some pain in my rotator sometimes, not like this or anything."

"At least it's the shoulder, right?" I said merrily as I passed.

"Shoulder's worse, dude . . ."

You *would* guess hip, if you just heard about a guy's leg getting clipped, but it's not that simple when the motions involved are professional-grade. You can't pull off an MLB-level play without making the very most of your frame, which means getting all sorts of body parts sincerely involved, which also means exposing them to trouble. If this guy lost his leg platform in the middle of his throw, his arm suddenly had to bring the toss up to Show snuff on its own—his shoulder had to shoulder the burden, in a manner of speaking. And that's just too much to ask. This is also why pitchers are so adamant about seeing a pitch through, when a batter calls time and steps out of the box late. Non-fans are always curious about this. "Why did that guy keep going?" they wonder. "And deliberately fire his baseball into the ground, or over the catcher's head?" Why not stop? It's because he doesn't think about his motion in segments. It is a complete thing. The first retreat from the rubber literally isn't over until a ball is airborne.

Last year, on the last Friday in August, I had one of the best games of my career. A 4 for 5 at our home park, two home runs and two singles, multiple RBI, a great deal of runs scored. One of those games where you look at the box score in the paper the next morning and your row is just deliciously clogged with numbers. Twos and threes all down the line, sticking like lumps in your throat. Like something you could eat with a fork. Only on the far right side, where the negative categories live, do the digits finally trail off. K's: Zero. LOB: Zero. Fuck-ups: Zero. After the game, I was the one surrounded by microphones, giving all the answers to the press. I was the shirtless guy with beer in his hair, wondering whether it was really appropriate to undress in front of all those people, if they shouldn't have a real locker room inside the locker room. When I got back to my apartment, I looked at myself in the hallway mirror and saw I still had a smear of shaving cream on my left ear. It's the main ingredient in pie.

Is algae a problem in any of these lagoons? Whatever happened to the manatee? When I first started coming to Miami to play baseball games, seven years ago, you saw concern for this sea creature wherever you turned. License plates, billboards, public service announcements at the stadium. Entire elementary schools were given over to its welfare. Young children sketched it again and again, loving its blobby shape. No animal had ever been so easy to draw. Their work filled special display cases at the airport, it was how we knew we'd arrived. The manatee: it came from nowhere, didn't seem to relate to anything else. Literally, in the animal kingdom, or as an idea. But then at some point, we showed up for three against the Fish, and the outcry just seemed to have faded. You don't really hear about the manatee anymore. And I just wonder: Are they extinct? Are they fine now? It would be good to know how that worked out.

## Saturday August 28

I have broken my number two bat. I went over to the college this afternoon for a little extra session. Not technically within the rules, but I knew their pitchers would be over there, getting their work in as we say, and the swings have been feeling good, the knee feeling good. So I hopped in a Volvo and got myself to the field. Upon arrival I found several game young aces, and off to the races we went. Only this wasn't the diet BP I've grown fat on. It hadn't occurred to me that these guys would do their damnedest to make me whiff. Quickly it became show-up-the-major-leaguer day. Full fastball heat started coming my way, along with a whole range of "experimental" pitches. You want to watch out whenever some arm says, "And this is just a little something I've been working on." Like he's some sous-chef with ambitions. These without fail won't live up to their billing—the world's first knuckle-fastball!—but the exotic spins and angles of break will wreak havoc on Kentucky hardwood. And today, on some sort of Phillips-head screwball, the ball bored an inch too far down my barrel, where the fragility starts in earnest, and I sent two long shards of ash scissoring out toward right, like they were still trying, again and again, to hit the ball that dribbled beneath them, the catcher manning short doing a little jig to get out of the way.

So you see, all the more reason not to use your top stick. Not till the fourteenth inning of a Game Seven, and only if you've fallen behind. Only if your franchise hasn't taken a title in at least two decades. Broken bats have become a real problem in our league, or so they'll tell you. Former players have begun calling it an "epidemic," but I'm not sure the real epidemic isn't former players saying that. And now, if some expert comes out, announces that he's pored over the stats, the break rate hasn't changed one iota, he will be called a so-called expert. One time, Willie Stargell broke a bat just swinging it. Fifty times, a former player has told that story.

But it always makes for a dramatic moment, the shattered Louisville. Maybe you saw that game, a few years back, where Roger Clemens fielded a bat segment, then threw it at the guy running to first. He got ripped for that in the press, labeled a "dangerous player." He said he thought it was the ball, he was just fielding his position. But when I watched the replay, his expression, the boomerang flip of that ex-Slugger, I understood. He was just disgusted, fed up, tired of it all. I mean here was this detail that didn't even relate to the game. He was Roger Clemens. He didn't want to pick up someone else's trash.

No one calls the house phone anymore. I guess this is it. This is how long it takes for the overflow of a modern life to finally flush away. For your personal data halo to fade out. In the majors, of course, we have another category of phone: bullpen. When a skipper wants to make a change, he just places a call, unless he doesn't. I've never been in on one of those calls, and since in the minors they just gesture with their hands, when I first got to the Show, I asked one of our veteran relievers what they say. I mean, do they say "Hello?" when they answer? And then does the skip go, "Oh hey—it's the skip. You know . . . from the dugout." They clearly have to say *something*, and I was just wondering what it was. And he just looked at me.

*Monday August 30*

Baseball. Where you can make the mistake of thinking a thing's too obvious to actually happen. That sheer likelihood is protective equipment. When a Cy Young candidate is going up against a journeyman on the sixth stop of his journey, and everything says he'll just wipe the floor with him—because after all his off-speed pitch is faster than the guy's fastball, which announcers have made the mistake of calling a changeup if he throws it first, because 84? their instincts buck at the radar gun: *really*?—this never seems to actually pan out. Something turns, and the outcome is so inevitable that it also becomes sort of impossible, and you just count on the big upset. This is how it seems. I guess it's seemed this way since 1951, when Bobby Thomson took his miracle swing and the Giants won the pennant, the Giants won the pennant. But really, when you look back on the stats, you realize the Cy Young candidate did wipe that floor, seven out of each eight. What was supposed to happen is exactly what did, Ralph Branca actually shut Thomson down, in every version of history except the one we wound up with. It's like your mind, or anyway mine, just blew up every exception, and forgot to remember the rules.

This afternoon I lost my job.

Let me back up.

This afternoon I was informed, in the call set up by my Assistant General Manager and agent, that when I arrive next year for spring training, I'll be expected to compete for my place in Carolina's left field. To "compete." Baseball code. You have to break it before it breaks you. Because what our AGM said after he said that, Jeff seeming to actually purr on his end of the line, the smooth transition of power, indicative of a free society, was that with the team making this run, and obviously given the uncertainty about my knee,

I can understand of course, they wanted Roy, only they used his real name, to enter September not trying to play for next year's job. In other words, he won't be competing. So who will this competition be with? This is my game. They take your job without taking it. They take it so it takes you a minute to realize what they just said. This afternoon I got fired. When he made that comment about September, my very first thought was, *But it's only August 30th! You still have one more day!* The thirty-one-day crowd.

But then of course it started to sink in. It started to sink in, and as it did, it was like the phone became this little shortwave radio, picking up voices from somewhere very far away, and at the same time I found myself unbelievably aware of my immediate surroundings, even though you'd think they would sort of fall away in that variety of moment. And it was like that day in A ball, when I looked around and suddenly understood an outfield for the first time, saw that it wasn't something I was on so much as something I was *in*, contained by, populating. I was in the living room for the first time. And as our AGM's voice buzzed on in the background, like he wasn't speaking in words, I found myself extremely interested in the texture of the couch, which I suddenly noticed had a super fine grain, so that if you dragged a fingernail across it very slowly, you could actually feel these tiny grooves. And I thought about how that's true of baseballs, too—you think of them as dead smooth, but actually there are these microscopic rivers and tributaries of rivers running all over the surface of a ball. And I thought about how it can take you an entire career to notice this, to see the basic nature of the basic object of your sport, and the fact that that is just crazy, and no one talks about how anything actually is.

# SEPTEMBER

*Wednesday September 1*

I wish you could see Bill right now. He's mowing again, and has his shirt off, and in addition to his hat is wearing cutoff jean shorts, high white socks, and sneakers by some company whose logo I can't quite make out. Our generation lost this—this urge to slice off our jeans when it became hot. We didn't want to destroy our pants. We were fine buying shorts of the same material. Of course, I can't really hold it against a guy that he's wearing high white socks. I mean, the White Sox, and whatnot. Though all ballplayers own about thirteen pairs of flip-flops and are practically pulling off their pale hose with the final pop-up still in the air. You get sick of socks. You get sick of being identified by socks.

I want to tell Bill, "Hey, if you like lawn-mowing so much, you should consider seeking the employ of a major league organization." Maybe we can apply together. They are always looking for someone who can execute that brushed look. God forbid we have to play on a field that all looks the same, that isn't striped like a jersey-knit from Lands' End. Lord help us if there isn't a team logo carved into shallow centerfield, folded artfully into the initials of the local agribusiness concern. As recently as ten years ago, when I was first coming up, you hardly saw any advertising inside the playing area of a major league park. That was what getting to the Show meant—relief from the money-grubbing, the neon car sales of a minor league fence. In the fifth year, the ballplayer ascended into heaven. He was seated at the right hand of the bench coach. And I don't really understand what changed. About capitalism, I mean. Why they would have that signage now, but not then. Although in European soccer, where you think they'd have team crests going back three hundred years, and where supporters actually wear *scarves*, they are that tasteful, the clubs just shill outright. They change entire color schemes between home and away, even sometimes breaking the most sacred rule, which is that they change the *type* of color. Go from navy blue to royal, crimson to maroon. Can you imagine if the Yankees threw in the occasional azure, the puce? Half of those FCs don't even have the team name on the uniform. It just never quite makes it on there, an airline slogan is already in the prime real estate. But maybe that system is just more honest, I don't know. You have to figure that when they axe you from a job mowing a major league field, they just come out and say it.

I've been thinking. It's a fascinating thing, the way a baseball firing works, a truly compelling concept. A ballplayer doesn't lose his job like you might. He loses it in pieces. If he's lucky, he'll slot into a platoon— that is, sub in against pitchers with the hand the top guy doesn't like to face. For a hitter, this is always the opposite of his own—an R for an L, or an L for an R like me. Then if that doesn't take, it's down to straight pinch hitting, plus occasional work in day games and on travel days. While the starter mentally travels, he gets his shot. The last stop on the road back to AAA is defensive-replacement and pinch running duty— the dregs of a game, its duties and errands. Imagine if all this was true of other lines of work. If they put you on accounts run by people who were left-handed, then accounts nobody wanted, then had you come into the office when everyone else was off on Christmas.

So sure, there are stops below me, outs to give in the inning. But anyone who's been around knows the gaping holes in that logic, and this is the reason I've been trying to count the rotations-per-minute of the ceiling fan, gluing my fastball eyes to the end of one blade, that's the trick, and around and around I go. It has to do with baseball, how it works. And with me, how I work. Because what happens with not starting is, it suddenly becomes April every time you're at the plate. A summer of Aprils, everything cold and raw, momentum gone. So you don't hit. And then they give you fewer chances, and then it's even more April, and you hit worse still, and Opening Day starts approaching fast from the wrong side. Not starting feeds itself. And then there's the opposite problem, the flip side of the coin: since everyone knows pinch hitting is that hard, it's also that valuable, and if you *do* start tearing the cover off the ball, well great news, you'll never get to start again. All of which is to say, the more I think about it, the more I can't see how anyone undoes the damage once it's been done, ends up north of the Mendoza Line, much less lines named for other people, least of all this here July hitter, I mean I just can't see how that story gets itself written, and it's like seriously, that grass is short enough.

*Thursday September 2*

They went with chin straps. One of our vets decided it. Churchy says the guy claimed it was the most intimidating look, but I'll wager anything he just couldn't grow a moustache. Nothing on the upper lip is needed for this, the most postmodern of beards. No cheek is involved. Just a thin line forming a U from ear to ear. A little pencil drawing on the face. From a distance, it's like the members of the Carolina Birds just have really strong jaws.

Churchy has been calling every day, seeing where my head is at. Baseball GPS. Lord knows, he's been at everywhere. I think he's now played on eight teams, maybe nine. He has switched leagues midsummer, been traded from one city's AL team to its NL team. Moved clubs without moving apartments. He's even fought on both sides of a division battle inside a single season, which is the mark of a true journeyman. The truest of the species have fought on both sides within a single *series*. Friday and Saturday a guy is pinch hitting for the Cubs, then boom, a deal is struck Scotchily at the hotel bar, and come 1:05 on Sunday he's playing the rubber match as a Brewer. It happens more often than you'd think, and for less valid reasons. And you wonder if a guy has ever forgotten. A freshly swapped first baseman hits a single, then takes his lead off first, and he looks around at all those familiar uniforms, familiar faces, and for one play forgets which side he's on, that he's standing there on offense rather than de-. And so he doesn't run at the crack of the bat, is thrown out by a millisecond. Baseball has a long history, is my point. You have to think it's happened once.

I wonder how the sport starts to feel to you, when you get traded around that often. To be like me, on one franchise for my entire time in the majors—that's a rarity in this day and age. It's because I am exactly how good I am. If I were any better, I'd be targeted by contenders on stretch runs. If I were any worse, I'd just be traded casually, they would throw me into deals, hey maybe I'd put something together, a 4 for 1 barter sounds better than a 3, if teams throw enough numbers at a wall something will stick. If I were better or worse, I'd have been on either side of a fire sale. But I've slipped into a middle ground where I don't get given away, but I also don't get desired. And I just wonder what that's like, to represent so many different cities that you have to peek at your hat before you take the field. An L slicing an A? Hey great, nice weather. I mean, does it purify the game somehow? Reduce it to its essence? You're not fighting for the Red Sawx, or the White Sahx, but for the sport. You play unaccented ball—the drag bunt and the speared liner, all the sweet things it allows, with nothing in the way. It's like you're on a team with history itself. Abner Doubleday is on the hill.

Maybe it's the hired gun who really has it made, who can just kick back and enjoy this thing of ours. I've roomed with Churchy for two seasons. Well, a season and a month. Since he showed up shrugging at the Carolina doorstep—the Birds it would be, until it was someone else. He could be a defensive replacement, or veteran presence, or just a clubhouse guy. Whatever your club needed. Me, I've only played baseball like a congressman. The state of my game is the state of my game. I stand in a spacious shower thinking about meaning. That guy gets straight in bed, watches the National Geographic Channel for fifteen minutes, then sleeps without stopping till it's time to wake up.

There was a brawl in the Phils–Reds game last night. A bench-clearer—is there any other kind? The highlights came on while I was finishing up at PARC. The Philly pitcher went in with a high hard one to a backup OF on Cincy, nicked him on the forearm, and the guy jogged almost all the way to first before veering off and charging the mound. Some guys do that: the fake-out blasé trot, like "Oh, no problem, just kidding it actually upset me *a great deal*." So of course the dugouts emptied, the relievers had to do that awkwardly long trot all the way in from the bullpens. All so everyone could hold everyone else back. Brawls. Talk about the weirdness of belonging to one team, then another, then another. Here you are resorting to violence for the sake of a guy who might have been a mid-season acquisition, all because he now has the same letter on his cap. He may have a short fuse, a primitive sense of justice—and you have to pretend you want to punch other people on his behalf. Imagine how it is for Churchy. It's like every year he has to alternate who he attacks and who he defends.

I've been in a few brawls in my career. Some are more authentic than others. Every once in a while two teams do really hate each other, they "have a history." But actually, in plenty of cases even the mound-charger himself isn't actually pissed. It's like he knows the guys just need a break, a change of pace, so the game doesn't feel like one game going on for weeks, even back at the hotel, on the plane, going on and on. Like how a manager will get himself tossed on purpose, for a spark, a jolt, and when they show the replays you can actually read the ump's lips asking, perfectly politely, "Do you want me to kick you out?"

My first year in the league, we got into an especially transparent scuffle with the Cubs. It just went on too long, was the thing. This is the easiest way to ruin the charade. At a certain point it became obvious that guys weren't delivering blows they could. My parents were at the game, and my mom was baffled by this. "But why would you want people to think you wanted to punch someone, when you didn't?" she asked me back at the hotel, as I wasn't nursing no wounds. Her point was that this is sort of the opposite of how things work in society, and with juries. And she was missing key things about baseball. But baseball was missing things as well.

Jenn was standing with me as I watched the flailing on the screen above us. Without realizing it, I must have balled up my own fists, and I can only imagine the look on my face. Even the most affable ballplayers can look ferocious when the moment is right. I noticed her staring at my hands.

"Old habits . . ." I mumbled.

"Or maybe you just want to punch someone, Blake." And then, looking me squarely in the eyes, she reached over and, quite slowly, unwound each of my fingers from its coiled position. There is no labrum in the hand.

When I got home I was still itching to take a swing at something. So I took bat three over to the college, and I really got her firing on all cylinders. I mean I started hitting lights-out. Actually, the term is pitching lights-out, but I've never understood that. You can't pitch a light out, but a smashed stadium klieg on a walk-off dinger is the model of a home run, the very symbol of it. A ball struck with such force it turns off the overheads on its way out, like it's sealing its own moment. Ending the game and saying goodnight. And I was hitting at midday, under fierce sunshine, but still, I was turning the balls around with such force that I could practically hear the glass raining down in the outfield. That's what you're really doing when you hit a baseball. You are redirecting it. You're rejecting it. I don't think my stroke has felt that good in about three years. But of course no one was there to see it. No one but a tired old career farmhand, stuffed sadly into a too-small Cane warm-up shirt, with its three-quarter sleeves just because. *Which Cane?*

Afunny thing happened at the intersection of sports and greed. When an owner decides it is in his fiscal interests to uproot a beloved team, and sets his sights on a fresh location, he is often faced with a name customized for the old town. An Astros, say, or a Twins. Yet he's reluctant to retitle, because he understands certain key things about branding. The result being that we have all these teams named for attractions not available in their cities. Look at the NBA. A move from my pond-drenched commonwealth gave us the Los Angeles Lakers. New Orleans to Salt Lake City produced the Utah Jazz: a nonexistent music. The Birds specifically *don't* have this problem. There are birds everywhere, especially since they didn't mention a species, though granted it would be a strange point to highlight in New York City. And I've wondered on occasion if our team name wasn't picked for that very reason. It would be a snap for the owners to move. No Tennessee Oilers to worry about, no LA Trolleydodgers. No, you know, Tulsa Knickerbockers. The bigwigs have learned their lesson. What would happen if they had to move the Phillies?

I didn't say it was hilarious.

The Birds are at the Braves this weekend. Three games head-to-head, huge swings possible, when you win it's really good, when you lose it's really bad. No fancy math, no getting off the hook. It's not clear to me if the Braves count as one of the weirdly misnamed teams. There aren't braves in Atlanta, but there weren't in Boston either, and if there were some in Milwaukee, stop two for the franchise, it was probably just a coincidence. Who knows why they were even called that to begin with? I guess in the early twentieth century, the easiest way to name a team was just to pick an insensitive term for Indians that started with the same letter as your city.

Three games means the teams will have to jump their recent standings groove (Birds up two), it's arithmetic, they have no choice in the matter. The Braves cut it to one last night, the Birds will win tonight (our CF will "fall a triple short of the cycle"), and then tomorrow will be an absolute rubber tree, a hockey puck, a pair of galoshes. I wrote awhile back about the standings needle getting stuck. I guess a season is really like one whole vinyl record. You look back and see a series of shinier rings, at sort of regular distances apart, where the needle finally gets comfortable. And in baseball it's these slick lines that are the point—where things feel fixed for a while, where you seem to have really gained or lost something, where there's quiet. And in between is just all that noise, rising and falling, just the endless music of faltering OBPs and swelling WHIPs and tags beaten or not, almost none of it getting anyone anywhere. I'd like to commission a study on how many plays in baseball actually make a difference.

It's 11 a.m. right now. I couldn't sleep in this morning, and around 7 I decided to quit trying and get up. I figured I would get my walk in while the heat was still at Massachusetts levels. And my knee ended up feeling so tragically good, which is to say, feeling like nothing at all, like a puff of breeze between my shin and thigh, that I just kind of kept going. At least I finally found the perfect walking outfit. Cargoes, a wicking T-shirt in a subdued color, and Saucony Jazz Originals. On and on I went, around fake curves, up and down *all* the cul-de-sacs, and by the time I got back to my front yard made of stones, it had been two and a half hours. Short for a baseball game, long for a stroll. And after I got back, I felt a little better, and there suddenly just didn't seem much point in waiting till it was time to go to the writing clubhouse. Where had my routine gotten me? I'd like to commission a study on the outcomes of superstitions. So I mixed myself a smoothie, spun the blender off its base to keep as my stein, and brought it outside to write.

I took a shower before that, of course. I wouldn't mention this except that I was low on laundry, so I dried myself with the Panthers beach towel. Which is a team name that sounds local, but hopefully isn't. Are there big cats around here? Do I have to worry about that, too? You know technically, historically, a team name is actually just its nickname—the thing you always heard locals calling their boys. The city name is the real name: the club is "Cincinnati." But some eagle-eye 130 years ago picked up on their repeated wearing of red stockings, so they got "known as" the redstockings, and after it was said aloud enough times, this got capitalized in print. The Red Stockings. Probably with a hyphen somewhere you wouldn't expect. Redstoc-kings. In a newspaper called *The Defender*.

*Monday September 6*

Jeff's been calling every day, I usually let them go to voicemail. What do you say in your outgoing message? Are you more of a minimalist or an explainer? Remember how when everyone got cellphones, they used to say, "Hi, you've reached so-and-so's cellphone," instead of just saying their name? You could understand where they were coming from, but it also made no sense. It wasn't like when you called a landline you'd reached something other than the telephone itself.

I just go with a snappy "Hey, this is Blake, leave me one." If they want my last name, it's on the back of my away jersey. Some teams put names on both grays and whites. The Yankees put them on neither, they figure you should know who they are. I recorded it two years ago, in a hotel room in Chicago, after my previous phone fell out of a faulty shorts pocket in the back of a cab. Right before I say the word "leave," you can hear a car alarm start turning in the background. That alarm went off repeatedly that night, and, I've always felt, adversely affected my performance the next day on the field. Wrigley didn't get lights until 1988, and they still don't like to use them. They are purists about illumination. So most contests start at 1:20, and if you don't nod off quickly, you're sunk. Make sure you're a heavy sleeper before signing with the Cubs.

This morning I let the phone enjoy a few rings, but eventually I just picked it up. It seemed like that was what it was there for.

"Hello?"

"Xandy? Xandy it's Jeff!" And off he went to the races. My agent is thrilled about my prospects as a backup major leaguer. His new dialect centers on terms like "role" and "chemistry." "Veteran" and "depth." And you can tell he never made it past JV. It's like Jeff doesn't understand the story aspect of baseball. He thinks a season, a career, can just bounce from word to word, that you don't need action verbs and subjects and objects, topic sentences and overarching themes. You can't just hop onto the noun you want, like it's one of those lily pads in the lagoon. "Matchup!" he chirped from Coldwater, Laurel, Benedict Canyons. "Mentor!" You have to blaze a path to it in language. "Presence!" You have to make the grammar work.

Roy's ROY candidacy trucks along, so far he's shown no signs of a drop-off. He does have some competition. The new SS they've got on DC, the Venezuelan National, turned in a fierce August, batting acceptably but dazzling everyone at short. He fields an unbelievable number of balls with his bare hand. Watching him on the 1 a.m. *SportsCenter*, I've started to suspect he limits his range on purpose, just so he can make more spectacular plays. Which is actually pretty brilliant, from a career perspective. Watching him, you think back to the game a hundred years ago, when the mitts were just thin coverings of leather. In the beginning, gloves were really gloves. Guys were still playing with their hands, they just had a little extra protection. Like baseball was winter.

They never actually give the award to a great fielder, though, not unless he's also a great base-stealer. Those skills are expected to go together. They pay lip service to it to get rid of guilt, but if Roy can hold 'em, he's in. But any former player will tell you: you learn a lot about a candidate a week into September. He's never experienced a season this long before. How will he handle it? Will his body start to break down? Will his mind? Everybody waits for it, because of alliteration: "the September swoon." Roy went to university for all those years. Who can yet say what this has done to his head? Will playing ball in the month of September confuse him? Will he try to go to the bookstore and buy used textbooks? Maybe we can look at the course catalog together.

For the moment, his play is alarmingly normal. He's hitting .290 over the last two weeks. Only .200 or .350 would make sense. Birds–Braves was the ESPN game last night. Regional rivals in a divisional showdown, an obvious choice, cancel the meeting. The Treetop

Flyers took it behind our SP5's 6.1 innings with two earned (a Lovely Start), leaving them up three. They may be pulling away. Or they may just be up three. I like the Atlanta stadium. Though it was built in the heart of the retro era, they alone didn't try to simulate the old parks. There are no fading warehouse walls to batter, no olde tyme berms in deep center. Allowing us a vintage twisted ankle. Instead, they just made it really fancy. There are gleaming season-ticket boxes for red-colored executives, and these are lined with unbelievably expensive bourbons, poured by game coeds. The outfield dimensions are mere feet away from symmetrical. The grass is natural, but it's not natural grass. And of course, they called it Turner Field. A human name that's also the name of a billionaire. Not suspiciously uncorporate, like Dodger Stadium, or changeable by the year, like San Francisco's yard. The whole thing is just so straightforward.

Hands. It's hard to imagine a time when a glove was just about hands. The glove is everything now, what baseball is, you break it in to catch the game itself. Cutting a bead up the third base line. Work in the leather, work out the stiffness, guard against bobbles and snow cones. The interesting thing about your glove is that it's the one piece of game equipment that doesn't get better with your level. You can't just shell out for the best, the shiniest, because mitt newness is not valued, in fact is a problem. So you're in the same boat as the American Legion player, and in fact he may have a better pocket than you do. This, of course, is the baseball pocket to end all baseball pockets—the ball-shaped depression where palm meets webbing. This song in the key of calfskin. And it's the youngster who can shepherd his with tenderness, with ecstasy. He doesn't have other things to distract him.

I guess what he really has is a good calendar. He's got the luxury of developing his snagger on a healthy schedule. In what you could call irony, the majors feature the worst gloves, because of all the games. We burn through them at about six times the normal speed, they go from stiff to broken-in to broken in just a few months. And that just never quite works, to accelerate something's natural lifespan like that. It's like marathoners, wearing out a pair of shoes a month. They're still out-of-the-box white, but they're already dead. Part of what a glove needs is just time spent alive. And you can feel the difference between a piece that's been out in the world a little and one that's been rushed through the paces. It will catch, sure, but there's no nuance, no sense that the ball is being welcomed back to its home.

The best glove I ever had was in eighth and ninth grade. I remember it clearly. It seemed to *come* broken-in. I pulled it off the shelf and it just fit, was right away flexible and soft to the extent that I always had suspicions, wondered if it had actually been pre-owned. If someone had returned it after a season, snuck it in with the new jobs. And yet the leather looked totally fresh. It was just an old soul, I guess. But I'd cheated the system, and I got punished. Midway through my freshman schedule, some keystone string popped in the webbing, and I knew I should just let the thing go, I'd had my run. But instead I tried a quick fix, some sort of round turn and a few half hitches. And in the middle of a tight contest I took a liner out in center and the ball blew right through the pocket without even being appreciably slowed down, only by luck thudding off my left collarbone and not my face, my confused hand stuck frozen in front of my eyes, the whole infield suddenly visible through this opened window.

I'm looking again at my hands. The fists have stayed gone since Jenn dissolved them. A stunning thing, to see a major leaguer with two naked hands. You'd never guess he'd look so exposed.

Gloves, mitts, getting some leather on it. My latest red Rawlings by my side, still stuck one majors week short of truly broken-in, a textbook case of suspended animation. Do you call it playing catch, or having a catch? Is it a game for you, or something you own? My dad and I used to say "have," so I'm biased that way. And really I've never understood "play," even though it's what you hear more often. If there was no baseball, then it would make sense for catch to be a game. And if there was no baseball, it would probably seem like a pretty fun game, this flinging of an object and retrieving it with oversized paws. But there is baseball.

*Wednesday September 8*

U nknown Legend" came on the radio again today, as I was driving to PARC. "Somewhere on a desert highway," Mr. Young crooned with feeling, "She rides a Harley-Davidson." And so on. I've always thought the key to that song was that he listed the brand of motorcycle. And didn't just say Harley either, but gave its full Christian name. Harley-Davidson. Like Janis, with her Mercedes-Benz. There's something respectful about it. Something about not just mailing it in.

My brace came off this morning. The value of its gentle squeeze on my right knee no longer outweighs the mild irritation of the fabric. Basic math. Jens insisted on slipping it off himself, after which he set it dramatically on a mahogany end table, where it kind of flopped to one side. "Voila!" he said, of course. *What if I hadn't worn it in?* I thought.

You might think I'd stop putting in the effort over at the Center. That I'd no longer give it my 110%, or even my 100. That a reporter would call, and I'd tell him I was putting in about a cool 75. You might think I'd think about not even making the drive over, no roots rock songs at all. But the thing you have to remember is, my knee is also a part of my body. Which is obvious—but I mean *my* body. And when you get your head around that, it's the kind of thing that will really make you clean and jerk. Extend an extension as far as it'll go. Today I even coaxed some encouragement out of Erik. "Sick," he said, as I grunted through a step set. Gushing praise.

It's the kind of thing that will make you really open your eyes, look around. When it's you yourself in a room. When your slot in the lineup has detached from your person, floated up into the sky like a metal balloon. And PARC is actually an interesting place, when you step back and really gaze at it. I was watching them all today—all the receptionists, and the various stretchers and experts, the ortho-pods and the bipeds, all spread out through suites, this very defini-tion of the metaphor of a well-oiled machine. And I noticed all of a sudden how impressive it was. All these individuals doing certain jobs, and doing them well, maybe not perfectly but certainly well enough to earn a living wage. Everyone talks about what gets a guy like me into this kind of room, they pore over film of the incident. But what about what gets *them* here? These folks have all at some point made a determination about what interests them, graphed the point at which their skills and their passions and the going salaries intersect. They've compared and contrasted, applied their interests in some fashion to the world, and here we have the result.

And I got to thinking about how this is just so different from baseball. Everyone looks with such longing at the life of the pro ath-lete, it's just assumed that if you *can* make it, you should. But what if you wanted to do something else? It's like ballplayers never stopped to do what the people at PARC did—to weigh their options. In baseball, getting "optioned" actually *means* getting fired, which should tell you something. Sent down to the farm. The option to wear a hat with worse penmanship. Not to mention this notion of the "non-tender candidate"—Jeff talk for not getting a contract. Well, I may be many things, but I'm no non-tender candidate. And if you think about all this for a while, it can start to seem like a thing got stolen out from under your nose. Like instead of having an opportunity, you missed an opportunity. Just if you think about it for a while.

As I was finishing up my final set of the day, I looked to my right and saw Jenn across the room. Jens had said she was out, but there she was, working with the damn Met again, who was doing some benching of his own. "Cool team name," I mumbled under my breath as I told Erik to add another plate, I wasn't done yet. "'The Metropolitans'—real fucking concise." I was on my back, and grunt-ing pretty hard now, so I was seeing things kind of sideways. But sometimes that's a helpful perspective to get—new patterns come into view. And as Jenn moved her hands up and down, shadowing the Met's bar, the motions fell into this rhythm, and I suddenly understood she wasn't spotting—she was gesturing. And even though she was supposed to be watching the Urbanite, I saw that she was looking in my direction. Which everyone knows is fine, he's not actually going to drop the bar. And moving her hands like that, looking at me—it was like she was standing near third base, giving me signs. Trying to tell me something important. And I felt so close to piecing the whole thing together. Only I didn't know what the signs meant, because I hadn't been taught the indicator. That's the sign that really matters, the predetermined belt tug or crotch jostle that says "Everything from here on out, pay attention to. Translate starting now."

But of course, you don't always get an indicator. Sometimes you were at the far end of the dugout when they explained how everything was going to work. Sometimes you just have to do your own assessments, decide to make the turn.

Before I could clear things up, Jens appeared and swept them down the hall.

*Thursday September 9*

You probably think you have a nifty little knuckleball, and if you could only get a pro scout to see it, who knows? It's just something you fiddle with on the side, you're not quitting your day job yet, but maybe I know someone who could give it a look after the season? Really you'd be fine with a nice little career in AA, you're not greedy. Maybe a late-season call-up to eat innings, save the ace for the playoffs. Well that's sure charitable, but I will say this: Have you stopped to consider whether this ball of yours actually knuckles? I know, it *should* knuckle, you're doing everything right. No spin, pushing the ball instead of whipping it, almost like you're putting a shot. You have read the Niekro brothers' memoirs. You've followed the instructions to a tee. But for some guys that thing dances and for some it just doesn't, and I'd urge you to take a hard look at which camp you fall into.

Our AGM has faxed me my options for the 20th of September, when my rehab ends, and along with it, a few hours later, my time in this state. Quick: to the airport! There is one—one options. I am to hop a flight back to Carolina, careful now, watch the knee, where I'll have three days to collect my personal items and personal thoughts before heading to Arizona for a fall league assignment. "Assignment" is sort of like "options." You want to keep an eye out, be careful you're not getting designated for it. Watch for subject-verb agreement. "Fall league" is sort of like "Lo, how the mighty have fallen." I have no idea why he sent me this by fax. I got two sheets of paper: content, and cover describing content, which I discovered about an hour ago on the kitchen floor. They must have spit from the machine while I was out on my morning walk. Each riding its own thermal and see-sawing its way to the tiles, one landing faceup and one down. I have no idea why I'd left the fax machine on.

November hitting, December hitting. I can't offer my code for these, don't own a guide on how those months get baseballed. By December any ballplayer worth his salt is up to his elbows in elk blood, teaching his son Walker the finer points of field-dressing. He is paying $2K to stock his pond with bass and $10K on the goods to fish them back out. The Arizona Fall League is known as a hitter's league, which is a bad thing pretending to be a good thing, because then if you don't hit in it, well sweet lord, you couldn't even hit in the Arizona Fall League. Baseball, this game of odds, averages, potentialities, lined up like ducks in a row. This game of situations and fixes and pickles.

The lagoon looks so inviting right now. The surface in between about eight shades of blue. Almost like a Birds hat. An unlikely noon onshore pushing ripplingly in my direction, no bloodthirsty reptiles visible. It's crazy, isn't it? How you can spend all this time in front of a body of water and not even take a dip? Of course, we are supposed to suppress this thought, put it right out of our minds. But do enough business travel and the tendency starts to become a theme— this way we tease ourselves with water, stick it obsessively in front of our eyes. People building where they can stare at rivers and harbors and lakes, paying top dollar to stare, just so they can never go in. From my apartment in downtown Raleigh-Durham, I can make out a reservoir in the distance, which will one day help with the resale. Baseball does it too, like with the Royals' waterfall, behind center-field in Kansas City, Missouri or Kansas. You'll be racing after a tailing liner and suddenly hear the sound of a rushing river. And I mean, what are you supposed to do with a noise like that, at a time like that? Though the opposite is also concerning. Out in Phoenix, home of the Arizona Fall League, Snake management decided to build a swimming pool just over the right field fence. Children can be taken all the way to the ballpark, just so they can ignore the game.

*Friday September 10*

Yesterday was my final day at the pool. The water polo team left last week. Went out in a blaze of earflaps and hole men. Both of which we have in my game, but which mean different things. They left last week, but they didn't take their lane divider, which by the end had been moved down so far that I would have had interference if I'd tried a breaststroke. And at first, on Tuesday, I didn't think about it, I just quarantined myself in the usual lane and got to work. There wasn't another soul in the aquatics center, yet there I was, remaining pent up for a good ten minutes, until finally, on a rightward breath, my goggles cleared and it occurred to me that I could do whatever I wanted. And so I rolled myself over the line, whose discs rolled with me, and headed for open waters.

On the way back to the house, my suit and flotation belt and shower shoes making their final trip home from the locker, making a puddle in a Publix bag on the passenger side, I found the Birds game on deep AM, fuzzing through three states' worth of clear weather and southbound breeze. It is amazing what AM radio is capable of when nothing gets in its way. They've started doing this in a number of cities, scheduling day games on Thursdays, calling them "Businessperson's Specials." You know, "Salaryman's Treats," "Office Drone's Delights," things of that nature. The whole league gradually moving Wrigley-ward, restoring the original notion of the ballgame, an excuse to play hooky and drink. By 2030 all the overheads will be back off, there will be nothing more to smash. Aces will throw lights-on. Though I'm here to tell you that the real reason the teams are doing it is so they can schedule earlier flights. Oh, their passion for departure.

The game was in the sixth inning when I got to it, quivering on landfill. The Back Bay of Boston, the Marina of San Francisco. Great real estate till there's a temblor. And big surprise, things started going to seed within about ninety seconds. We were down 5–2 to the Picaroons, our SP4 still in the game, and you could practically hear the wheels turning in our skip's mind: Do I hang him out to dry, save the pen? Keep our 6:30 wheels-up in order? Do I really have to fight for these outs? So he was on edge, I'm here to tell you, because strategic or not he was thinking about giving up on a game. And as I approached the causeway, there was a bang-bang play at first, not even an important one, don't let anyone tell you all plays are created equal. But he started barking, and according to the announcers "He said that thing you can't say." (Do you know what it is? I do.) And by the time I was back on land he'd gotten himself axed from the contest. They should cut sixth innings entirely, like thirteenth floors in hotels.

We won anyway, behind the steely guidance of our bench coach. He drafted the relief corps, and our bats really stepped up to the plate, and the division lead became padded. Does it shock you that we were able to win without our manager? Are you laboring under the impression that it makes a large difference who is calling the shots at the end of a baseball game? To double-switch or not to double-switch, that is pretty much the only question. You hear tell of skippers who can really move an outcome, swaying events with some genius blend of infield substitution and mound visitation and ball/strike lamentation, but ours is not among their number. What I mean is, there's a reason I've barely mentioned the man, that he hasn't fought his way into my pages. I suppose on some level I think the things I write down should be what you couldn't figure out on your own. That's what writing is, right? It's surprises. Our skipper has a paunch, and chews things, which he later spits out. He is dead words, a wash, a fielder's choice.

I learned about the game result later, though. About a mile past the causeway, there is a sign I'd been noticing with some curiosity all summer. It says "waterslides," and has an arrow pointing to the right. White writing on brown metal, surrounded by larger and more important signs. Doesn't clarify the point, just "waterslides," somewhere to starboard. And yesterday, given that I had my suit with me and everything, I decided it was high time to investigate. So I made the turn, and literally five hundred feet down the road, around one bend and behind some sort of mangrove grove, I came upon these two huge blue plastic chutes corking into the sky. It was like the opposite of a development inside a development, like discovering some *un*gated community. Well, you didn't need to tell me twice. I paid my admission and got into line with the after-school crowd, and for the hour allowed on my plastic bracelet I slid and I slid.

And during that hour my mind started to drift, in a way it hasn't in some time. Like I was at a supermarket, but better. Like in an MRI tube, but way better. These slides were open air, not that covered kind that trap you just because. So there was a sense of privacy, as your healing body took the turns, but also of being out there. Like you really were taking a curved ride through your world. And maybe it's because I'd just been driving, like we did once, or on account of the presence of children, or the fact of red hair, but I found my mind drifting toward Jenn. One thing I just can't get over is how she still hasn't moved into nickname territory. I know this to be physically difficult, the body gets urges over a long season, it wants to go there. "*XANDY!*" it just begs to come out.

And then, still sliding, periodically plunging, my mind started rolling around yet another strange phrase we have in my sport. It's the term for when a pitcher wings the ball in close: chin music. I always believed that was a terrible way to describe a feeling that's got no melody at all. But the phrase stuck because the phrase is good. The phrase is the music. And yesterday it occurred to me that they should keep the idea, but just apply it to something else. Forget baseball: take this one back for life. Just think about the things this could describe. Folks playing that chin music. People writing those chin songs.

Last night I made up my mind to ask Jenn about this. I made up my mind to make the turn. Had she heard of the concept of chin music, and would she mind if I called her Jenny? But when I showed up to PARC, there was Erik, stretching his hammies by the stacks, Jenn nowhere in sight. Finally, as I was finishing up a dead lift, I worked up the nerve to ask him where she was. He looked down.

"Let it go, dude. Just let it go," he said.

"But how? How can I just let it go?" I pleaded.

"The barbell, Xandy. Let it go."

*Sunday September 12*

You're holding it correctly and everything. You know that it's actually gripped with the fingernails, not the knuckles. You've familiarized yourself with all the ones who made it, Wilhelm down to Wakefield. In the years after the Niekro brothers' retirement, it fell to Tom Candiotti to keep the craft alive. His nickname was "The Candy Man"—"Candy" to his friends. He pitched for the Dodgers for the better part of six seasons. In a twelve-knot wind at Chavez Ravine, he was the second coming of Koufax, his ball would literally blow away from bats. In a fifteen-knot wind, he couldn't get out of the first inning.

Lightning struck the birdhouse in the wee hours of the morning. It lies in ruins. Splinters of baseball coloration spread tragically across the flawless lawn, like the storm heaved and spit up a ball. One whole white wall drifting around this end of the lagoon, Bill nowhere in sight, presumably in mourning. Ironically there are now birds everywhere, feasting on the explosion of seeds. Doves and finches, robins and wrens and terns, all these perfectly common birds that for some reason have been passed over by thousands of sports franchises, why every other team got called the Cardinals I do not know, it's not like they ran out of breeds. Birds everywhere, and of course one more right here, in a dun patio chair, still a little soggy in front where the rain snuck past the eave. A weirdly even stretch of his right leg paler than the cushion he sits on, except for a perfect circle of tan in the dead center, where the last brace had its hole—the kneecap's own cap.

The storm system, which finally cleared out of here around noon, has been wreaking havoc on a Sunday of baseball. Extensive delays in both leagues, staggered all the way up the seaboard. Synchronized tarping. None of the contests where they should be by now, time of day no longer any guide to time of inning. Most ballplayers hate rain delays, seeing as we don't receive an hourly wage, but there's something I've always appreciated about them. It's the sense of community, the way you all take your turn experiencing the same weather. Watching the out-of-town scoreboard from the dug-out, you can almost see the storm coming. You'll be in Queens, and spot the ^2 taking weirdly long in PIT, and then see a DEL pop up. And then a little while later PPD's flip next to BAL and WAS, came down hard for a while there, they couldn't escape the fourth, and then a DEL after six in PHI, okay, at least it's slowing up a bit, and Oh look, they're onto ^3 now in PIT. By this point you know the speed, intensity, and width of the storm, you've sketched out a mental map complete with isobars and color-coded rainfall totals, and if you're really good, if you've been in the business for seven years, you can pinpoint practically down to the third of the half of an inning when the grounds crew will show up in their khaki shorts.

I actually saw it—the lightning strike that took out the bird-house. I got woken up maybe half an inning of night earlier, the cracks getting close, and I was lying there ticking off the fifths of a mile between flash and thunder. And then suddenly sound and light collided, the whole lagoon lit up, and I heard that sick sizzle of a tall wood-based object, which is nothing at all like the crack of a bat. The birdhouse. One year it looked like our stadium was going to be affec-tionately called that by locals, but it never panned out.

Afterward it took me awhile to fall back asleep. As a ballplayer, you learn to understand sleep well. That is, you not only get good at doing it, you get insightful. And you don't have that confusion of non-players, over whether they actually drifted off. "Was I out?" they wonder, ask nearby lovers. You develop this sort of ability to hear yourself as you hook-slide into dreams. It's the breathing you have to listen for, with-out listening so much that you get in your own way. That's your clue. You listen for that sharp scrape at the end of each breath, almost like you're shoveling dirt, like you have joined the grounds crew, you are secretly padding the first base line to keep your star drag-bunter's balls fair. For a second that is your audio visual—and then you are out.

Like instead of having an opportunity, you're missing an opportunity. Like instead of riding it till the bitter end, backed up against an endless April Fools' Day till the process spits you out, of being one of those guys whose card mashes up three teams in one season, then skips the next entirely—02 CHI, 03 CHI/MIN/SEA, 05 HOU—you can not.

My sport does this so beautifully, in cahoots with Topps: convinces you that any year like that is a black hole, not even worth a mention. Tells you to see your world as a bullpen, a place to wait for phone calls that might or might not come. Imagine if the card was honest about a guy's missing season—if that fact made it on there too, where the club and stat line would have been: 86 CLE, 87 *The player, always a marginal major leaguer, just wasn't good enough that particular muggy summer*, 88 TEX. Some relievers wear running shoes with their uniforms, that's how uncertain they are about getting called into a game. That's waiting in the bullpen for you. It's not an attractive look.

All I mean is, I'm thinking about a number of things. I'm not like Churchy, who can receive those messages on his answering machine, those faxes and mimeographs, like he's a freelance consultant sitting in his home office. He is a specialist. Some years he bills more hours than others, but it evens out in the end. I guess I am a generalist. What I bring to the game isn't a skill so much as an approach, a way of being inside a ballpark, of addressing situations. A sort of attitude I spread like fertilizer over the field. And it's just, when you get down to it, who's to say there aren't other fields I can bring this to, other than left? Not only center or right, or even infields, but other fields entirely?

The Sox game was on this afternoon. Red ones. I watched it all the way through. They were hosting the Halos, a Monday afternooner at The Chapel. A Monday afternooner? Every once in a while this will happen. Not an ESPN game or a holiday special or a Truant's Classic, but a game that's just . . . on, when you turn on the TV. Like it slipped past the schedulers. On some regional cable channel that you're not even sure why you get. A Sox game is always worth watching, because so many things can happen inside Fenway. Every twenty feet you proceed along the wall, there is a drastic change in conditions, not only in degree but in style. Centerfield is endless and sharply angled. Right features a short fence that is also a short fence, plus a funny curve at the end that leaves the foul pole inappropriately close to home. Then out in famous left, which I've patrolled six times in my interleague-era career, the field is actually two things at once. The Green Monster makes it both the truest hitter's and truest pitcher's alley in baseball. Hit it high and even a little chip shot will go out, you can score yourself a 280-foot home run. But drill a liner with all your might a good twenty-five feet off the ground, and all you'll make is a lot of noise. In fact, the harder you hit it, the more you hurt your chances of extra bases, because it will just bounce back that much faster. The biggest home runs in Fenway history have gone for singles off the wall.

Anyway, as I watched I started considering how really, Fenway makes my point. About fields of grass and fields of study. About foul lines and lines of work. I saw Seraphim sophomores erring doubles into triples because they never considered, till the moment the ball was in the air, what material that great wall was made of. You could see their eyes suddenly ask the question: How springy is a Green Monster? From the minors they have come and to the minors they shall return. By contrast, the hometown Hose were literally playing the indentations off the scoreboard numbers. They knew about all the little data their park makes you process. Good old misshapen Fenway—it's packed with details, with choices, is really just a huge pile of 0s and 1s, yeses and nos in the very architecture. You watch a game there and you can't be under the illusion that baseball is anything but a sport of decisions. And what I mean is, this is ironic. We got to the Show being excellent decision-makers, but it's like we never applied that skill to the big picture, just never even noticed there were calls we could make.

This morning Jens called me in after my session with Erik and handed me a folder containing the program I am to follow this fall. A sort of moveable Center. The folder was beautiful, made of heavy, textured paper stock and emblazoned with the PARC crest. This crest is pretty abstract, but seems to feature a nude man bench-pressing fig leaves. The man, if that's what it is, is muscled but lean, in the ancient way. He probably has about nine labrums. The color of the folder was a darker take on burnt sienna—sort of a charred sienna. As I held it I became increasingly certain that the next expansion team in baseball would adopt it as their own. The South Dakotas, of the AL Plains.

Jens was in a nostalgic mood. All the squat series we'd recapped together. All the times he'd compared my knee to honeydew. He openly pouted for about a week after I got my news, which was sweet enough, though I suspect he was mainly annoyed that he wasn't included on the call. That he'd have to reprint his promotional materials, put some sort of asterisk next to my name. Like I'm the Roger Maris of cruciate ligaments. Today, though, that was behind us, and the doc was waxing reflective. He rubbed a hand across his gorgeously shaved chin. "Xandy, Xandy, Xan—"

"Where's Jenn, Jens?"

"Jennifer is . . . We have new clients now, Blake. In need of our best people."

"The Met? Jesus."

"I don't know what 'it' is, but that kid's got it."

I've been laying out on the grass behind the patio all afternoon, down by the coast of the lagoon, working on my tan. Two pillows beneath my head, laptop on my lap, gallon of orange juice like a trusty steed by my side. I'm not doing this out of vanity. I've been trying to bring my knee into the fold of my tan. My goal is to have it pretty well blended by the time I leave, which means I've had to get on the accelerated program. But I don't want to burn my leg in the process, and also I need to really stagger the pacing, so I've developed a mixed sunscreen regimen: Bain de Soleil 4 in the affected area, then sweatproof 70, the hard stuff, infant formula, on quadricep, calf, foot. I can already see the first effects. The whole knee region is still much lighter, but the edges are starting to blur. It's gone from something exact to something hazy, like I'm literally watching it fade into memory.

At first I didn't think it would work to write out here, because in the sun I couldn't see the computer screen. But I needed to shake up my routine somehow. And I figured out how to do that thing where you turn the color inside-out. Blues become orange, purples green— reds show up as some sort of turquoise. I'm just reporting what I see right now, and trying to remember what they were before. And your document turns black, so you are actually writing with white letters. It's like you're uncovering the words instead of producing them. It's almost like you're reading instead of writing. It's almost like, for a moment, I am you. So whatever I put down comes as a slight shock, even though of course I know what I'm going to say. And I almost want to keep on typing and typing, just to find out what happens next.

## Thursday September 16

I've started to pack up the house. This is an involved process, it's not like throwing together a roller bag for three in Cleveland. Staging areas have cropped up all over the residence. The tricky part is the medical equipment. If I was bound for the Hall, they'd probably cordon off the whole living room, take note of where I'd left each brace and crutch, build a to-scale replica in upstate New York. If I was Hall-bound. As it is, I spent an hour this morning at Mail Boxes Etc., trying to find the right boxes for a three-foot walker boot and crutches the height of my armpits. Mail Boxes, and so on and so forth. I'm shipping the gear ahead to Sam at the park. Our field has its own zip code. The street address is 1 People's Park Way.

The team has been pulling away, there's no mistaking it now. Nothing else them winning and other teams losing could mean. Their "magic number" for a playoff spot has started getting printed in *USA Today*, below the division standings. There's no magic to magic numbers, I can explain the principle right now. The number is the sum total of Good Things that need to happen for your club to get in. For example, a win is a Good Thing, but a loss by a pertinent competitor is just as Good. And if you actually beat the competition yourselves, that's downright Great—two points for the Birds with one stone.

They're now in the spot every team longs to reach, with a playoff spot "in their own hands." This is "all they can ask for," a guarantee they'll win it as long as they don't ever lose. None of which has ever made a lot of sense to me. A World Series victory is in your hands whenever you're up a single game. Build a division lead of one in May and it's all up to you, you're in charge of your destiny. At the beginning of the season, don't you have all you can ask for? You are holding the free-will pennant.

Roy's stat line has stayed so flat that you start to suspect he isn't thinking through the math. I mean he is consistent down to the level of the week, the series, the half-game, it's like he doesn't understand that an average gets made over the course of a whole season, you have a .432 week followed by a 2 for 23, and in the end it just works out. Even Tony Gwynn was Dan Brouthers one fortnight and Bill Bergen the next, to be a ballplayer is to be one other ballplayer after another, a league of schizophrenics as I've said, and eventually Elias just takes the mean of all your mood swings. But our Roy—it's like he has to go 2 for every 7. The club had the Wednesday game last night. I flipped it on for a time. He produced the most representative line available with 5 plate appearances: 1 for 4, but that one being a double, and as he added a walk his OPS barely budged. The alternative would have been a 2 for 5, but with no walks, and both hits just bloop singles. He's cutting it as fine as you can with small numbers.

It's probably time I mentioned the young man's real name. It's Carey. And no, that's not a nickname they fashioned out of Care. He was born with the letter already in place. I know, I know: What happens in a case like that, when there's a pre-existing "y" condition? Because even ballplayers know you can't call a guy Careyey. But they also can't very well call you by your name, just because it sounds like their own concoction. So they've come up with a backup plan. They replace the "y" with an "s," turn your handle into a concept that comes in quantity. Which means in Roy's case, they call him Cares. Did you really think they wouldn't have thought this through?

Jennifer. Jenn. Jenn-y.

I can't get the box holding my crutches to close. I angled them, went hypotenuse. But they keep pushing at the corner of the cardboard, eventually peeling up whatever tape job I try. One thing I learned today is that you can't find a box that's long enough for crutches that isn't also way too wide, it's like the shipping people think that all objects expand in proportion, that there is one universal "thing" and as it gets bigger it adds bulk evenly on all sides. So in spite of the fact that this container is too large for its cargo by far, I'll probably end up giving it a puncture wound. I've tried duct, electrical, double-wide Scotch. No dice. Packing tape, of course, with its camouflage. It is sneakily the color of a box. At one point I even introduced a layer of athletic, for entertainment purposes mainly.

*Friday September 17*

At the Center this morning, someone had brought in a bunch of balls for me to sign. I had a long shower and a shave before I confronted the pile, so I wouldn't smudge the ink with my sweat. Talk about leaving your individual mark. This happens when you're a ballplayer, you periodically just get confronted with balls, whole passels' worth, and asked in essence to name one after another after yourself. What I find interesting is that obsessed as people are with autographs, no one seems to care what the signature actually looks like. I mean they're begging you to personalize this thing, you wouldn't believe the lines that are liable to form, and then they don't even pause for a compare-and-contrast. Of course players play into it too, make no effort. Rookies inscribe with care, but by year three everyone's just scrawling little mountain ranges. Though God forbid they don't pen the bible verse clear as day. ~~~~~~~ GENESIS 1:1.

I've certainly been guilty of the squiggly line myself. But today, as I caught myself drifting over the letters in my name, I resolved to focus, I buckled down. I didn't know who was getting the balls, often as not you don't, but that wasn't the point. My handle, I decided, was going to be readable on these particular horsehides. I even added a little #29 to each, like it was a flourish. They're not actually made of horses anymore.

Jenn's ex-husband pulled up right on time, to drop off his son. My little delay tactic had worked. I'd set aside a couple balls for him, the last two of the batch, which I gave my most exacting signature. I know he doesn't really care, or at least would probably rather I ink some different sporting surface, but hey, maybe they'll have resale value. It's a gift I can give. And as I crouched down to give them to the kid, look, no pain—there, coming out of the front doors, was Jenn.

She walked up slowly, three red wisps trailing from her face like pennants in home run weather. "Blake . . ." she said, accurately. And then she touched my arm, and not in the way she does when she's spotting me. It was more like she was spotting me. I could feel each of her fingers individually, like she was wearing a batting glove. "What do you say?" she asked her son.

Yeah, kid—what do you say?

On the drive home, I got to thinking more about baseballs with my X on them, what that could do for anybody. It seems obvious that the most interesting balls are the ones marked with nothing but game. Which isn't even visible, that's the interesting part. One thing I'd do, if I was involved, is position the stadium in question such that when you hit a home run out of the park, it would actually go out. In my mind this is what old venues like Fenway and Wrigley, and yes, a few new ones but you don't see it much anymore, really do right. A longer long ball departs the sporting grounds and enters the city. It starts bounding down the street, and if people aren't paying attention to exactly where it left, and there's some slope, it may roll a good quarter-mile before coming to rest behind a car tire. And maybe the next morning some passerby notices it lying there, and it's a pretty clean ball, darkened only by mud he doesn't know is from the Delaware River. So he sticks it in his briefcase, then on occasions brings it to a park to throw with a preferred nephew. Time passes, and it's a good nine years later when, married now and with his own child itching to possess a catch, the former passerby pulls the baseball from a drawer and suddenly notices for the first time six words in fading black script: "Official Baseball of the American League."

## Sunday September 19

You'll never guess who I talked to this morning. That's right, if you guessed right: the brother. I was in the kitchen, eating cereal and working on the *Herald* crossword. The paper had been sitting on the front path when I opened the door to greet the day, the first time that had happened, a subscription kicking back in I guess. So I brought it inside, shook it from its cobalt rain bag onto the kitchen island, flipped to the Calendar section, and located a golf pencil, which is a pen as far as crosswords are concerned, because of the lack of eraser. There is a single piece of baseball trivia you need to know for crosswords: "NLer Mel." It appears in a good one out of three, and I always start by scanning the clues for it, and if it's there, I have my starting place, my foundation. Sometimes you'll see the hockey equivalent instead, "Icer Bobby," and this was the case today. And I had written ORR down, and was working on the across clue, "Shaft trove," and was just starting to get the puzzle-maker's joke when the phone rang.

I was surprised, I'd almost forgotten it could do that, and without thinking I answered. And lo and behold: the owner of this home. He wanted to make sure I knew where to leave the keys tomorrow. I hadn't, so I guess it was good that he called. A notably friendly guy, as it turned out. Not that I thought he wouldn't be, but I think you know what I mean. He asked if I'd enjoyed my stay, if the house had suited my needs, and I told him yes, yes indeed, that I'd gotten particular use out of the patio.

After I hung up the phone, I finished my cereal, and made a little more progress on the puzzle, but pretty soon was forced to abandon. I run into problems when the clues involve old movies, or multi-line quotations, and today the multi-line quotations were from old movies, so I could see quickly it was not going to be my day. The remains of my effort, some downs in the upper left and lower right, the rest of the action around the middle, formed a strange-looking symbol on the grid—a sort of single houndstooth check. Like something you'd see on the suit of an ex-ballplayer.

I decided to bring my laptop out to the patio and put on Zeppelin's *Houses of the Holy.* One of my all-time favorites, but an album I've hardly been able to listen to outside of locker rooms for the last decade, because it's in my pre-game rotation. That's pretty much ruined it for lay purposes. It's like the music you use for your alarm, it just means waking up, you can throw it on on a Saturday at the beach and all you'll think about is your boss's breath. But I must have finally cleaned out the associations, because this morning I savored the whole thing without any shreds of game-prep poking at my mind. "The Crunge," and the pitch I'm looking for in a 2–2 count. In fact it sounded so fresh, so original, even though I was just running it through the computer speakers, that when it ended I went inside, made a sandwich, and came right back out and started it again.

Now it's 2. In Minnesota, my own brother should be just settling back into his stadium seat, ready for halftime of the Vikings game, having sacrificed the final minutes of the first half for short bathroom lines. He is a season-ticket holder, the renter with like-minded colleagues of aisle seats about a third of the way up the lower bowl, on the home-bench side. If you continued painting the thirty-yard line up into the stands, swerving just a little toward the twenty-nine or twenty-eight, you'd intersect him, drinking nothing more harmful than a too-big Sprite. His seat wouldn't exist if the park were rigged for baseball. He has always been candid about his preference for pigskin over calf-. "More strategy," he'll say when pressed, and I do sort of see where he's coming from. Just to view it in terms of quantity.

Now it's 2:05. The brother told me that when I leave tomorrow, I should hide the house keys under a rock to the right of the front door. A rock that is supposedly bigger than the ones around it, and of a slightly different color. I didn't remember it offhand. In a few minutes I'm going to investigate. Then I'm going to head back out onto the grass and finish off my tan. The experiment has been an unqualified success. So much so, in fact, that I had to tone down the SPF differential. I was finding myself in danger of not having a less tan knee but a tanner one. So last night, on a break from packing, I went and dug through the bathroom drawers, and I located a tube of 8 and a 15 that was three years expired. The oil and cream actually came out separately when I did a test squeeze in the sink, so I figure it's probably more like a 12, which is ideal. And by my calculations, if I spend the next ninety minutes under bright sun, everything will come together perfectly.

The Birds clinched a spot in the playoffs yesterday afternoon. They don't know yet what kind of spot it is. They actually lost their game, beneath a pile of uncharacteristic errors. Point me to the place in the history of baseball where there occurred a characteristic error. But their magic number was down to one, and everyone seemed to lose yesterday, there are days like that, days the league is full of losses and days it's full of wins, even though this isn't possible.

Because they didn't actually win it themselves, they had to sit in the locker room for fifteen minutes, then watch victory get beamed in from Milwaukee. At which point they ran *back* onto the field to celebrate, which they did by firing champagne corks at each others' eyes and punching each others' sternums and rubbing faces into the dirt by third base. I saw it all on a *SportsCenter* this morning, even the clinching moment: twenty-five guys sitting around a flatscreen, gripping sealed bottles in one hand, flat-brimmed playoff hats in the other, which they held just above their heads, until the instant they could legally don them. The quality of the champagne increases with each tier of playoff victory. You get Korbel for a wild card or division title, then something authentically French but not actually from the Champagne region for a divisional series win, followed by Veuve for a pennant, and at long last, Dom for the Series. Of course, this is mainly for pouring on heads. For actual drinking, guys stick to Wisconsin.

After *SportsCenter*, I washed my cereal bowl by hand and set it upside down in the drying rack, then drove over to my final session at PARC. They had me do about a two-thirds workout for my last day, the remaining .333 taken up by exit paperwork, basically me saying that anything that might seem to have happened here, didn't. After which I did a brisk round of goodbyes, because I've never seen the point in lingering on things like that, then hit the Center's showers. I had brought a change of clothes so I could just wash up there, rather than leave a soiled towel at the house. And as it went, when I stepped out of my exercise articles, and pictured stuffing their sweat in my suitcase, I just walked over to the trashcan under the paper towels and threw them away.

There were a few Florida Atlantic basketball players drifting around the locker room as I got dressed, looking straight past me with those stoic faces, that particular lack of interest that means interest. They knew who I was, had probably watched the same ESPN broadcast as me, were wondering what it would be like for a professional to view his team in that circumstance. And I can't blame them, because a thing like that makes for an intriguing story. But even if they had asked me directly, I didn't have time to stop and chat. I was in a hurry, and I jogged across that shining asphalt to the Volvo with the damp heat of shower water and sweat gluing my button-down to my back. By the time I saw those highlights, my own plan was well underway.

It came to me last night, as I stood out here, sipping a pale ale and grilling up some monkfish. Or should I say, I came to it. Instead of heading back to my Carolina, or even the other one, there *was* something I could do. A way to put my salary to use. What are we supposed to do with all this money, anyway? They just give it to us, without a single suggestion. Figure we'll work it out, there must be stuff we want. So what I did was, I went online. And once there I booked first-class tickets to every great American city I could think of without a major league ballclub. Nashville. Austin. New Orleans. Portland, Oregon. Indianapolis. Portland, Maine. There are so many the league has left untouched, so many I hardly know at all. Memphis, hell. Vegas, for God's sake. I did it all through one airline, and I requested they overnight paper tickets, so I could see how they all looked, because a thing like that is important.

The delivery envelope was sitting on the front step when I got home from the Center. Now it's lying by my feet. And after I write one more paragraph, I'm going to shut my laptop, and I'm going to lay all the tickets out on the ottoman, and I will pick the one that seems to have my name on it. And in approximately ten minutes, when the Town Car driver rings the sound of the doorbell, I'm going to step outside, slide the keys under the rock, and head to Palm Beach International. Then I will board the airplane heading to the town of my choice, and upon arrival check in to a downtown hotel, one with a full name. And that's when I will get out the second envelope, the one now cooling in my carry-on. The one that says "J" on the front, and is likewise filled with cities, one soon marked with an "X." And I will send it back here, and not media mail either.

So it's time for me to get off my computer. Anyway, my battery is running low, and the charger is packed. But there is one more thing I got to thinking this morning, seeing those shots of the guys on the basepaths. You asked. It's just: How would I look if I were to step on a diamond right now? I mean to you, the casual fan? Because there's this phenomenon that happens. When you see a young player on the field, he looks like an adult, because he is on the field. But if you think of him by his age, he looks way younger, like an innocent kid. And there's this weird doubling as you watch, this flipping back and forth—now a grown-up, now a kid, now a grown-up, now a kid. And over a few years, the difference gradually shrinks, the player and the young adult only looking slightly different. And then one day, one moment, it's suddenly just over, the kid option no longer exists, and the age he looks is just the age he is. It seems to happen extremely late in a guy's twenties, right around the age I am now. You look down for a second, fish a cracker jack out of your beer. You scan the out-of-town scoreboards, guess the number of the crowd. And you look up and he's just a man.

# ACKNOWLEDGMENTS

I'd like to thank Morgan Clendaniel, Claire Cushman, Nathan Deuel, Henry Finch, Laura Goode, Vanessa Hope, Carmen Johnson, Jonathon Keats, Michelle Latiolais, Allison Lorentzen, everyone at McSweeney's, Anna Noyes, everyone in Scriblerus, everyone in Sotesville, and Brianna Spiegel.

XL thanks to Andrew Leland. Decade-long and newfound thanks to Ed Park. Special thanks to Mom, Dad, Amanda, Henry, Kevin, and Rachel. Endless thanks to Zoe.

# ABOUT THE AUTHOR

Theo Schell-Lambert's essays and fiction have appeared in *The Believer*, *McSweeney's Internet Tendency*, the *Village Voice*, *Day One*, the *San Francisco Chronicle*, and other publications. This is his first novel. He lives in New Orleans.